What the critics are saying...

෪

"Tense drama alive with excellent characterization and conflict." ~ *Coffee Time Reviews.*

"Taking you to the darkest corners of your mind. A great read." ~ *Lighthouse Literary Reviews*

VELLA MUNN

WHITEOUT

Cerridwen Press

A Cerridwen Press Publication

www.cerridwenpress.com

Whiteout

ISBN 1419954849
ALL RIGHTS RESERVED.
Whiteout Copyright© 2005 Vella Munn
Edited by Martha Punches
Cover art by Syneca

Electronic book Publication June 2005
Trade paperback Publication October 2006

Cerridwen Press is an imprint of Ellora's Cave Publishing, Inc.®

Also by Vella Munn

&

If you are interested in a spicier read (and are over 18), check out the author's erotic romances at Ellora's Cave Publishing (www.ellorascave.com) written under the pen name of Vonna Harper.

Captive Warrior

Dangerous Ride

Dark Touch

Equinox *(anthology)*

Equinox II *(anthology)*

Forced

Hard Bodies

Her Passionate Need

More Than Skin Deep *(anthology)*

Refuge

Scarlet Cavern

Storm Warnings *(anthology)*

Thunder

About the Author

≈

Vella Munn has published more fiction books than she can keep track of; the last ten or so for Ellora's Cave as Vonna Harper. One of her Native American historicals earned her finalist status in both the Women Writing the West Willa award and the Pacific Northwest Booksellers Association. Before discovering romances, both erotic and otherwise, Vella penned more than forty confessions. She still writes the occasional nonfiction article, worked for a small town newspaper for four years, and created three association newsletters.

A longtime Oregon resident, Vella also works part-time as a writing instructor for a national correspondence school, holds memberships in Novelists Ink, RWA, Women Writing the West, and Willamette Writers. She's president of her local writers' association and has spoken at a number of conferences.

She's also working on a biography of her grandparents and her absolute favorite gig - being a grandmother!

Her first Cerridwen book, *Whiteout*, came to life while she was alone at the family wilderness cabin during an unexpected snowstorm. Fortunately, unlike one of her characters, she lived to tell the tale.

Vella welcomes comments from readers. You can find her website and email address on her author bio page at www.cerridwenpress.com.

WHITEOUT

᭐

Dedication

❧

As a child I lived in and embraced the wilderness.
When my in-laws bought a mountain cabin for the family, my soul embraced the setting, as did my sons.
Doc and Evelyn, thank you for the gift and the years you were in our lives.

Trademarks Acknowledgement

The author acknowledges the trademarked status and trademark owners of the following wordmarks mentioned in this work of fiction:

Beretta: Beretta

Bronco: Ford

Chevy: General Motors

Discover: Novus

Dodge:Daimler Chrysler

Doppler Radar: Belo Kentucky Inc

Eddie Bauer: Eddie Bauer

Goodwill: Goodwill Industries

Home Depot: Homer TLC Inc

Lexus: Toyota

Mastercard: Mastercard

MTV: Viacom

Plexiglas: Rohm & Haas Co.

Teflon: DuPont

Visa: NBO Systems

Prologue

ᔓ

Snow captured the sun's rays and threw them back to spear the lone skier's eyes. Isolation permeated everything, lived and breathed, and still the man pushed himself. Forced his body so there would be nothing else.

Last night's storm had packed another five inches on the Cascade Range, and Cherokee Moya embraced this moment when nothing mattered except being part of that glory. Work be damned. The U.S. Forest Service that all but owned him be damned. Most of all, Suzanna be damned!

He *needed* to be here, to breathe in the icy air, to feel the silence and stare at snow pillows and massive ponderosa pines that hadn't been buried under winter's weight. To become part of nature.

His skis hissed with each turn. He wasn't a born skier, knew just enough to meet the job requirements at Crater Lake National Park, but the siren's call of the forested slopes and the end to what he and Suzanna once had took him beyond caution.

He'd begun at Phantom Run, which meandered north from Crater, thinking to reach either Bailey or Thielsen. Then it hadn't mattered which mountain was his destination, but that was before he'd come across his friend and coworker Jace Penix and Jace's fiancée who were also on the trail. Jace, his arm around Kailee and hip pressing against hers, had kept after him with sober tone and eyes that said he knew what he was going through and hurt for him, reminded him that rule number one was that no one skied alone. Feeling trapped and angry, he'd said he was heading back.

Instead, once the pair was out of sight, he'd looked down and onto the hill to his right—and entered it.

Well-dressed for the elements, his only regret was that he'd worn shades instead of goggles which were better designed to cut through the deep shade cast by endless trees, but the goggles, like his heart, had gone with Suzanna.

Rhythm, he thought, *find the rhythm,* but the randomly spaced trees made that next to impossible, and in places, the slope was so steep that disaster teased. Although he was tempted to focus on the surrounding trees and what maybe crouched behind them, he knew enough to keep his head up, instinct and peripheral vision would keep him from sideswiping the trees as he passed.

It had begun to snow, the flakes large and lazy. Most of the time, the branches caught and held the fat globs before they reached him, and he didn't mind the few that landed on his exposed nose and cheeks and chin. What, after all, was wrong with a little numbness? It wasn't as if —

A pine, so large that maybe it was old growth, loomed ahead and slightly to his left. The sheltering and snow-packed branches were in the way, and he couldn't see the trunk, but he knew not to get too close to the snow-free pit at the base.

Jerking sideways and slowing at the same time, he felt first panic and then soul-deep pride as his athletic body took him past the potential danger. He was twenty-eight, intelligent, a full-time and permanent Forest Service employee, making decent money, loving the out-of-doors and what he was doing in it, ready to settle down and start a family —

No, damn it!

Reaching a berm, he planted his poles and stopped. Profound silence closed in around him. For a moment he felt disoriented, then remembered the compass strapped to his wrist. He was facing northeast, and if he kept going in that direction, he'd eventually reach little-known Lake Wolf with its ten private cabins. A small, nagging voice told him to retrace his tracks, but that would mean slogging uphill.

No sweat. Decision made.

If a tree fell in the woods but no one was there to hear it, did it make a sound? He angled left around one grove, then right to avoid another. The question wasn't quite as earthy as the one about the shitting bear but good enough, not that he'd learn the answer to either today because the few resident black bears were in hibernation and there wasn't enough of a wind to test a tree's stability.

He was up and over the edge before he'd known it was going to happen. Ahead yawned the steepest slope he'd seen today. Half scared and half reckless, he calculated his options. Either he could skewer the snow with his poles and find another way down or he could see just what the hell he was made of, take it to the edge.

In the time it took for his skis to travel ten feet, the decision was no longer his. Momentum packed on momentum. The treeless slope was exposed to the sun, which meant the snow melted during the day and froze at night, creating something too damn close to an ice field.

His mind snagged at options. Plant those poles. Drop his butt to the ground. Wrench his hips—and hopefully his skis—sideways even if that meant throwing himself ass over chin or was it the other way around?

Too fast. Humps of white that marked buried boulders but made him think of albino bears skimmed past. He hit one and his skis plowed into it and he thought he'd found an inelegant but manageable way of stopping, but then the tips broke through the downhill side of the mound and he was off again.

"Shit! Shit, shit!"

Terror, excitement, his life not quite flashing before him, hot energy, all those things slammed into him, mix-mastered into swirling confusion and still his skis sucked up the yardage. The slope was ending, finish line in sight. Maybe he should lift his arms in a victory salute like some Olympic racer, but how the hell did they do that without losing control?

What control?

Trees, angel white but with the devil's intent, sped up and at him. One lurched at him from the right, and he threw his body away to avoid it. He felt the ground begin to level out and waited, not breathing, for the slowing to start. Instead, his left arm was yanked back. He snapped his head around and stared, only half comprehending that what he'd thought was a lifesaving maneuver had brought him too close to the trees, and one had snagged his pole. Because he had the strap around his wrist, he couldn't break free.

His forward motion did just that and although the fight with the tree had slowed him, he was now off balance and still going too fast, sunglasses fogged, mouth open and teeth and gums freezing, tasting snow, yelling maybe.

Barreling, knees locked and then broken-jointed. Arms flailing.

A tree stopped him. Hard. He went at it all wrong, knees first with his feet bent back. When he hit the trunk, his upper body whiplashed forward. His forehead smacked into frozen bark.

So this was what a rear-ender felt like, he thought as his body vibrated to a stop. Just call him a crash test dummy.

At least he hadn't split open his head. Could still feel his arms and legs. Spine intact.

And…

Oh God, his knees smashed.

Both of them.

It continued to snow.

Chapter One

🕾

At first, the small, white cross on the side of the narrow dirt road made no impact on Dayna Curran. Then her gaze went to the rearview mirror where the marker stood out in contrast to its green and brown surroundings, and she tapped the brakes.

Although there was little chance another vehicle would come along anytime soon, she pulled over to the side of the little used road, careful not to let her tires get too close to the loose pine needles and pumidust that made up the forest floor.

Not sure why she was doing this, she got out and walked back to the solitary crucifix. She'd nearly reached it before she realized she hadn't grabbed her jacket from the seat beside her. The wind was break-dancing with the tops of the ponderosa pines this fall afternoon, the sound a swishing whistle that warned of winter. There was no snow on the surrounding peaks, and yet she shivered.

Despite the wind's song, she felt a certain sensory deprivation. She buried herself in her solitude, inhaled the scents of pine and dirt, pitch and cold air. The woods she now lived so far from called to her, and for a moment she forgot who she was and why she'd come back.

There was a cross, similar to this one near where she lived in Auburn, a small town in the northern California gold country. Those reminders of unnecessary death made more of an impact on her than traffic fatality statistics ever could, but what conditions could have resulted in a vehicular death out here? Not that she'd done a study of it during the summers of her childhood that she'd spent at the not too distant family cabin, but she'd be surprised if one car every half hour traveled this road.

A spider had left veins of web to hang from the cross stick and dirt had crawled up the two-by-four stuck into the ground so that it appeared more gray-brown than white at the base. Pinecones lay heaped on the ground around it. A faded blue woolen ski cap had been draped over the top and was held in place with wire. Written in black on the wood was a name and birth and death dates, and since she'd tried to wipe the dirt off the lettering, she now knew that Cherokee Moya had been twenty-eight when he'd died in February of last year.

Crouching, she rearranged a few of the pinecones. The gray day and heavy clouds might be responsible for the bone-deep sorrow she felt, but more likely it was an accumulation of everything she'd been through lately. Still, it was easier to think about someone she'd never met than herself.

Had this twenty-eight year old been alone at the moment of his or her death? Still squatting, she took in her surroundings. The country around Crater Lake, Oregon was an awesome mix of dense forest and rocky outcroppings. Ancient lava flows had covered the soil in many places, but this area belonged to the close-packed trees and shrubs, which provided a home for deer, occasional bear, chipmunks, birds and other wildlife.

Still, a sense of isolation permeated everything.

Sighing, she tensed her leg muscles in preparation for standing. As she did, her foot slipped and struck the base of the cross. Regaining her balance, she saw that she'd kicked aside several of the largest cones, exposing a slab of rock. She used the hem of her sweatshirt to wipe the surface clean.

I'm sorry had been written in neat cursive.

During a brief phone conversation last week, Dayna and her older brother Park had made plans to meet at North Junction some six miles from Crater Lake Rim Village so they could drive to the Lake Wolf cabin together. Dayna had pointed out that having just the trunk and backseat of her car would severely limit what they could haul out during their last trip before the new owners took possession in the spring, but Park had informed her that other than some fishing gear he intended to sell, he had no interest in anything and couldn't imagine what she'd want. He was right.

Now, a good hour before her brother was due, she once again pulled over to the side and turned off the motor. This time when she stepped out, she grabbed her jacket and planted her shoes on pavement, one of the benefits of being on the only road circling Crater Lake. Not that it had mattered during the nightmare years of her childhood, but she'd grown up with the world-famous lake in her backyard.

With time to kill, and her mother's death and her brief as possible visit to the nursing home where her father languished on her mind, she trudged up the slope leading to Crater's rim. To her left was a wind-crippled white bark pine. Nearly needleless, its stunted branches served as host to rust-colored moss. Much of the root system lay exposed and was bleached almost white. She traced the swirls and knots with a minimally tended nail.

To her delight, she found pale green false hellebore or corn lily growing in the white bark's moist shade and nearby, a mass of yellow rabbit brush. Although spring's fawn lilies and summer's purple lupine and white American bistort were done for the year, she'd driven past a high meadow filled with foxtail barley and yellow groundset and had picked several of the foxtail's seed heads. Now if she could just dig up a little stonecrop—

The great lake lay below her, not startling royal blue the way it could be on a summer day but icy and brooding. The heavy clouds were responsible. No longer a solid weight the way they'd been when she'd stopped at the cross, there were now a few holes in the curtain where the sun shone through. As a result, the lake's hues reminded her of a careless watercolor with shades from near black to palest silver swirling in random, changing patterns.

The nearly two hundred thousand surrounding acres were under the management of the Department of the Interior, but from where she stood, she saw no signs of civilization. She should know how deep the lake went, the details of its formation and current attempts to keep it unspoiled but she didn't because Crater Lake, like the cabin, was part of a world she'd put behind her.

Only, she reminded herself as a large Clark's nutcracker approached, her mother was dead and her father the next thing to it and everything had changed. Maybe.

The gray and black bird opened its mouth and loudly announced something—probably a demand for a tidbit.

"Sorry," she told it. "I don't have a thing worth eating on me."

After a moment, the nutcracker jumped from the ground to the denuded white bark pine and began rooting in the moss. Glad to have something living around, she waited as the bird tore out and discarded chunks of moss. The lake made a breathtaking backdrop and if she had a camera and knew more than the rudiments about working with lighting, she might come up with something worth framing.

What was it she'd heard about Crater? That Indians had once considered it sacred and, superstitious, had refused to come near. Looking at the pristine body of water cradled in a rock caldera some six miles across, she understood why. The deep, massive depression had once been a mountain, but it had been blown apart, leaving the world's largest rain and snow catch basin. If there had been Indians around when the ancient eruption occurred, they must have thought the world was coming to an end. To have the pattern of one's existence suddenly disrupted, to feel utterly helpless—

Another vehicle was approaching. It was still too early for it to be Park, and she gave a fleeting thought to ducking behind a boulder, but whoever it was would be more interested in the lake than her. Besides, she hadn't had to hide in years. Recognizing the four-wheel drive as belonging to the Park Service, she watched it pull in behind her car. The ranger—she guessed that's what they were called—who got out was a little over six foot tall with broad shoulders, a somewhat wilted dark green uniform, and a stare that caused her to drop her gaze. She placed his age at close to hers, late twenties. According to the tag above his right breast, his name was Jace Penix.

"You're okay?" he asked.

"Okay?"

"Not many people stop out here. I thought you might be having car trouble."

"Oh. Yes, I'm fine. I'm just waiting for someone."

"Hm."

His disinclination to say more made her a little uncomfortable. Maybe he'd seen her collecting the foxtail seed heads and was going to fine her. Stumbling a bit, she asked how long he'd been working here. Other than explaining that he was going into his second winter, he didn't say anything.

"I suppose you've seen the lake so many times you hardly notice it anymore, do you?" she said in an effort to keep the conversation going.

He shrugged.

"It's beautiful," she admitted, his silence beating at her nerves. "I love the fact that man hasn't tried to change it into something else."

"No, at least not yet."

Finally releasing her from his stare, he stepped past her so he could gaze out at their shared world. The wind again made its impact. There were fewer trees for it to torture here, but that still left the tall, sharp spires and dikes on the long slope to her left. The outcroppings gave the wind something to bounce off and skittle around, and the result was an eerie whine that both set her on edge and filled her with energy.

Jace Penix stood with his legs spread and his hands behind his back as if he'd been handcuffed. He leaned forward from the waist, still except for the clenching and unclenching of his jaw.

"Are you looking for something?" she asked.

"What? No."

"Then…uh, before you showed up, I was thinking about the Indians. When the mountain blew, it must have terrified them."

"It did."

Now that she'd had time to take her measure of him, she wondered if he might have Native American blood in him because his face was rounder than would be expected on someone with little body fat and his hair and eyes were black. There was solidness to him, the kind of physique an Indian would need to survive an unforgiving world.

"Why don't you have a camera?" he asked abruptly.

"What?"

"Most visitors, that's the one thing they wouldn't forget."

"I'm not exactly a visitor. Uh, my family has long had a cabin at Lake Wolf."

"Oh."

"Yes, but we're selling it. My brother and I are here to close it for the winter."

Not responding, Jace Penix turned his attention from her to the clouds. In the few minutes since she'd last looked at them, they'd multiplied and grown fat, once again blocking out the late fall sun. She felt a sense of urgency she hadn't before. Although her father had always winterized the cabin no later than the middle of October, the family had occasionally traveled into the mountains in the winter, and she knew what storm packed on storm could do. As a child trying to find her way to sleep, she'd often wondered what it would be like to be trapped by a blizzard. Only by telling herself she'd be alone inside the walls, which provided the sole protection against a freezing death, had she been able to keep her musings from turning into a nightmare.

With a mental shake of the head, she brought herself back. The ranger hadn't ceased his study of the lake. She mentioned that she'd already taken an exploratory run out toward Lake Wolf via what was more trail than highway. "I didn't go far, just a couple of miles," she said. "Do you think they're ever going to pave the road?"

"What? Oh, the project keeps coming up. But every time it does, it gets kicked to the bottom of the list."

"I suppose," she mused, "as long as people can get to Wolf by way of Diamond, there's not much point, especially since this end of the rim road isn't kept open in the winter."

"No, there isn't."

He slipped his hands into his back pockets and hunched his shoulders. He struck her as being alone, maybe not physically but deep down where the monsters lived. Monsters she understood all too well.

"Maybe you know the answer," she began. "When I was on the road, I came across a handmade cross. I can't imagine how a fatal accident could have occurred out here. I mean—"

"Cherokee wasn't in a car."

"Oh. What happened?"

"I don't know." Removing his hands from his pockets, he stared at them. "I haven't found his body yet."

"You mean he disappeared?"

"Yeah."

As the crow flew, it was about ten miles between Crater and Wolf, but the steep, tree-choked hills and valleys made a straight run impossible. By car, it was close to twice that, and she had no idea how many hiking trails existed these days.

"He was skiing," the ranger went on, his words soft and hollow. "He never came back."

A chill slashed down her spine. "But the marker gives a date of death."

"That was the last day I saw him."

"Oh. Did a storm hit?"

"Yeah. One that lasted the better part of a week."

She tried to form an image out of the little he'd given her, but too many of the pieces were missing. Her best guess was that when Cherokee didn't return, searchers had done what they could to find him, but with the kind of winter storms that hit the Cascades, they'd been severely limited. Throughout those frustrating, frightening days and nights, the searchers had had to ask themselves whether Cherokee was alive or dead and if alive, was he lost or injured or both. Dying alone.

I'm sorry, the rock message had said. Was she talking to the person responsible for the words?

"What a horrible way to die," she managed. "I-I hope the end came quick for him."

"If I'd been doing my job…"

"Your job?"

"Yeah, mine. He was my friend." The ranger walked past her, got into his rig and pulled back onto the road.

Both numb and alarmed, she stood where she was as she contemplated what little he'd told her. The truth was, she'd learned more from his body language and the look in his eyes than his words. Jace Penix blamed himself for Cherokee Moya's death.

What did it feel like to carry such guilt around? Was there anything she could do or say to help him past that point? Although she wished she could, she couldn't imagine that happening. They were strangers, two people whose paths would never cross again. Still…

As the low hum of an approaching motor penetrated her senses, she gave Crater a final look, bracing her legs and back to counterbalance the gusting wind. The lake still mirrored the dark gray clouds, reminding her of a bottomless quarry. The winter wilderness of the Cascades had killed Cherokee Moya. If she wasn't careful, Crater Lake might suck her into it.

Chapter Two

✿

Park Curran's cellular bleated at him. Eyes on the road, he punched the mute button on his CD player and picked up the phone.

"You've got it," the man on the other end said in response to his crisp "hello".

"What'd it come in at?"

"One hundred forty-nine thousand."

"I hoped it'd be less than that."

"The land alone's worth that, and once you get the lot divided, you're going to come out on top of the heap, again."

Jeremy was right. Besides, now that the appraisal and thus the selling figure of the property he'd made an offer on had sunk in, Park grinned. He took a moment to listen to the low panther hum his spun-silver Lexus RX made. He wanted to see if the two hundred and thirty horsepower engine really could go from zero to sixty in eight point five seconds, but the twists and turns of Highway 62 made that impossible.

"So," Jeremy said. "What now? I thought the owner rejected your offer."

"That's a mild way of putting it. I'll let him sweat a few days."

Jeremy chuckled. "You're a real bastard."

"If I am, I learned from a master. Look, I appreciate the call."

"No problem. By the way, how long are you going to be on this little vacation of yours?"

"This is no vacation, believe me. What my sister and I have to do shouldn't take more than a couple of days, but then I've got business in Grants Pass. All I accomplished today was to confirm a rumor."

"Rumor?"

"Yeah. The nursing home our old man's in changed hands, and they're jacking up the rates. We shouldn't have chosen the first place that'd take him, but we were up against it trying to warehouse him somewhere and putting their place on the market."

"You really loved him, didn't you?"

"There was nothing to love. Look—"

"Wait a minute. You let someone else sell your folks' house?"

Park briefly let go of the steering wheel and pressed the heel of his left hand against his temple, the gesture one that had followed him—like too many things—into adulthood. After telling Jeremy he'd managed to unload his parents' three thousand square foot, riverfront place in less than a month because he'd had the local agent offer it at a fire sale price, he said goodbye. He'd like to know the particulars of how Jeremy, another real estate investor, had heard about the low appraisal on the diamond in the rough Beaverton property, but their connection had begun to break up.

Park ticked through what he needed to accomplish once he got home. His rule of thumb was to hold onto a property for the better part of a year because it usually took that long for the former owner to get over the fact that he'd been taken, but this time he was willing to take the chance since the place had appraised out far below market value—thanks to a favor owed him by one of the local appraisers. Flipping it could net him over eighty thousand.

As he slowed to accommodate the lumbering fifth wheel ahead of him, he contemplated what he'd tell the owner—a thirty-nine-year-old bachelor salesman who was making no more than he had when he'd started his so-called career. Park knew this because he'd had a credit check run on the loser. He'd also learned that the man had fallen behind in his mortgage payments and run up several thousand dollars worth of dental bills.

Park would give him a week to stew over the deflated appraisal before getting in touch with him. The conversation would be short and to the point. The offer he'd made stood but would be withdrawn in twenty-four hours.

His old man would be proud of him, or at least as close to that emotion as the bastard was capable of feeling.

Irritated because the driver of the fifth wheel wasn't pulling over, Park tried to call his investment broker, but the mountains must be causing interference because he couldn't get through. Frowning, he patted his soft and relentlessly expanding belly and tried not to think about the gusting wind slamming into the Lexus. Staring forty in the face was the pits. His sister was ten years younger than him, which meant they'd never really lived in the same world. Before he'd broken free at seventeen, she'd been a proverbial drink of water with a collarbone that jutted against her skin, but the girl could run. Lordy, could she run. Took first in who knew how many district and state meets and had set a regional record in the three thousand meter. He'd sometimes wondered if what drove her had been her need to run away from, not toward anything.

A van pulled up behind and slowed, like him, unable to pass the fifth wheel. Through the rearview mirror, he saw a youngish man was driving it, with a woman around the same age next to him, and an uncountable number of children in back. His sister hadn't yet married which seemed strange because with her looks, the men should be panting after her. Maybe, conditioned by what passed for a marriage between their parents, she'd decided to have nothing to do with the institution. If that was the case, she was smarter than him because it had taken two failed marriages for him to wise up.

Two divorces and a twelve-year-old son he barely knew.

＊ ＊ ＊ ＊ ＊

Dayna was leaning against her car when Park pulled up behind her. His first thought was that there wasn't much of a shoulder and he hoped the Lexus would be all right. His second impression, that his sister looked like a windblown gypsy with a faded denim jacket wrapped around her and her long legs accented by equally faded jeans, briefly chased away his concerns about his vehicle. The third thought didn't hit him until he stepped out.

"Damn, it's cold!" he said by way of greeting.

"And getting colder. I was beginning to think something had happened to you."

"We have to talk. What's it called, Farmhill, where the old man is, they're jacking up the rates. That's where I've been, getting the particulars."

"Did you see him?"

"Yeah. Briefly." Glancing up at the sky, he took note of blue-black clouds. "He had no idea who I was, kept calling me Mr. Bond."

"That's what he called me when I was there yesterday," she told him. "Maybe he's thinking about those 007 movies."

"Who knows? You didn't notice that the management was new?"

She shook her head. "I-I don't know what I expected, maybe that he'd recognize me."

"What would the two of you have talked about?"

"Nice car," she said after a silence of several seconds.

Using the sleeve of his Eddie Bauer jacket, he scrubbed at what remained of a bug. "Two layers of topcoat," he told her. "I hope it'll do the job."

"Hm. I'm glad you're here."

She'd been worried about him? Given how seldom he thought about her these days, he found that hard to believe. "Learning what we're up against with him was important. Now…" He could get a little further off the road, but he was tempting fate. He asked if she'd been on the spur to Wolf, and when she said she had, he pondered the advisability of leaving the Lexus there.

"It'll get dusty," he grumbled. "And covered with pine needles and pitch. Damn it, leaving it there might make it more appealing to vandals."

"If you had an old beast like mine, you wouldn't have to worry."

Her Dodge wasn't exactly a beast, but neither was it the first choice of car hijackers. He couldn't remember what she'd been driving when he'd seen her in June, but they'd been so busy that half the time they'd forgotten to eat.

"The way I look at it," she said, her voice soft against the wind, "we can drive back to headquarters or the lodge, or we can look for a place to hide it once we're on the dirt road. There's just not much of a turnout here."

Her first suggestion would add at least another hour to their day when he wanted to be settled in before dark. His words clipped, he said he'd follow her until he spotted a place both inconspicuous and secure. No way was he going to risk damaging the undercarriage on the dirt track that led to their cabin.

"You really should see the lake before we leave," Dayna said as he started toward his car. "It's spectacular."

"What for? I know what it looks like."

She winced almost as if he'd struck her, stirring a memory. "I thought I did too," she said. "But back then I took Crater for granted when I shouldn't have."

As children, neither of them had taken anything for granted. Instead of reminding her of that, he contemplated his surroundings. He'd tried to catch the weather report as he was leaving Portland this morning, but what he'd heard was for the northern end of the state, and once he'd gotten on the road, he'd spent most of the time on the phone. He wouldn't be surprised if it started raining before the day was out, although at this elevation they were as likely to get snow. Fortunately, it was the first weekend in November, not yet winter.

"I thought you were going to bring Scott," his sister said.

"So did I. However, his mother saw it differently."

"Not living with him is rough, isn't it?"

Instead of answering, he trudged up the rocky slope, took a deep breath and looked out and down. The great, yawning hole had always overwhelmed him, awed him, and in ways he didn't understand, frightened him. He knew what it was to be alone, but staring at that inhospitable body of water kicked the emotion into overdrive. Why had he thought he wanted to show this to his son?

Sensing his sister beside him, he concentrated on her. "It's not as clear as it used to be. I'm sure it isn't."

"Pollution." She sighed. "No matter what it is, man has to muck it up."

"That's called progress. Civilization."

"I guess. Park, do you ever wish you lived in the past?"

"It's not going to happen so why bring it up?"

"Maybe because I think I'd be happier living a few hundred years ago."

"Without antibiotics, 911, and MTV?"

A slight nod was her only answer. She'd glanced at him while talking, but now she looked at Crater again, and after a moment, he forced himself to do the same. There was a brooding quality to the view, perhaps the doing of a vengeful god, he thought, surprising himself. Once, thousands of years ago, this had been a mountain but something—maybe that vengeful god—had blown it apart and allowed this monument to nature's strength and power and whimsy to form.

"It humbles me," Dayna said. "Puts me in my place."

He, too, felt humble, not that he'd tell his sister that.

"Look at it, Park. Not just the lake, but everything here. We think we've accomplished something because we've paved over half the world, but would any of us survive if we were alone out here?"

"It's not going to happen."

"I know that. I just—"

They'd wasted too much time here, and with daylight threatening to fade, he should have already pointed that out. Instead, he pulled the clean, free air deep into his lungs.

* * * * *

"Yes, it's possible for the lake to freeze. I'm just saying I haven't seen it and neither has anyone I've ever talked to."

The elderly woman who'd waylaid Jace Penix on his way to the storage barn repeated what he'd just said to her husband who kept a hand cupped to his ear.

"Why not?" the man demanded. "Everything else around here does, doesn't it? Otherwise, they'd keep the whole road open, wouldn't they?"

"A couple of reasons," Jace explained. "For one, the rim protects the lake from the worst of the arctic air. Also, there's so much sheer volume in the lake that its heat dissipates slowly."

The man nodded, but his expression made Jace wonder how much he'd heard.

"You stay here year round?" the woman asked.

"We're pretty well self-contained, and there's always something that needs doing." As he said the last, he was struck with the feeling that he should be doing something other than what he was, but whatever it was eluded him, not that that was anything new.

Because the elderly couple was interested in learning more about what winter here was like, he mentioned that most weather patterns originated in the Pacific Ocean and after building in strength and moisture, storms were pushed inland. Over one hundred inches of rain fell on the coast each year with around thirty descending on the Rogue and Willamette Valleys. When the systems reached the Cascade Range, the mountains pushed the air to elevations in excess of ten thousand feet. As a result, the air cooled, changing water vapor into clouds, and if conditions were right, as they almost always were in the winter, snow was the result.

"It sounds pretty technical," the woman admitted while her husband stared at her. "With the clouds looking so ominous today, I'm glad we're leaving in the morning." She reached out and patted Jace's forearm. "I'll be thinking of you in January when we're in Arizona."

He chuckled, and then ended the conversation by reminding both them and himself that he was on duty. As he stepped inside the dimly lit shed, his nostrils filled with the smell of rubber and gasoline. A case of oil next to an inoperable forklift reminded him that his Bronco was overdue for a change. He could either schedule a time with the resident mechanic or do the job himself. It wasn't—

"Jace? Jace, you in there?"

"What? Yeah."

"What the hell are you doing?" Henri Lansky demanded.

"Looking for…"

"I don't give a damn," Henri interrupted. "I waited for you the better part of an hour. Tried reaching you on the PTT half a dozen times."

Henri had waited for him? What—? "Damn, I'm supposed to be at Pacific Crest."

"Were. It's too late now."

Henri, who refused to give his age and was somewhere between thirty-five and fifty, was a big man. At the moment, Jace's fellow ranger stood at the entrance to the shed, one shoulder against the open door. When he'd first met Henri, Jace had decided to avoid crossing him if possible. After a tentative start, he'd learned that neither he nor Henri had what could be called a religious belief and were fascinated by all things scientific. As a result, their relationship had deepened and become solid. At least it had been that way until recently.

"I'm sorry," he apologized. "It slipped my mind."

"Like too damn much these days. We talked about walking that trail just last night."

"I know." Leaving the shed's inner recesses, he started toward the older man. "It's just that I—"

"We both know what it is. Cherokee. It's always Cherokee."

He waited.

"I kept telling myself you'd get over your obsession or compulsion or whatever it is, but I have to tell you, you're running out of time. Either you get your act together or—I don't have to spell it out, do I?"

No, he didn't. "Has he said anything?"

"Yeah, he has."

The *he* they were talking about was Paul Soffin, park superintendent. Although Paul had more to concern himself with than just the conduct of the men and women under him, he expected results from them.

"What did he say?" Jace made himself ask.

"Nothing you haven't heard from me." Henri shifted his weight so his left shoulder now appeared to be supporting the doorframe. "You're not doing yourself any good the way you are."

"So you've told me."

"Don't get defensive. It keeps you from seeing what's happening to you. You're losing it. Hell, maybe you already have."

He did his job, damn it! Worked a lot more than forty hours a week and had more stamina than most. There wasn't anything he wouldn't tackle, any job he refused to do.

"I'm telling it the way I see it," Henri went on. "And I'm not the only one who's noticed the change in you. What is it? You think that if you keep on looking for Cherokee eventually you'll find him? Damn it, there isn't anything left. Animals…"

Teeth clenched, Jace struggled to reject the image that went with Henri's words.

"I'm not going to tell you to quit blaming yourself because I've already said that so many times I've turned blue and you still won't listen."

"I don't blame myself."

"Yeah, you do. Jace, you can't bring him back. He's dead."

Chapter Three

ॐ

Beacan Jarrard slid the key into the deadbolt and turned it. He gave a half thought to stepping back so the girl could enter first, but he'd been waiting too long for this moment. Propelling his professional baseball player's body forward, he inhaled new wood smell and what had been used to seal and varnish the peeled logs. Although he hadn't seen his cabin since the remodeling had been completed, his hand easily found the light switch.

Yes!

"Beacan!" the girl gasped. "It's fantastic!"

Instead of reveling in her admiration, he resented her intrusion. The last eight months of his life had been an incredible ride beginning with a spring training packed with hungry rookies wanting but not claiming his position behind the plate and ending with a seven game World Series that had given his team the championship. What he found even harder to believe was that he'd held together through the nearly 150 games he'd caught.

Now the roller coaster was behind him. He felt exhausted. Spent.

"The way you talked about it," the girl said. "I thought I knew what to expect, but this is fantastic."

If she said that word one more time— "It needs furnishing. All this stuff is from before the remodeling."

The girl, Kandi something, nodded but didn't continue her gushing. Instead, she walked into the large, open room with its exposed rafters, polished oak floor, and large picture window. He turned his attention to the place he'd bought two seasons ago.

Originally, there'd been a wall between the kitchen and living room, but that had been removed so the two flowed together. The final bill hadn't yet come in, but whatever it was, he didn't care. When the time came when he could no longer do the only thing he'd ever wanted out of life, he'd need a place to go to.

Kandi shivered but didn't complain about the cold. A new cast iron stove had been installed near the doors that led to the two bedrooms. Someone, either the workmen but probably Gus Withers who he'd hired to supervise the work, had left a supply of wood and kindling. When he opened the stove door, he was relieved to see it stoked since he had only a rudimentary understanding of how to start and maintain a fire. As he lit a match and held it against the crumpled newspaper, he noted how the materials had been laid out. Then he stood, listening to the whoosh of flames and catching the first hint of heat. Holding his hands over the stove, he absorbed the weight and reality of his first and probably only World Series ring.

Kandi, her arms locked around her slim waist, stood at the base of the steps leading to what had been a bat-infested attic. "What's up there?" Her voice echoed a little.

"A loft."

"Not another bedroom?"

"No."

"But I thought— Then there's just two bedrooms?"

"One for me and one for my folks or sister and her husband when they come to visit. If we're all here at once, I'll sleep upstairs."

Kandi slanted him a look, then trailed a finger over the banister. "It really is a getaway, isn't it? I thought you might be, oh, I don't know, entertaining a lot."

He had a three thousand square foot house in Castro Valley for that. "The cabins here are on land owned by the Forest Service," he told her. "I was able to increase the size from what it was originally but not much. Besides, I didn't want to overwhelm my surroundings."

She started toward him, her head cocked to one side, her large, lavender eyes on him, his magnificent body calling hers. "Why did you choose here?"

The week after the World Series had been insane. Although he'd been in desperate need of sleep, he'd gotten sucked up in the hoopla and had fed off it. Lived in the moment and denied the pain locked in his back. There'd been a different woman every night, strangers until he'd singled them out of the crowd with no more than a wink and a nod. Then he'd been at some hospital charity function and Kandi, who worked there and was photogenic enough that the press had pulled them together, had asked him to speak to a young man who'd been paralyzed in a car accident. The patient's eyes had burned with despair and envy and he'd fled after less than a minute. Kandi had said nothing, but her expression let him know she'd seen.

Instead of walking out of the antiseptic-smelling building, he'd asked her out—a confrontation of sorts. She'd said yes, and although he waited for her to bring up what had happened between him and the kid, she hadn't. That, maybe, was why, after two dates during which he'd bedded her each time, he'd invited her here. As for why he had and why she'd accepted—

"There's good fishing," he said, belatedly remembering she'd asked a question. "And I've always wanted to try cross-country skiing and snowmobiling. I had the loft finished with a door to the outside so I can ski or snowmobile from the cabin in the winter."

"The snow gets that deep?"

"Not often but sometimes."

She turned so her back was to the fire and stared out the window. He looked in the same direction wondering how long it had been since he'd seen anything except baseball complexes and airports. How long had it been since he had heard anything except the sounds of crowds and bat against ball, thought of anything except making it through another game?

"I was thinking." Her voice was so soft he had to strain to hear her above the fire. "About the Donner party?"

"The what?"

"The pioneers who spent a winter trapped by snow in the Sierra Nevada Mountains. About half of them died."

"Oh yeah. They became cannibals, didn't they?"

She nodded. "It was either that or starve."

"Forget that. To eat."

"What if your child was starving?"

He didn't have any living children. Still, in the silence that followed, he all too easily imagined a wasted youngster in his arms and despair filling his heart. "I never thought about it that way," he told her.

"I did after I read a couple of their diaries."

"You read diaries?"

She nodded again, her gaze serious. "I love the human part of history."

He wanted peace and quiet and a quick and easy lay, no journey into certain aspects of his past—one chapter in particular. Just the same, caught by the pensive look in her eyes, he waited for her to continue.

"I took some college history night classes thinking they might help me understand…certain things. They didn't."

"What things?"

"Just— What was in here before? The logs used for the walls are all new, aren't they?"

The stove gave off enough heat that he felt the need to step back, and after closing down the damper, he did so. The gray day had seeped in, and even with the overhead light on, shadows clung to the room's edges. "Yeah," he answered belatedly. "I had the logs trucked in from a place out of Medford."

When she didn't say anything, he walked over to the new stereo. Although it consisted of both tape and CD players in addition to the radio system, he hadn't brought along any CDs and had only about a half dozen tapes in his Bronco. When he turned on the radio, he found it tuned to an easy-listening FM station. Sound wafted to him from several speakers, the bass tones enhanced by the twelve-inch diameter logs that acted as their own insulation.

Kandi, with her eyes half closed, swayed from side to side, in time with the beat. Her long, dark hair reached to her shoulders and half covered her features. Maybe because she was dressed in muted colors, he had trouble distinguishing her from her surroundings, not that he tried all that hard. She worked in the hospital's billing department, at least he thought she did. She hadn't said anything about how much time she'd taken off. In fact, other than being pretty sure she wasn't married and that she liked history, he didn't know much about her. Oh yeah, he knew one other thing. She was on the pill.

Gus had stocked the kitchen. His agent didn't expect to hear from him for at least a week, and his back wasn't going to be cut into for three weeks.

He crooked his finger at Kandi. "Come here," he said.

There were two windows in the bedroom Beacan had taken her into. The blinds were drawn up, exposing them to the world. Amend that, Kandi thought. Because of the distance between the cabins and the fact that each lot held dozens of trees, she'd barely spotted the place to the left as they drove in, and there'd been no sign of a vehicle.

When Beacan touched the base of her throat with the finger that bore his World Series ring, she jumped but stilled the reaction, hopefully without his being aware of it. His hands were broad and she imagined them wrapped around her neck, squeezing, but a co-worker who was proud of her standing as a baseball groupie had told her that Beacon Jarred didn't go the domination route. That was why she'd said yes when he'd asked her out following his visit to the hospital, one of the reasons anyway.

Despite the deep chill in the room, she didn't object when he pulled her sweater over her head and removed her bra. His chuckle and rough fingers on her breasts told her he approved of what the cold was doing to them.

"I'm going to have to warm them, aren't I? I don't want you getting sick on me."

"I don't get sick."

"Never?"

"Never. Beacan…"

"What?" he asked with his hands now clamped around her waist.

"Nothing." An instrumental she didn't recognize began, and she became one with the music, took herself away from what was happening to her body. Hovering between the nothing place where she needed to be and what she believed he expected of her, she ticked off the seconds, her appraisal of his mood and needs and pace never wavering.

"I watched you on TV," she told him when he tried to kiss her. "It…bothered me."

"Bothered? What the hell for?"

"I don't know. They'd do those close-ups of you behind the plate and I wondered if you were nervous or…"

"Or what?"

"Afraid you'd miss the ball."

The admission hung in the room. "I shouldn't have," she said when she couldn't take the silence any longer. "You were great."

"Yeah? How would you know?"

"I love sports. Especially baseball. The poetry and complexity of it, the power and the danger."

"Danger?"

"A ball moving a hundred miles an hour coming within inches of a batter."

"After you've caught as many as I have, it gets routine."

He slipped his fingers under the elastic on her bikini briefs and slid them down and off her hips. When he crouched so she could step out of them, she buried her fingers in his thick hair and for a moment let his strength and competence become hers.

When he raked his teeth over her naked belly, she tried to pull away, but he pressed his hands against her buttocks and held her in place. Slivers of sensation trickled deep into her pelvis, surprising her. His tongue trailing over her belly button set off ancient memories. Still, she knew to move as if trying to deal with what was an overwhelming impact on her nerve endings.

"Ticklish?" he asked, his question muffled because he was now trying to find enough loose skin to close his teeth over.

"Ticklish."

His laugh, accompanied by a burst of air, felt like fine sandpaper against her flesh, but she curled her body around him. He was rock-muscled, swift and aggressive, a man who took no prisoners and daily pitted himself against other strong and competitive men.

"You're freezing," he observed. "Fortunately, I'm ready to warm you."

That said, he stood and lifted her in his arms. She caught a glimpse of a royal blue flannel sheet, and then he dropped her onto it, slipped out of the rest of his clothes, and covered her naked body with his.

His hand slid between her legs and she obediently spread them, lifting her pelvis off the bed and making herself accessible to him. Foreplay, such as it was, consisted of a brief finger exploration of her inner recesses. She paced her breathing to his movements, moving, always moving. Pressing her fingers over the muscles at the back of his neck, she took her pulse of him. He was plunging downstream, caught in the current of his pulsing blood. Opening herself even more, she worked her hips so that he slid into her. His urgent grunt reminded her of a bulldog with its nose stuck through a fence opening, but she killed her revulsion and became the actress she needed to be.

Still, even as her body rode the waves with him, she remained locked in her cage, half hating him, hating herself even more.

Alone and lonely and yet warmed by him.

The sound of an approaching vehicle caused Beacan to stir. Taking advantage of his heightened awareness, Kandi slid out from under his weight and sat up. Spotting a blanket at the foot of the bed, she wrapped it around herself and walked into the living room. Alone, she measured its space and workmanship against her own apartment. On the rare occasions when she stepped beyond reality, she dreamed of living in a place like this without neighbors nearby, high, white ceilings, enough room that she could spread her arms wide and dance if she so wanted. A yard.

She couldn't see the vehicle she'd just heard but dust puffs rose up from the driveway leading to the nearest cabin. Wondering whom they might have as neighbors and whether Beacan would welcome or resent them, she checked the fire. The three small logs were nearly burned down to coals. Going to the stack of wood, she picked up and then discarded a pitch-filled slab. After gathering an armload she'd determined to be safe to burn, she managed to carry them over to the stove and hold onto her blanket at the same time. She'd just opened the damper when Beacan, naked, came out of the room.

"Do you know what you're doing?" he asked.

"Yes."

"Hm." He gave her an appraising look. "Can you split wood?"

"Yes."

"No kidding, a woman of many talents. Speaking of talents…" Stepping up to her, he flipped her blanket off one shoulder. "What are you doing up? I was just catching my breath."

"I heard a car drive in. I think our—your neighbors are here."

"Damn. Who are they?"

"I don't know. I didn't see anyone."

After a glance at the window, he pushed the blanket off her other shoulder. "It doesn't look as if they can see us either which means…" Slowly, deftly, he eased the covering down off her body until it lay puddled at her feet. "What a body you have." He whistled. "Your leg muscles…"

"I'm a runner."

"I should have known."

Maybe, but for him to know anything about her, he would have had to ask and she'd have to be willing to answer and neither of those conditions existed.

They'd have sex again—making love was beyond her experience—and this time the sex would probably take longer because his urgency had been dulled. She'd survive, and later offer to fix him something to eat. They'd listen to the stereo and maybe look through the books here and he might tell her what this year of his life had been like. For a few insane moments she might even pretend to be part of his world of domination and force.

Maybe.

* * * * *

KYGH meteorologist Homer Harkins took what he expected to be a quick look at the data just in from the U.S. Weather Service. He'd already given his forecast during the five o'clock news and was looking for confirmation that he'd be saying essentially the same thing at six o'clock. However, something in the updated computer images caused him to frown.

"Home, you want to give me your okay on these satellite photos?" a technician asked. "The quality's not as good as what they sent us earlier. I think they'll work, but I don't want you wondering what the hell you're looking at while you're on the air."

"In a minute."

"That's about all we've got."

Homer waved off the technician, then peered at the data again before turning to the information brought in by the station's Doppler radar. Fronts were stacking up in the Pacific like bumper cars, not that he hadn't seen enough of them in the ten years he'd been forecasting the weather. What had given him pause was how much a still developing cold front had grown since he'd last looked at it.

Turning to the network computer, he speed-read through the latest printout from a Weather Service office in Washington. In cryptic sentence fragments, his Washington counterpart had made the observation that it looked as if Mother Nature might be gearing up for an early celebration of winter.

Might be, Homer mused. He wouldn't say anything on the air right now, but by eleven o'clock, he could have something to expand and expound. If nothing else, the prospect of an early snow would get the area's skiers' juices flowing.

Chapter Four

೫

Trees crowded around the cabin like the curious at the scene of an accident. No other vehicles had been on the route between Crater and Wolf, and Dayna had been torn between unease at the prospect of not having anyone around while they were closing up and a sense of freedom.

The barely single-lane dirt track, which connected the graveled road to the cabin, had been inundated by tree roots. Consequently, she hadn't dared look up until she reached the parking area behind the cabin. The metal roof had been put on three summers ago. Her father had fought the Forest Service over that ever since the old shakes had started to disintegrate. Insisting that a rustic structure needed a natural-appearing roof, he'd opposed the regulation calling for metal even though manmade materials decreased the fire danger and snow couldn't cling to it.

"Looks like he scored what I'm sure he believed was a significant victory," she acknowledged. "But bright blue? That's disgusting."

"That's what the new owners said." Like her, Park remained in the rapidly cooling car. "The Service fined him every year since he did that. Five hundred dollars a pop, not that he cared."

Suddenly exhausted, she leaned her head against the seat back and stared at the wooden siding that first Park and then she had covered with water sealant every year. "Why did he go through life fighting every step of the way?" she asked. "Everything was a confrontation with him."

"You're asking me?"

But you're like him in many respects. "Mom called him a bulldog, but that doesn't scratch the surface. How did she...? Why...?"

Sighing, she opened the car door and stepped out. Pine needles crunched under her feet, and she concentrated on where she was walking. A number of tiny, perfectly formed pinecones lay under the tree to her left. Pausing, she reached down and picked up a handful. Bringing them to her nostrils, she inhaled the rich, clean aroma of pitch and pine.

"What are you going to do with those?" Park asked.

"I'm not sure, maybe I'll leave them beside the cross." She'd told him what she'd learned about the white marker but not about the connection she felt, not just to Cherokee, but also the ranger who held himself responsible for Cherokee's death.

"What for? It's not like anyone's going to know."

"I will," she said, tucking the cones into her coat pocket.

"Fine. It just doesn't make any sense to me."

"I know it doesn't. And I'm sorry."

"Sorry?"

She took a deep breath, pushed it out. "That you don't get it."

Because she didn't have a key to the cabin, she stepped back when Park produced his and placed it in the lock. Instead of stepping inside, he stood with his hand on the knob.

"Are you ready?" he asked.

"As ready as I'm ever going to get."

* * * * *

"What the —? There should be more food than this."

44

After putting down the kindling she'd just brought in, Dayna joined her brother in the kitchen. He'd opened the cupboards where canned and packaged foods had always been kept, revealing a pitiful supply. A quick appraisal told her that if they were willing to subsist on tomato soup, canned tuna fish, and rice, they'd be all right. Fortunately, she'd gone to a grocery store after leaving her father, and if the refrigerator was still running, they'd have milk, eggs, butter, hamburger, and a couple of steaks.

"Mom was always in charge of that," she said unnecessarily. "But having a spouse with Alzheimer's changes priorities, doesn't it? Besides, I think she was sicker than we knew."

"Maybe."

"I'm just glad her heart didn't give out while she and Dad were here."

He grunted. "It would have served the old bastard right."

"He wouldn't have had any idea what was happening. If he'd tried to drive, he might have killed himself or someone else."

"Or gotten so lost we'd still be looking for him, not that I'd bother. You either. Go on, admit it."

Facing him, she spoke slowly. "It didn't happen, Park, so why are we having this conversation?"

"Because, someday, we're going to have to."

"No, we won't."

His look said he remained unconvinced, but he didn't challenge her. After asking him to go out for the cooler—Park could be as clueless when it came to the everyday details as their father had been—she closed the cupboard doors. Thinking about bringing warmth and thus a sense of life to the icy, musty room, she opened the door to the old potbellied stove. Unfortunately, it was heaped with ashes. After finding a short-handled shovel and a metal bucket, she started easing out the loose, gray remnants. She'd completed most of the job when she spotted something that looked like a small chunk of tin foil at the back. Sliding the shovel under it, she brought it out.

She'd zipped her jacket to her throat but suddenly felt hot. Picking up the ash-covered object, she rubbed it against her jeans and then held it up to the light.

Standing, she took in her surroundings. The small living room had a deceptively homey quality, the result of her mother's decorating touches with wildlife paintings on the barn board walls, rag rugs, old-fashioned floor lamps, and four easy chairs. Given how dark it was getting, it didn't make much sense to draw back the curtain over the large window facing the lake, but she'd done so anyway, thinking she'd at least get a glimpse of the lake before night.

"You wanna get that door for me? It's getting damn cold."

She hurried to close the door behind her brother, and then watched him carry the cooler into the kitchen and place it on the counter. He opened it and started pawing through its contents.

"Park?" She didn't recognize her voice.

"What?"

"You remember that we couldn't find Mother's wedding ring after she died?"

"Do I? The ambulance attendants must have taken off with it figuring the old man was too out of it to notice. I don't give a damn what they say, I'm going to sue."

"They didn't."

"How do you know?"

By way of answer, she held out her hand, her fingers cupped as if cradling the tarnished gold and dirty diamond.

"What...?"

"It was in the stove."

He dropped more than set down the carton of eggs he'd been holding and closed his thumb and forefinger over the ring. "What the hell...?"

"Oh Mom," she moaned. "I'm so sorry."

Park lifted the mess to the light. "Do you have any idea what this might do to its value? The last time the old man had it appraised, it came in at close to ten grand."

She nearly pointed out that neither the gold nor diamond had been destroyed, but she didn't care if it was worth a million dollars. More than once, she'd seen Judith Curran staring at her wedding ring as if reconciling herself to the fact that she wore chains.

"I can't believe Dad would do something like that," Park muttered. "Even with his mind going, he wouldn't have."

"Then Mom..."

Park stared at her.

By the time it was dark, the cabin was warm enough that Dayna had removed her coat and was cutting an onion to go with the steaks sizzling in the skillet. Frozen hash browns were in the oven and broccoli simmered in a pot she'd placed on the stove. Between the smells and warmth, she felt almost homey. Park emerged from the larger of the two bedrooms.

"Mice," he grumbled. "They've chewed on at least one of the blankets. It's disgusting."

"I don't remember mice being around when we were children, do you?"

"Just bats." Shuddering, he glanced up at the ceiling. "The old man insisted I crawl around in the attic and leave mothballs there, not that that did any good."

"That became my job after you left. The bats never bothered me, especially not once I saw how they went after mosquitoes."

"We have neighbors. I saw their light from the bedroom."

"Oh. I thought maybe all the other cabins were already closed up."

"All?"

It had been a long running joke that Lake Wolf was the exclusive place to have a cabin because it didn't have over a hundred of them like Diamond. The truth was that Diamond Lake sported a paved road, a resort and year-round accommodations and activities, to say nothing of Forest Service and law enforcement presence, thus making it more appealing to most people. "What are you doing?" she asked when Park reached for his jacket.

"There's been some major remodeling. If we have well-heeled neighbors, I want to know."

"But dinner's almost ready."

"I won't be gone long. By the way, you'd better check to see if there's an electric blanket on your bed. My sheets are so damp I thought I was going to have to wring them out. Hopefully, by cranking the controls all the way up, they'll be dry by the time I go to bed."

She wanted to point out that if there was only one electric blanket, the least he could have done was offer it to her, but before she could organize the words—not that she'd ever been any good at that sort of thing—he'd stepped outside.

Alone, she finished slicing the onion. Then, when a gust of wind rattled the ancient windows, she hurried over to the small radio that was all her father had allowed them to have and turned it on. The AM dial didn't pick up anything and on FM she had her choice of a religious station, hard rock, and oldies. She chose the last, wondering what it had been like for her mother once she and Park had moved away—escaped—and Judith had spent day after endless day here with nothing except the static and her husband.

* * * * *

Because the two flashlights he'd found didn't have working batteries, Park had to rely on what passed for night vision as he made his way through the evergreens that separated the two cabins. He walked into several branches until he caught onto the trick of holding his hands in front of his face. If their neighbors had a floodlight, they hadn't turned it on, a thought that gave him pause.

Dayna might wonder why, but he had no intention of turning theirs off when they went to bed. Not that he was afraid to be a million miles from civilization, but a man couldn't be too careful these days, not with all the crazies running around. In fact, as soon as he got back, he'd let his sister know he'd brought his Beretta along as insurance. If she'd been thinking—

Did his sister think? Of course she had to or she couldn't hold onto a job, but to think either of their parents would deliberately throw an expensive ring into the fire was ludicrous. His father hadn't so much as stepped over a penny in his life and his mother…

Frowning, he tried to come to some conclusion about what drove his mother. Judith Curran hadn't exactly walked ten paces behind her husband, but neither had she—as far as he knew—ever opposed Clifford Curran in any way.

Before he could throw up his defenses, thoughts of his mother turned to memories of his two failed marriages and from that to an image of his son. Scott, who was still young enough to embrace everything about life, would want to go fishing and hiking, activities that would have had to go by the board due to the press of time, but he'd been looking forward to having his son beside him, passing on selected images from the past, bonding with the lanky kid.

It hadn't happened. Scott's mother had gotten custody. Sudden, wrenching pain nearly brought Park to his knees, and unchecked tears blurred his vision. His mouth opened and a moan—high like a child's—pressed against his lips and it was all he could do to hold it back. Then, because this wasn't the first time he'd had to deal with the agony, he shoved Scott to the back of his mind.

The cabin to the east of theirs hadn't been this big before. He was certain of it. Built around the turn of the century, it had sat on rocks instead of having a foundation. However, what was there now held no resemblance to that listing old wreck. Gone were the weather-warped and unpainted walls and in place was...

After slipping closer and letting the inside lights fill in the blanks, he came to the not so brilliant conclusion that whoever now owned the property had major money. Log homes, and that's exactly what he was looking at, didn't come cheap. It sure as hell wasn't something a man or two could clabber together on weekends. No wonder they'd had so much interest in their place. Anyone with the least bit of savvy would come to the conclusion that the neighborhood, such as it was, was going upscale.

The wind cut through his jacket, and as he turned back toward his place, the rest of the wheels in Park's mind meshed. The contractors and subcontractors had finished their work, which meant that whoever was in there was probably the owner. If, in the morning, he walked over and introduced himself and suggested they share tools and labor, well, who knew what other conversations that might lead to. More than just conversations if he had his way. After all, a businessman, which he was, took advantage of the situations that presented themselves and a business contact made in the middle of a forest was just as good, if not better, than one forged in a corporate board room.

*　*　*　*　*

Wineglass in hand, Kandi settled herself on the couch and watched Beacan flip a switch near the front door. Light flamed away the darkness and revealed great shadow trees and beyond that the faint outline of Lake Wolf. She'd hoped the moon would be out tonight, but the clouds hid it.

Instead of returning to her, Beacan stood looking out the window, his hands clasped behind him, muscled forearms first tense and then relaxing.

"It's peaceful," he muttered.

Wind whipped the tops of the trees, and despite the heavy insulation, she caught the whisper of pine needles and the creak of branches. It seemed as if the log house was engaged in an occasional battle with the gusts, giving a little when it was struck, then instantly righting itself. Beacan had turned off the overhead light and the three-way bulb in the lamp near her was on its lowest wattage. Neil Diamond was singing about his attempts to find himself, the desperate-sounding *I am I said* reverberating through her.

"God, I needed this," Beacan muttered, his back still to her. "It's been insane this year."

"And yet you didn't want to be alone."

When he didn't answer, she vowed to remain silent. Even at rest, his body gave off an aura of strength, and she drew comparisons between him and what had happened to her one desperate night right after her fourteenth birthday when she'd stood at the side of a freeway, only her broken ankle stopping her from throwing herself under a semi. There'd been no fear, just fascination with speed and power and the promise of an end to everything. The difference between her and Beacan was that she'd been mesmerized by power while he couldn't possibly envy anything or anyone.

Fear anything.

Maybe that's what attracted her to him, by allowing him to have sex with her, she absorbed a little of his strength and power. Maybe.

"A man's got needs," he said as he returned to her and sat down. "It was either bring you along or take cold showers and play with myself."

She stared out the window. "You didn't have to choose me."

"You were the first girl who said yes."

"Girl?"

"Shit, don't get into that. You know what I mean."

"Yes, I do," she told him, then maybe because there was just the two of them and she couldn't think beyond that, she asked if he knew how old she was.

"Under forty." He wrapped his arm over her shoulder, his fingers inching down to her breasts.

"I should hope so. Come on, how old do you think I am?"

"Look, I don't play twenty questions. God, I'm stuffed. Where'd you learn to cook like that?"

"I used to work for a Mexican restaurant."

"Well, I have no complaints. Maybe we'll spend the winter here screwing each other and me getting fat on your cooking."

Although he'd worked his fingers under her neckline and was running his nails over her right nipple, her gaze and most of her attention remained on what she could see of the forest. She couldn't imagine ever getting tired of the view or the house, and other than a couple of co-workers, there was no one she'd miss. There were all those books, and even if some of them looked as if they'd been around forever, she wouldn't have any trouble burying herself in them.

"What do you think?" he asked. "Think we could go into hibernation, just you and me?"

Just you and me. "Your agent would never stand for it. You've got a new contract to negotiate."

"How do you know about that?"

"It's been in the papers."

"Well, don't believe everything you read. Twenty-six."

"What?"

"I think you're twenty-six. You've been engaged four times, but you fell out of love every time before the guys could get you down the aisle. You're still looking for Mr. Right and figure that when you find him, he'll sweep you off your feet and you'll live happily ever after."

He couldn't be more wrong.

* * * * *

"I've been watching this one for a few hours now, folks, and it's the real thing all right. I can't remember seeing a system this well-organized so early in the season, but that's what keeps the job interesting, trying to keep a step ahead of Mother Nature."

Homer Harkins paused while he shared a shrug with the female anchor. "I've been in contact with every source at my disposal, and they all say the same thing, winter's first storm is going to be a whopper. If you want a technical explanation of a whopper, I'm afraid I'm going to disappoint you, because it's still developing. What I can say is that by morning, even those of us living in the valley are going to be putting extra blankets on the beds, and if you have outside work to do, I'd suggest you get it done early. There's a doozey of a tail on this cold front which means it could be days before it plays itself out."

He took a breath. "And that's not all. There's another behind it."

After getting confirmation that he had another twenty seconds to fill, Homer went on. "To you I-5 truckers, make sure you have your chains with you before you head over the passes. I've missed some forecasts in my time, not many but one or two. This time you can take what I say to the bank. The next week or so is not the time to venture into the mountains if you don't know what you're doing."

Chapter Five

ॐ

Jace had been to the Mount St. Helens monument twice. Thanks to the wall-sized photographs that had been taken during the May 18, 1980 volcanic eruption, he'd felt as if he'd been there when the mountain erupted. At the time of the blow, he'd been too young to fully comprehend what was happening but had been fascinated by the great gray cloud spreading over his world. Then his interest had been captured by something else, and he'd forgotten that people had died as a result of the earth's determination to release underground pressure.

It wasn't until he'd started working at Crater that he'd understood and respected the incredible power involved in that explosion as well as the events behind Mount Mazama's ancient death and the consequent formation of the lake responsible for his employment. Now when visitors asked about comparisons between the two, he told them that three-tenths of a cubic kilometer of magma had erupted into the atmosphere when Mt. St. Helens blew compared to fifty plus kilometers for Mazama and during Mazama's death struggle, she had spewed ash over two hundred fifty thousand square miles. Once that had sunk in, the next question was inevitable. What were the chances that what was left of Mazama would come back to life?

It could happen, he told them.

Today he and Henri Lansky had Pacific Crest Trail to themselves, but Henri hadn't stopped talking since they'd hooked up this morning. Jace occasionally tried to remind Henri that they were here to document how much wear and

Vella Munn

tear the season's visitors had exacted on the trail, but as long as his friend didn't return to yesterday's conversation, he didn't care what they talked about.

When they'd started hiking, Henri had carried the clipboard on which to jot down notes on areas needing repair, but Jace had now taken over that chore. Although they'd been walking only a little over an hour, he was on the fourth page.

"You going to go see your folks next week?" Henri asked, picking up on what Jace had said a few days ago about his parents' car being in need of repair. "I don't imagine they're going to be able to get up here any time soon."

"No, they're not. I don't know. I'm thinking about it, but I only have two days off."

"Yeah, but they live near the fine lady you were going to marry." Henri gave him an appraising look. "You let a good one get away that time, my friend. Beautiful and intelligent to boot."

"Hm."

"Clamming up isn't going to change the fact that you screwed up big time. You know what my advice is?"

"No, but I'm sure I'm going to get it."

"I just hope you listen. Go after her. Beg forgiveness. Tell her you'll get counseling so you can start acting like a normal human being again. And even if she won't give you the time of day, get that counseling. You need it."

The wind was more than brisk this morning. He'd been watching it flatten the ground cover, and his ears ached from the pressure being exerted on them. During the night, most of the clouds had broken up and it had dropped to near freezing, but they were coming back and more purple than gray. His world was tinged dark lavender, everything feeling electric and alive.

"What's the weather forecast?" he asked.

"There you go changing the subject again. You've got serious problems, boy."

"I asked about the weather. That doesn't make me mentally unbalanced."

"Ha!"

Stopping, Henri looked around. He'd begun to lose his hair and wore it long at the top to downplay that fact. As a result, what he had now stood on end, adding another half foot to his considerable height. He tried to press it into place.

"We're going to have a storm," he said.

"You think?"

"Don't get smart with me, kid. I could take you with one hand tied behind my back."

He probably could. "What else does your crystal ball say? Or maybe it's your arthritis kicking up. Is it gonna snow?"

"I don't have no arthritis, boy, and don't you forget it." Henri stuck his finger in his mouth to moisten it, and then held it aloft. "Nope. No snow. Hail and two tornadoes but no snow."

The Crater Lake area was an insatiable mistress, who'd brought Jace under her spell the first time he'd come here. Cherokee's death had taught him how cruel she could be, at times he hated her, but he could never dismiss her. The awesome forces that resulted in her creation were what fascinated most people. Only a few concerned themselves with the reaction of the ancient people who'd been the only ones to see the immense explosion.

The woman he'd talked to yesterday, the one who'd asked about Cherokee's marker, had. She'd also left him feeling off balance. He'd had no intention of revealing anything of a personal nature around her, and yet he had.

And in the wake of what he'd blurted, her expression and big, lonely eyes had said she cared.

Henri's PTT went off, startling both men. The conversation with whoever had called didn't take long.

"Remember those engineers who were coming next week to inspect the lake boats' gas line?" Henri said as he placed the PTT back in its holder. "Well, they just showed up, and they want me around."

"What changed their schedule?"

"You got me."

"You want me to come with you?"

"There's no point in it since you, fortunately, haven't been involved in that particular bureaucratic mess, but if you don't want to be up here by yourself…"

"What are you talking about?"

"You know better than I do. Are you going to go all spacey again?"

Jace indicated his clipboard as proof of what was on his mind. As he did, the wind caught the pages and threatened to tear them free. "I'll see you tonight," he said.

"Hm. Your PTT works?"

"Yeah."

"And if I call, you'll answer it?"

"Yes, of course."

"I hope so."

The park's herd of Roosevelt elk left their summer home at Union Peak and headed for lower elevations. At the same time, golden mantle ground squirrels and chipmunks were in evidence everywhere, fat and sleek in preparation for hibernation. Jace's father sometimes complained about Oregon's rain, but he accepted it as part of nature's balance.

He couldn't say which was his favorite season because each had its own rhythm and reason. Winter was different from summer, not better or worse, simply different.

At least he'd seen the approaching season in that light until last year. Now he resented the warnings brought by the morning's harsh wind.

Cherokee was a ridiculous name for a blond Swede, but his parents had been hippies and for reasons that had remained hidden in hazes of marijuana smoke, Cherokee had satisfied their need to make some kind of a statement.

"You're the Injin," Cherokee had informed him one night as they sat drinking beer. "You wanna switch names?"

"Why not? Wrong tribe, but what the hell."

"Yeah? So what tribe are you from?"

"Klamath."

"You getting any of that government money?"

"Nope. My folks took one look at all the red tape and said to hell with it."

Cherokee had found that hysterical and Jace had joined in, their yucks punctuated with yeasty belches. It had been good that night, a sharing of hopes and dreams and a fair number of dirty jokes. They'd both been newly engaged and full of the wonder, excitement, and fear that went with the state, admitting things they wouldn't have if they'd been sober.

He'd never been clear on what had gone wrong between Cherokee and Suzanna, but if he'd reached out to his hurting friend, everything might have turned out different.

Spotting something out of the corner of his eye, Jace lost himself in the distraction. An eagle, and an immature one from the looks of it, circled overhead. The wind ruffled its feathers and gave a jerky quality to what for it was an effortless maneuver. The big birds had lost much of their mystique for him because despite their impressive wingspans, keen eyesight, and powerful talons, they were little more than scavengers. Still, watching this youngster was preferable to going back inside his mind.

Wondering if he could spot what the eagle was studying if he was a little higher, he scrambled up a crag. From here he couldn't see the lake's rim, let alone the lake itself, but rocks, trees, and sky all stood out in sharp relief. Except for the distant bird, he was alone and layered in silence. He needed to feel the weight of his pack, be aware of the boots snug around his feet, hold up the pencil he'd been using to make notes, have his PTT come to life, but none of those things happened. Instead, he soared and floated with the eagle, watched a nearby pinecone fall to the ground, heard his own breathing.

It was darker close to the trees than in the open spaces, and his mind went into that darkness. He couldn't say where one tree left off and another began and the line between trunk and roots blurred. The wilderness was relentless and patient. A sapling sprang from the earth, grew and reached for the heavens. Then it either reached old age or was felled by the elements. When it crashed to the ground, it was slowly absorbed until eventually nothing remained.

Like Cherokee?

Groaning, Jace tried to wrench free, but his mind and sight slipped deeper into the shadows and he saw.

Cherokee.

Waiting for him.

* * * * *

Dayna stood on the dock her father had had built several years ago. Longer and sturdier than what had been here while she was growing up, this one could be pulled out of the water before the lake froze over. She'd come out here this morning to determine whether she and Park could tie a rope to her car's bumper and snake out the two heavy sections, but this was her first opportunity to be at Lake Wolf's edge, and she allowed it to absorb her.

Thanks to the wind, its surface reminded her of wrinkled fabric. Ducks were swimming about in the middle of it, and she was careful not to disturb them. She'd found several old coats, but the one in the best shape had belonged to her father so she wore one her brother had used as a teenager. The arms were too long and the hem came to her knees. There was a hood she probably should be using, but if she did, she wouldn't be able to hear the ducks or fully sense the wilderness.

Alone. Although she lived by herself, the state felt different here than it did at home. Maybe it was because there weren't any power poles around Lake Wolf, the electric wires having been placed underground to protect them from the elements. Maybe isolation made more of an impact here because the wilderness was its own presence. And maybe the past had something to do with—

"Good morning."

Startled, Dayna faced the newcomer. The woman, around her age, was half buried in a leather coat. She'd caught her long, dark hair at the base of her neck, but the wind whipped the ends about her shoulders.

"I'm sorry," the woman said. "Did I scare you?"

"It's all right. I was just—communing with nature I guess."

Smiling a smile that didn't quite reach her eyes, the woman made her way down the bank and stepped onto the dock. "I can relate to that. I've never seen anything so—so peaceful."

Given the way the dock was rocking and the gray cast over the rippling lake surface, Dayna wasn't inclined to call their view peaceful. Energized, maybe. Potentially dangerous, yes.

"I was listening to the ducks," she explained. "They're getting ready to leave."

"Are they? I love looking at them, thinking how wonderful it is that they're free to do what nature intended them to do."

"In other words, not in a cage?"

"Exactly." The woman held out her hand, shrugging back the sleeve that threatened to engulf it. "I'm Kandi Ferber. I'm staying over there." She indicated the log home.

Kandi? It sounded like—like a stage name for an exotic dancer. The young woman's striking features were expertly made-up. Dayna shook hands and introduced herself, then explained what she and her brother were doing here.

"Beacan has to close up too," Kandi said. "I don't know how much help I'm going to be. Is there a lot to getting these places ready for winter?"

"Enough. The most important thing is not leaving any water in the lines. If there is, it'll freeze and burst the pipes. That's a beautiful place you have."

"Oh, it isn't mine. I'm just...visiting."

"Well, I hope you'll tell—Beacan did you say his name was?—Beacan that I'm impressed."

"So am I."

Before Dayna could think of anything to say, the ducks took flight with a great rush of wings. She and Kandi watched their loud and disorganized leave-taking.

"Are they gone for good?" Kandi asked once the sound had faded.

"Who knows? They gathered like that every fall when I was a child. Most times they were still around when we closed up."

"You haven't been here lately?"

"Not since I was a teenager."

"Really? If I had a place like this, nothing could keep me away."

Turning her back on the lake, Dayna stared at what she could see of the bark-brown cabin with its abomination of a roof. In deference to her brother's economizing, she'd turned off the interior lights when she came outside with the result that it looked more like a pen and ink drawing than a solid structure.

"It wasn't an idyllic experience," she explained. "My father wasn't easy to live with. That roof—I'm sure you noticed it—was his idea. Anything to give the Forest Service a hard time."

"And you could hardly wait to get away."

"Yes."

"You don't regret it?"

"No."

"Good."

They stood looking at the cabin for several minutes. It wasn't until Kandi shifted her weight that Dayna acknowledged how much she'd revealed to this stranger.

"Beacan?" she asked abruptly. "Is he strong?"

"Very. Why?"

"Because—" She laughed. "Park and I need to pull the dock out, but I don't know how we're going to do it on our own. Of course if your boyfriend's willing to let us borrow his Bronco…"

"I'll ask, and he isn't my boyfriend. He's... God, I love the air here! If I could, I'd bottle it up and take it with me. The stuff I have to breathe at work has been recycled forever."

"Oh? Where do you work?"

"A hospital. Crazy, isn't it?"

"Are you a nurse?"

"No. I work in the billing department. Spend my days trying to make sense of the insurance industry, as if that's possible."

"It doesn't sound easy."

"It isn't. What about you? Do you like what you do?"

Even with her brother's coat, Dayna was beginning to shiver. Still, she stayed. "The nursery I worked for just went out of business."

"So you're pounding the pavement?"

Instead of answering, Dayna allowed her attention to stray to the treetops. They swayed and bent, disorienting her and making her slightly sick to her stomach. She'd been nine or ten the year a ponderosa had torn a chunk out of the bathroom roof. Downed trees were always a possibility, and her father had spent years trying to convince the Forest Service to let him cut down several large ones close to the cabin. They'd declined his request.

Before she could tell Kandi that, Park called out, his tone irritated.

"Duty calls," she said. "Look, I'm glad you and your bo—your friend are here. You never know what might happen."

Kandi's gaze strayed to the bucking treetops. "No. We never do."

Chapter Six

ဆ

"Look at it. Just look at it."

Dayna did as her brother ordered. However, it took a few moments for her eyes to adjust to the poor lighting inside the workshop. Her father had always been fanatical about neatness. There was a place for everything and woe be to whoever left so much as a nail out.

In the past, the overhead light always held a three hundred-watt bulb, but what was in there now provided barely enough illumination to reach the corners. However, the greatest difference lay in the shop's contents. Instead of clean work surfaces and room to move about, the small space put her in mind of a jammed storage unit. Tools, many of them still in their original packages, covered every inch and were stacked nearly to the ceiling.

"What…?" she began, and then fell silent. She counted no less than four unopened radial saws, two identical and the others so close in output capacity that they might as well have been. Next to them was a bulky metal cutting band saw that could do both vertical and horizontal work although what her father would use it for was beyond her.

"Mom said the things he was doing made no sense, but I didn't realize it had gotten this bad," she admitted.

Park made his way to the far end of the workbench and picked up three new hammers, which he added to another five. "Neither did I," he said. "Mom asked if she could cancel their credit cards, even the ones that only had his name on them. I told her she'd better check with whoever had issued them, but when I asked her what was up, she didn't tell me."

"And you didn't ask."

"You think I should have?"

"No." She shook her head, the movement making her dizzy. "Or maybe the truth was, we both should have, but you know how things were."

When her brother didn't answer, she took his silence as confirmation that he hadn't forgotten what it had been like to grow up with a drill sergeant of a father and a mother who existed somewhere behind blank stares and tiptoeing.

Park picked up a box with a Home Depot sales sticker on it. "An arc welder? I'm going to return it."

"What?"

"All this stuff." Park indicated their surroundings. "As long as it hasn't been used, I can get my money back."

His money hadn't been involved, not that she'd waste her breath pointing that out. "I'm surprised the buyers didn't say anything," she mused. "They must have seen…"

"They kept their mouths shut because they hoped we wouldn't find out and they could do what they wanted with this crap. Well, they're wrong." He carried the angle grinder outside and came back for another armload.

"What are you doing?" she asked.

"Isn't it obvious? Come on, help me carry this to your car."

"What? Park, it'll never fit and even if it did, my car doesn't have that kind of suspension."

"What are you saying, that you're willing to throw it all away?"

"No. Of course not. But what if we take what costs the most and is the easiest to return? Besides, right now that isn't the priority. You came in for a ladder so we could work on that stove pipe, remember?"

Park grumbled something to the effect that he couldn't get to the ladder until he'd cleared a path to it. Working together, in silence, they uncovered an ancient wooden ladder. Although they hauled the wooden shutters outside in order to free up space, there was no sign of the extension ladder they both remembered.

"I bet the jokers working on that log home took it," Park snapped. "Go over and demand they return it."

"What we have here will work. Later, we'll tell them Dad wasn't responsible for his actions and have they seen anything that doesn't belong to them."

"They'll just lie. Dayna, you're such a coward. Always have been."

* * * * *

"Damn!" Releasing the ladder he'd just dragged over to the rear of the cabin, Park held up his hand. A sliver was imbedded in the web of flesh between his thumb and forefinger. He tried to pull it out, but his nails were too thin for him to get a decent grip.

"Let me see," Dayna suggested.

"You can't."

"Let me see," she repeated. Before he could point out that her nails were as short as his, she took his hand and squeezed so the splinter stuck straight out. He felt her nails clamp around his penetrated flesh, then a sharp sting followed by relief.

"How did…?"

"Strong nails." She held up her hand to demonstrate. "That's what I get from working in the dirt for a living, I guess."

The thought of what might happen if she had soil imbedded in her flesh gave him an uneasy moment, but from what he could tell, she kept her hands well-scrubbed. He wanted to go in for soap and water, but the wind had grown in strength since morning, meaning they'd have to get the roof work done as soon as possible.

After shaking the ladder to test its positioning, she scrambled up and onto the metal roof, the heavy rope they'd tied to a tree on the opposite side and thrown over the peak giving her something to grip. He climbed up the first four steps so he could hand her the length of wire he wanted her to wrap around the stovepipe, then reached in his pocket for the pliers she'd need to snug the wire to the eyebolt drilled into the roof.

"It's slippery," she said. "If I fall, grab me."

You won't fall if you're careful, he nearly pointed out, but didn't. More than just cautious in the way she moved up there, she handled herself with an innate gracefulness that held him in awe. He remembered a child who'd learned to walk at ten months and mastered a bicycle before her fourth birthday. Along with her competence as a runner, she'd started playing high school varsity softball and basketball while a freshman. That, if nothing else, had earned grudging respect from their father.

Because his attention was focused on her, he knew how much stress her muscles were being subjected to as she gripped the rope and stretched toward the pipe that would flatten under snow's weight if it weren't anchored in place. He breathed a little easier when she returned to a sitting position as she twisted the wire. Then she began inching to her left where the eyebolt waited. By wrapping the rope around her waist, she managed to free her hands so she could slip the wire through the eyebolt. Then she twisted the wire back around itself, using the pliers to stretch it even tighter.

"How does it look?" she asked without looking down at him.

"From here, good. Is the wire taut?"

She ran her hand over it. "Not bad. I might be able to haul on it a little more."

"Don't try. You don't have anything to brace yourself against."

"Okay. Look, I'm going to start back down, but I can't see where my feet are going. Will you guide me?"

"Sure. All right. A little to your left."

When, finally, her toes rested against the top step, she let out a long sigh. "This is a job for the young, the young and foolhardy. Now if your son was here…"

"He isn't, all right!"

"I was just making conversation, trying to calm myself."

"I wanted him," he heard himself say. "All that crap his mother gave me about him missing too much school was because she wants him to herself."

"I'm sorry."

"It's not your problem. You going to get down?"

"Yes. Park—" She flicked him a glance. "I know it's hard for you."

"The kid's happy, and he sure as hell doesn't want for anything. By the time he's ready for college, I'll have enough in investments that he won't have to borrow a red cent."

"Money doesn't make up for—"

"Damn it, I'm getting a crick in my neck. Are you going to spend the day up there?"

She stared down at him but didn't say anything. He couldn't do a damn thing about the look on her face, nothing except turn his back on her.

What happened next would remain a mystery to him. The wind might have slammed into her or instead of settling onto the middle of the step, she'd put too much of her weight on the side. Maybe the ground hadn't been as stable as they'd thought and the footing had given way. Possibly the metal overhang the ladder was leaning against had sagged and maybe—

Whatever the reason, one moment she was beginning her descent and the next, she and the ladder were tilting, tilting. His sister descended with the same grace she'd exhibited while running down a fly ball or going after a layup or pacing herself through a long race. Then she struck the ground.

Silent, Dayna felt her mind switch to slow motion. Park's fingers tore at her coat sleeve, his grip not stopping her but slowing her freefall and turning her so that she no longer followed the ladder's lead. Generations of pine needles had slid off the roof and piled up beneath it, turning it spongy. She had time to will her body to relax, and then she hit the ground, not with a bone-breaking thud but more as if she'd jumped into a mound of sawdust.

"Dayna? Dayna, are you all right?"

"I...don't know."

"Don't move. Damn it, what happened!"

"I fell."

Although she was still trying to assess her injuries, she steeled herself for his sarcastic retort. Instead, he dropped to his knees beside her. "Don't move," he repeated. "If you've broken your back..."

From what she could tell, all her body parts still worked. Judging by its throbbing, she guessed her hip had absorbed the initial impact. Her mouth had snapped shut, causing her to bite her tongue, and she felt a headache coming on, probably the result of her brain being rattled.

"I-I think I'm going to live."

"Thank God."

Park didn't believe in a higher power, at least she didn't think he did. He'd placed his hands on her shoulders, his fingers pressing, probing.

"How did it happen?" she managed. "Never mind. I know. I was always a klutz."

"You aren't a klutz! I don't know — the ladder — I thought it was stable but... Sis, I'm sorry."

He never called her "sis", never apologized for anything. "I want to get up."

"No! Not — "

"What happened?" a female voice demanded.

Dragging her attention off her brother, she spotted Kandi Ferber and a tall man hurrying toward them.

"We heard a crash," Kandi said, sounding breathless. "Oh my God. You fell."

Was God going to come up in every conversation today? Now that she'd been here awhile, she realized how cold the ground was and that her right leg was folded tightly against itself. Taking the remedying of that as her first goal, she started to straighten her leg.

"Don't!" Park ordered. "Damn it, Dayna, don't move!"

"Sis" hadn't lasted very long, had it? Still, she was grateful for its brief appearance. The big stranger squatted beside her, his bulk forcing Park to lean away.

"Tell me what you feel," the newcomer said. He sounded calm, almost unconcerned. "Starting at the top of your head."

"I-I'm all right. You don't have."

"Where does it hurt?"

Her tongue where she'd bitten herself, she admitted, burned. The sudden, fierce headache was already receding and her hip would sport a colorful but far from life threatening bruise. She was cold and getting colder.

"How many fingers?" The man held his hand in front of her face.

"Five."

"Good. Now I want you to track my fingers as I move them around."

"Are you a doctor?" Park asked.

"No, but I've had enough heavy objects run into me that I know what it feels like." The man moved his hand in a semicircle and she followed its movement as much to satisfy her own curiosity as because he'd ordered her to.

"Good. Now, how's the head?"

"Fine. Really. Can I get up?"

Although Park hissed a protest and Kandi shot her companion a questioning look, the stranger slid his hands under her shoulder and helped her into a sitting position. Her hip spoke to her in a no uncertain tone.

"Thank heavens for soft ground and a substantial coat," she said. Catching sight of the harried look on her brother's face, she gave him a small smile. "And thank you for pushing the ladder out of the way."

"I didn't think. I just reacted."

"So did I." She took a deep breath, and then eased away from the man.

Standing took effort and concentration. Dizziness made a brief appearance. Not waiting for approval, she took an experimental step and had nearly accomplished the second when her hip gave out on her, and if the man hadn't been so close, she probably would have ended up on her knees. Although she tried to pull away, he picked her up and carried her into the cabin. Her brother and Kandi trailed behind them.

"We've got to make sure you don't fall asleep for several hours," the man said as he deposited her in the nearest chair. "A concussion is nothing to fool around with."

"I appreciate everything you've done," she said as she sank into the recliner. "Please, what's your name? I can't thank—"

"Beacan Jarrard. Don't thank me. I'm just glad—"

"Jarrard? The baseball player?" she asked, flustered. "Of course. I'm sorry I didn't—"

"You had other things on your mind," Beacan said while Park stared at him.

"I know…but…"

"Baseball?" Park echoed. "Major leagues?"

"Yes," Beacan said.

Stepping forward, Park pumped hands with Beacan. "If you hadn't been here to check her out—if there's anything I can do, anything at all, please don't hesitate to ask. "Ah," he cleared his throat, "I invest in real estate, mostly in the Northwest but sometimes in California if the price is right. There's always room for more players so if you're interested in—"

"No." Beacan stepped away from Park. "I'm not."

"Just because you've never flipped properties doesn't mean it isn't something you shouldn't consider," Park continued. "I'm not into risky ventures and my track record, well, let's just say I've done well for myself. Well indeed."

"I already have a financial advisor."

"But is he diversified? Most are experts in one, maybe two areas but they can't possibly know everything. I'm simply offering—"

"I know what you're offering, and I'm not interested. Look." Beacan's tone dropped a notch. "I already have more money than any one man could possibly need or want."

She'd seen Park's mouth drop open before, but never had his eyes held such a look of incomprehension. "Well, I, for one," she said in an attempt to work past the awkwardness, "am glad you bought a cabin with some of it."

Beacan shrugged. "What I gave you was a layman's assessment. You really should see a doctor."

"Maybe I will once I'm back in civilization." She held out her hand, but when he engulfed it in his massive one, it was all she could do to not to pull free. "Thanks," she managed.

* * * * *

Beacan and Kandi hadn't stayed long. They'd left after making Park promise to come for them if her condition deteriorated.

"I can't believe it," Park muttered after she'd filled him in on exactly who Beacan Jarred was. "His share of the World Series bonus alone has to be more than most people earn in a year, years. Damn, I wonder who his agent is? That might—"

"Park. What are you doing?"

"Thinking." He paced from one end of the living room to the other. "The sharks must already be around him. I've got to find…"

"You're one of the sharks."

He stopped pacing. "Just because you have no ambitions, don't try to tell me how to live my life."

"Park, I don't want to be having this conversation." The little she'd said exhausted her, but she sucked in air in an effort to revive and calm herself. To ignore the wound his words had opened.

"What's wrong?" he demanded.

"Nothing."

"I heard you gasp."

"I was just… Never mind."

Park stared at her for so long that she dropped her gaze. A moment later, she heard the sound of the liquor cabinet door being opened. She thought to tell him that it wasn't a good idea for her to have alcohol right now, but when he rejoined her, he carried a single glass half full of amber liquid. He sank into the couch opposite her and took a healthy swig.

"You didn't cry out," he said. "Why not?"

Chapter Seven

🔊

The cloud, a dark and tattered blanket, settled over the lake and covered the gray surface like a shroud. Deep inside, the ducks continued their restless movement, but now when they gave voice, the cries and calls were muffled.

Dayna, who'd been tearing the covers off old paperbacks and stuffing the pages into the fire, looked up. Because the cabin was situated deep within the trees and her view of the lake limited, she couldn't tell if anything had changed about the nearby water. Just the same, she felt compelled to take a closer look—either that or there was something about disposing of musty paper that demanded distraction.

After getting her assurance that she felt fine, Park had returned to the workshop. She considered telling him what she had in mind, but her motive wasn't easily explained, even to herself. After putting on her coat, she stepped outside, noting that the wind hadn't let up its attack on the landscape. For the first time she felt, not kinship with the wind, but flickering unease.

She'd been to Wolf a hundred times as a storm blew in and saw its energy as a playful thing. And even if play sometimes turned into battle, that was for the dead of winter, not now.

She wasn't afraid of her surroundings. Surely, coming across Cherokee's cross and finding her mother's wedding ring, which she'd kept in the ashes, each played their own role in her fitful mood. That and knowing that except for their immediate neighbors, she and her brother might be the only human beings for miles around.

A thin sliver of water showed at the edge of the bank, but the end of the dock had been swallowed by cold mist. Beacan had agreed to use his Bronco to haul the dock out, but first she would have to walk out onto the barely visible dock and unfasten the bolts securing it to the metal poles driven into the lake bottom. At the moment, setting foot on something that flimsy and nearly no longer existing was the last thing she wanted to do.

Instead of refuting or reinforcing that statement, she opted to head east. She wouldn't go far, just enough that she could settle the question of whether the other cabins had already been boarded up. As a child, she'd occasionally slipped away from her father, but even when she found other children to talk to, she hadn't dared stay long.

She'd traveled just a short while when she realized the mist had consumed the water. Although it had yet to reach the path she was on, she half believed damp tentacles were curling around her ankles. The wind pushed at her, forcing her to alter her posture to accommodate the constant change. Several times, she wiped grit out of her eyes. What entered her nostrils felt cold and alive, and when she looked upward, it was into a heavy, ashen weight. It had begun to snow.

After rubbing her cheeks to increase circulation, she opened her mouth and stuck out her tongue, capturing a few flakes. They tasted newly minted, and even when flakes slapped at her face, her sense of excitement remained. Why shouldn't she live in the moment, it wasn't as if she had anywhere else she wanted to be.

Maybe ever.

The first cabin she reached had been built in a small meadow. Although seedlings took root there every year, none lived long enough to grow to any height. As a result, she could easily make out the small covered porch with wood stacked around twin windows covered with sheets of plywood. Knowing that those people had no intention of returning soon stopped her in mid-swallow, stilled and silenced her childlike mood.

After working moisture back into her throat, she forced herself to walk closer. The foundation, as such, consisted of rocks piled one against the other with four by fours laid over that. The timbers served as the subflooring. She'd been inside.

Once.

Frowning, she stopped with a foot on the first of three stairs leading to the porch. A memory flickered just beyond capture, teasing and haunting her. Trying to pull the threads into her conscious mind didn't work, but instead of abandoning the past, she stepped onto the porch and ran her hand over stacked lodgepole that served as firewood. Then she turned her back on the cabin and stared at the lake or rather the gray mantle over it. Fat snowflakes swirled this way and that, defying gravity. Children were sometimes like that, all fitful and aimless energy, oblivious to any constraint.

She'd started to shake her head at the thought when the not-quite-a-memory solidified. She couldn't say how old she'd been at the time, maybe eight or nine. She didn't think Park had been at the cabin, not that it mattered. Maybe she'd grown tired of doing whatever task her father had given her and had wandered off. She should have known better than to give into spontaneity.

And maybe she'd run away—a child hurrying down a dirt path to the neighbors because there was nowhere else to go. There'd been a dog sitting on the porch, large and lanky and black. As she hesitated, it had gotten to its feet, jumped down, and headed toward her. It had had its mouth open, long youth-white teeth exposed. Curiosity and fear had warred inside her, but she'd remained where she was, small pink hands held in front of her.

The dog's tail had begun wagging, and although she'd known little about dogs, she'd taken that as a good sign. It hadn't growled but tilted its head, regarding her.

"He won't hurt you," someone had said. "He loves everyone."

How could that be, she'd timidly asked the elderly man who'd spoken to her. The dog didn't know her so how could it like her? The man—his expansive belly had been his most notable feature—had explained that dogs' emotions were uncomplicated. They were hungry or full, rested or tired. As long as someone didn't mistreat them, they loved and trusted.

She, who had never seen a dog in her house and knew she never would, had wrapped her arms around the creature's strong neck. In response, its dark, damp tongue had flicked out and over her cheeks and neck. Sobbing, she'd buried her face in its fur and felt loved.

* * * * *

"It's snowing."

"Is it?"

Kandi forced her attention off the view from the picture window and onto Beacan who sat at the table, his head bent. Whoever had been in charge of the remodeling had left a packet of material for him and he had been pouring through it for the better part of an hour.

"It's beautiful," she said. "Don't you want to see?"

"What?"

"I said…" she started then stopped because Beacan was getting to his feet. Not for the first time she noted that his every movement was deliberate and although he was in his early thirties, something about him seemed older.

"You must be glad the season's over." She stepped to one side to afford him a clear view.

"What?"

"All that physical activity. After a while a person needs to rest."

"I'm fine. Not a damn thing wrong with me."

Isn't there? "I used to waitress, gave it up when I pinched a nerve in my neck from carrying heavy trays so I know a little about what the human body is and isn't designed to do."

He continued to stare at the snow.

"Do you want to go outside?" Part of her wanted to touch him, but the emotion was alien and easily denied.

"It's not going to last long."

"No, it probably won't. But don't you want to, I don't know, commune with nature. Get some exercise."

"I guess."

He took longer to get ready than she did, making her wait while he propped one foot at a time on a chair in order to lace his boots. As they stepped outside, she wondered what they'd talk about—or more precisely, what she'd come up with in order to keep the conversation going. If she'd left him to his reading, she could have stepped alone into the wilderness.

By the time they reached the lake, she'd amended her observation regarding his mood. His voice animated the way it had been when he'd first seen the remodeling, he told her about the time he and several teammates had gone duck hunting in northern Idaho. The temperature hadn't once gotten above freezing, but the expedition had been successful with everyone bagging his limit. She turned her head so the heavy flakes struck her cheek.

"Don't tell me," he said. "You're one of those anti-gun activists."

The wind tore at her hair, raked her forehead and scalp. "I've never been any kind of an activist. I just can't understand how someone can shoot anything for reasons other than survival."

"It's legal."

"I know it's legal." He'd stopped to stare at the mist coating the lake, and she did the same, standing far enough away that she couldn't feel his heat. So their surroundings could speak to her. "It's just something I'll never do."

"A pacifist?"

If she had been a pacifist, she'd probably be dead. "What was it?" she asked. "A male bonding thing?"

"Whatever. So what do you and your girlfriends do if you're not into shooting Bambi? Shop?"

"I don't have many girlfriends."

"Why not?"

"I just don't." The lake had been home to uncounted ducks earlier, but maybe they'd flown away. "Did it snow when you were hunting?"

"Not that time, but it's happened more than once during elk season."

This man she'd given her body and several days of her life to saw nothing wrong with tracking down and destroying a creature capable of surviving the harshest weather. If she wasn't careful, she might wind up hating him.

"Has it ever been a problem?" she said to silence the thought. "I mean getting caught in a blizzard would make everything else unimportant, wouldn't it?"

"Yeah, it would."

"And then what? There's nothing a person can do until it's over, is there?"

Reaching out, he took hold of her coat at the shoulder and drew her to his side. Then he began working his fingers under the opening at her throat. "Don't worry your pretty little head about that. I'll take care of you."

"The great white hunter?"

"You can call me whatever turns you on. So, you want to go fishing or are you opposed to that too?"

Although her breasts filled her bra's cup, he'd managed to find room for his forefinger in there. When he raked his nail over her nipple, she sucked in a deep, icy breath.

"Beacon." She clamped her fingers around his wrist. "I don't…"

"Lighten up. No one's going to see."

"That's not the point."

"Then what is?"

"You don't own me. All right." She jerked away. "You do not own me!"

"What the hell is your problem?"

"I don't have a problem! You're the one who thinks he can do what he wants with me, when he wants."

"You're the one who came here with me, sweetheart."

He stepped toward her, long and powerful legs erasing the distance between them. Unable to stop herself, she shrank away.

"What the—? I'm not going to hit you."

"Go to hell."

"Did you think I was going to?"

She didn't, couldn't answer.

"You did, didn't you? Why?"

* * * * *

Beacan didn't know where Kandi had gone, but she wouldn't be gone long. After all, the snow wasn't letting up, and she hadn't dressed that warmly. He used a few minutes of his time alone to remove the outside lights and wrap plastic around the exposed sockets. He thought about splitting some wood, but the idea of repeatedly swinging an axe in the cold gave him pause. He could wander over to the brother and sister and ask about draining water pipes, but the brother might start in on his investment schemes again.

Going inside, he opened a beer and took a long pull. Then he scooted a rocking chair near the window and sat down. He couldn't really call what was happening a storm because the flakes were taking their own sweet time reaching the ground, and there weren't that many of them. They twisted first one way and then the other, reminding him of a blender in action.

"She's going to freeze her nose off," he said, surprised because he'd spoken aloud.

What did he need with a broad with an attitude? It wasn't as if he couldn't have his pick of women who knew better than to cop an attitude about hunting or fishing or a little foreplay. Okay, so he'd made a mistake by bringing her up here. As soon as they got home, they'd go their separate ways. It wasn't as if he hadn't done that before.

He'd started to take another drink when he spotted movement at the window to his left. He made the brother wait fifteen, maybe twenty seconds after knocking before responding.

"I don't mean to interrupt you," Park said as Beacan opened the door. "But I've been trying to get my cell phone to work. I'm wondering if you've been any more successful."

"I didn't bring mine."

"You didn't?"

The not too gracefully aging man continued to stand in the opening, letting in the cold. Although he figured he'd regret it, Beacon invited him in, then explained that his primary motive for coming here had been to get away from everything, including phone calls.

"Are you sure that's wise?" Park glanced at Beacan's beer, licked his lips. "I mean, considering what almost happened to my sister…"

"She's okay?"

"I think so, but even if she wasn't, she wouldn't tell me." He shrugged. "We brought Dayna's car. It's useless if conditions go to hell."

"You can leave before the road becomes impassable, can't you?"

"I don't want to pack up until the cabin's ready for the new owners. There's no way I'll give them anything to complain about. Your place is really something." He indicated his surroundings.

Resigning himself to the inevitable, Beacon offered to show the other man around. "I'd love it," Park said as he figured he would. "But I'm not disturbing you? If you and your lady friend…"

"She's gone for a walk."

"So has Dayna." He shrugged. "This isn't easy for her."

"What isn't? Selling the place?"

"Hell no. My guess, she can hardly wait to be rid of it. Our childhood was no cakewalk. Having to come back here is probably bringing it all up again."

"Oh," Beacan said. Then because he didn't want to hear more, he indicated the spiral staircase leading to the loft. "I debated having something that could be pulled up out of the way when it wasn't in use, but this doesn't take up that much room."

Park whatever his last name was, seemed fascinated by everything that had been done, and although Beacon wondered whether Park's interest was an attempt to ingratiate himself, it didn't matter. Kandi had listened politely when he told her about the project, but he could tell she didn't know squat about foundations and load-bearing walls and modern electrical requirements. Park, on the other hand, knew more than he expected.

"Like I said," Park told him when he asked how he'd become knowledgeable about installing thermo pane windows, "I invest in property."

"Is that what your cabin is, an investment?"

"Once, maybe. Not anymore."

"That's right. You're selling it."

"You're damn right I am."

A wind gust slammed into the side of the house, shaking the structure. It occurred to Beacan that this was the first time he'd heard anger in his visitor's voice. Park walked over to the door and pressed his weight against it, maybe assuring himself that it wouldn't fly open. "Let me ask you something. You don't have to answer if you don't want to, but— Do you love your father?"

"What? Sure."

"Well, I hate mine."

* * * * *

The buck's legs trembled, but the doe he'd been following no longer refused him by lashing out with sharp hooves. Instead, she'd lifted her tail high, and when he stretched his nose toward her, she extended hers. After nibbling the side of her neck, he moved behind her. She was ready, the smell of her heating his blood and swelling his organ. She sucked in air, her body spasmed a sharp spasm, and yet she held her ground, her rear end still offered.

He was in his prime with five winters behind him. The season for spilling seed was upon him and he'd run off the young bucks with their puny antlers and immature muscles. Although he knew nothing counting success, since the need to mount a doe had come over him, he'd lost over twenty pounds and impregnated a half dozen.

He nipped the doe's hindquarters, ordering her to open herself to him. She smelled of fear and excitement, and he rose on his rear legs, settling his front ones on her back. His head roared. Even as he thrust himself into her, something new reached him.

Cold. Snow. Wind.

Winter. Hunger and starvation waited if he remained high in the mountains.

Chapter Eight

ଲ

The storm's strength increased as morning marched into early afternoon. Like a grizzly freed from captivity, it hurtled itself through the sky, and yet its full power was felt only in the atmosphere. Near the earth, it manifested itself alternatively as tiny, deadly, driven ice crystals and fat, lacy snowflakes that covered the mountains with a fine dusting of white.

"I don't believe it!" Park yelled. "Of all the stupid luck!"

"Then don't stand out there!" Dayna yelled back.

Her brother grumbled something she couldn't hear, but although he gestured that he wanted her to join him on the heaving dock, she couldn't force herself to take the necessary steps. He'd been the one to insist they take a look at the tire sections that protected the sides of the dock. Her observation that the condition didn't matter if they were going to pull out the dock and responsibility belonged to the new owners anyway had fallen on deaf ears.

Ignoring her suggestion that he retreat to safety, Park got down on his knees on the wet boards and leaned over the side. His bare head and upper back were already covered with snow.

As his form lost definition, she allowed her attention to turn to what she could see of the trees. They were dancing, not a graceful waltz but wild and hard and angry. The cutting wind was coming from the north. As a result, shouldn't the trees all be bending in the same direction? But there was no order or rhythm and those growing close to each other occasionally slammed together. The resultant scream set her nerves on edge, and she felt sorry for the punished limbs and pine needles. Still, she couldn't deny the energy coursing through her.

Life was like this storm. The world closed in around her, diminished her and at the same time made her part of the tempest. Either, she thought, she'd change into something she'd never been or become nothing. At the moment she cared only about the journey.

"Dayna!" Park bellowed.

"What?"

"I want you—need..." Whatever he said after that, she couldn't hear. Hoping to make that clear to him, she cupped a hand over her ear. The gesture earned her a look of exasperation or maybe anger.

"Park, get off!" she said with the wind driving her words. "If you stay out there, you're going to get hurt."

He shot her another annoyed glance, but either her warning had penetrated or he'd come to the same conclusion—more likely the latter. She'd been squatting near where the dock butted against the shore, now she stood and backed away. As she did, the wind pushed against her back with enough force that she stumbled. She started to whirl around, but before she'd completed the action, the force was gone.

"Park, if you fall in..."

"What is he doing?"

She shook her head at Kandi's question. "I wish I knew."

Kandi still wore the oversized man's jacket she'd had on earlier and had put on a stocking cap that covered her ears. Wondering how much the other woman could hear, she turned her attention back to her brother.

By walking straddle-legged, he'd managed to get closer to shore. If he fell into the lake, he'd risk frostbite, but this close to the shore, the water was less than waist-deep. She knew that, and yet falling snow and mist had changed the lake, made it both less and more, taken it out of one realm and into another beyond her comprehension.

Without saying a word, Kandi scrambled onto the dock and extended both hands toward Park. He lurched more than reached for her. Much of the color had been stripped from his face, and Dayna wondered if he too was questioning everything he'd believed about their surroundings.

"I've got you," Kandi said, her voice fighting the nature-made sounds, looking strong and sure and determined. "Come on. You can make it."

Looking like a drunken sailor, Park managed to flounder and stumble his way off the dock, but even when solid ground was under him, he continued to grip Kandi's hands.

"I had no idea." He sucked in a breath. "If I'd known it was going to get that bad, I'd have never gone out there."

"I told you," Dayna couldn't help saying.

Ignoring her, he stared up at the gyrating treetops. "This is insane!" he yelled. "I've never seen wind like this."

Instead of following his gaze upward, she took in her world at eye level. Snow was everywhere, painting everything. Although the wind drove the flakes and turned them into shotgun pellets, eventually they found a place and way to land. What a couple of hours ago had been a fine white sheet was now a thick quilt.

From where she stood, she could barely make out the cabin.

"Dayna," Park said abruptly. "We have to move your car."

"What?"

"If that tree falls, it'll land on it."

Which tree, she almost asked.

"I don't know why you left it where you did," he grumbled as he set off. "Damn it, the old man staked out his parking place for a reason."

Their father had insisted on that spot because he'd determined that the fewest number of pine needles would reach his car there and no destructive chipmunk could drop — maliciously of course — a cone on the precious surface. She, however, had chosen at will and obviously poorly.

"What do you guys think of the storm?" Kandi asked as the two women hurried to catch up with Park. "Has your brother said anything about wanting to leave today?"

"If I know him, he won't until everything's done."

"Thank goodness."

"What?"

"Nothing. I was just thinking…" She tugged on her stocking cap. "Oh, I don't know what I was thinking. Like Beacan said, this can't last long."

It better not, Dayna thought as, hoping to forestall a lecture from her brother, she went inside for her car keys. Although she guessed the snow depth to be only about two inches, she wasn't sure about her tires' ability to break trail now let alone later if the storm continued.

With the cabin door closed behind her, she was struck by how more comfortable with herself she now felt. True, the old place grumbled and groaned, but she was insulated from most of the storm's vigor, sober again after being drunk on it. Just the same, she could hardly wait to walk back into it, to inhale its raw courage.

The lights flickered, and then steadied again. In that brief time, the kitchen clock lost its tempo and began blinking a line of zeros. Finding her keys didn't take long because she didn't carry much in her purse. With a grimace, she recalled she had just this one set with her and if anything happened to them…

Park and Kandi were standing close together when, fighting the wind, Dayna rejoined them. Both stared upward. Following their gaze, she saw that one tall, slender lodgepole was whipping back and forth.

"My God," Kandi gasped. "Just look at that. I keep thinking the wind has to let up but—"

"Where're those keys?" Park demanded. "Some of those gusts have to be fifty to sixty miles an hour. We're fools for standing out here."

Agreeing, she handed him the keys and remained with Kandi as he made his way to her vehicle. Given his mood, now was not the time to tell him she was capable of getting behind the wheel. From what she could tell, the skinny lodgepole was far enough away from the car that if it fell, it wouldn't land on it. However, other whiplashing giants surrounded her hunk of plastic, rubber and metal. Park was right. The car would be a lot safer in a more open area.

Kandi touched her shoulder, startling her. "I keep telling myself it's like this a lot in the mountains in winter," she said. "That we're not seeing anything all that unusual. But I'm impressed."

"It is unusual, particularly for this early in the season. And it's beautiful."

Kandi frowned, the gesture barely disturbing her flawless features. "I was thinking." She paused, took a breath, and then continued. "If a man ever made me feel like this, I'd understand what all the shouting was about. Hell, I'd even be a willing participant."

Whatever Dayna might have learned from the other woman's comment was lost in the sound of the car's engine. The windshield wipers slapped this way and that but left uncleared streaks in their wake. Park had wiped snow from around the door handle, but the rest of her vehicle seemed part of its surroundings.

"Better step back," Kandi warned. "The wheels might kick up mud and stuff when he takes off."

She'd begun to follow the other woman when a powerful gust crashed into her, spun her back around toward her car. Beside her, Kandi struggled for balance. Overhead, massive evergreens shrieked and slammed together, fought to separate themselves.

Kandi said something, but the force stole her words. Dayna couldn't think to speak, to act, could barely comprehend.

"Park!" she screamed.

She'd started to take a step toward her brother when Kandi grabbed her and nearly jerked her off balance. Still, she fought to remain where she was. The trees bent and straightened, twisted and bent again.

"Dayna!"

Her world became a roar, a nightmare of exploding bark and wood. As she watched, horrified, one tree broke free of its roots and seemed to hurtle itself into the air. Like a giant javelin, it briefly speared the air, and then landed.

Inches from her car.

Above and around her, the monster that was the wind continued to tear at the surviving trees.

Run, run, run! Instead of heeding her mind's terrified demand, her legs danced and trembled, accomplished nothing.

"Oh God!" Kandi sobbed. "Oh God!"

The cacophony grew in intensity. She didn't know which way to go, didn't trust her footing and should look where she was racing, but that required concentration when there was only room for flight.

For survival.

Snow sucked at her inadequate boots and the uneven ground forced her knees and ankles to accomplish things God—if there was a God—had never intended. Still, she ran because the instinct to live allowed nothing else.

When the second crash came, she screamed and stumbled, seeing in her mind thousands of pounds of dying weight biting through cushioning layers of snow.

Even as the ground shuddered, she whirled around. She'd been in a couple of car accidents—one a fender bender, the other as the middle driver in a three-car pileup—and knew what tortured metal sounded like. The thunk and crinkle of breaking glass went on and on.

"Park!" she wailed.

Blind to everything except what she needed to do, she fought snow and fear until she'd gotten so close to the dying tree that the smell of pitch filled her nostrils. Still-shuddering branches lay between her and her brother, and she began pushing them aside. They sprang back the moment she released them, some slamming into but not stopping her. The flesh under her jeans and jacket felt flayed.

Finally she spotted what remained of the driver's side window, but the limbs here were so thick that they held her prisoner several feet away from the wreckage. Whether she was glad she couldn't see or touch her brother she'd never know. She stood her ground, calling his name over and over again.

The trunk had landed more on the passenger's side than where her brother was or had been sitting, but from what she could tell, no part of the roof remained intact. Pine needles and other debris had rained over everything, making it difficult to distinguish blue metal from its surroundings. When she shifted position, she heard glass crunch under her boot.

"Park?" Her throat throbbed. "Park, are you all right?"

Finally, after a lifetime, she spotted him. Motionless, he stared through the shattered windshield as if determined to steer the vehicle on the course he'd set for it. Glass fragments and pine needles littered his coat sleeve. The collapsed roof had forced his body forward.

"Park," she whispered. "Park, Park, Park."

"Get back!" Beacan ordered.

She accepted the baseball player's presence without thought but didn't move until Kandi pulled her away. Beacan set about hacking off the limbs that kept them from getting to Park. Surrounded by ruination, barely able to move in the confining space, he swung and swung and swung a three-foot long axe. His attack was relentless and beautiful, muscled perfection obeying its owner's command.

When, finally, he'd cleared a path to what remained of her car, he stopped and leaned against the axe, faced her. Sweat ran down his temples and small bits of wood covered his cheeks and chin. His eyes looked a thousand years old.

"I don't know if he's alive," he said.

"He hasn't moved?"

"I don't think so. Look, you want to go somewhere until I'm sure?"

She didn't want any part of this, but instead of telling Beacan that, she heaved a branch out of the way and stepped over the cluttered ground so she could grab the door handle. The door remained sealed so she put her weight into it, groaning with the effort. It released a little of its grip on the frame but not entirely until Beacan took over the task. She resented his greater strength. Then, despite her heart's racket, she heard her brother's ragged breathing and only that mattered.

"Don't move," Beacan said. "Damn it, man."

Silent, Park surged upright and he half propelled himself, half fell into Beacan's arms. His coat sleeve had been torn nearly off. Dayna became aware of other things like the long, bleeding gash on the side of his neck, the way his left arm hung at his side, his legs' inability to support his weight.

As Beacan lifted him into his arms, her brother threw back his head and squealed. His mouth hung open, his tongue protruded.

"Park!"

* * * * *

When Beacan carried Park into the cabin and settled him on the couch, it was Kandi who hurried into the bathroom and came back with a damp towel and began wiping blood and other things from Park's face. After the storm's thunder and roar, the quiet interior felt both wrong and safe. Beacan, his tone emotionless, asked Dayna where she kept the knives.

"Don't-don't cut off my coat," Park managed through white lips. "It cost…"

"You can't move your arm," Beacan said, his explanation aimed at a frightened four-year-old. "We have to learn the extent of your injuries."

Dayna, glad to have something to do, rummaged through a utensil drawer for what she hoped would do the job. Her brother looked like what he was, an accident victim. She tried to absorb his disheveled appearance, the fact that he was bleeding, that he'd begun to tremble and his teeth clattered when he tried to speak, but what made the greatest impact was the look in his eyes.

He was a man in shock, her big brother grown suddenly young and afraid.

Feeling too close to tears, she dropped to her knees beside him and gripped his hands. "It's all right," she whispered. "We got you out of the car. At least he did." She indicated Beacan who didn't turn from his attack on Park's coat.

"I heard — I felt…"

"Don't talk. Please. I know you're cold. I'm sorry, so sorry. I'll do something about it, but first — "

"There," Beacan interrupted. "That's got it loose. Park, you're going to have to sit up so I can get this off you."

Dayna wasn't sure Park should move, but before she could question Beacan about that, her brother righted himself slightly. His features contorted and he gasped.

"My chest."

"What-what does it feel like?" she managed.

He didn't answer but hung there like a broken doll while Beacan and Kandi peeled what remained of the coat off him. In the few moments she'd been kneeling beside her brother, she'd absorbed the fact that he needed her touch. She gave it to him willingly, gladly, holding his hand when she could, stroking his forehead while Kandi slid the ruined sleeve down his arm. She was aware of talking to him and that her whispered words had a singsong quality. This man, in essence, was her only living relative, the only one who knew where she'd come from and what the journey had been like. Because he'd been there too.

The front of her brother's shirt was stained with blood. She looked up at Beacan and he returned her gaze, his eyes still ancient, too dark.

"Wha…?" Park started.

His eyes locked on hers and she gave herself fully to him. "I think—maybe you hit the steering wheel."

Park touched his chest and then looked at his hand. He seemed puzzled by the blood. "My head hurts."

Chapter Nine

ဢ

Park struggled to stay in the here and now, but someone would say something and he'd miss the response—either that or the conversation defied his comprehension.

The smell, sight, and feel of his blood sickened him, and he muttered a thanks when Kandi wiped off what she could of it. He refused to acknowledge that fresh blood replaced what had been disposed of. He hated sprawling on the couch like a just-landed fish. Every breath sent pain shivers through him. Landed fish. His-his bladder felt full and yet he feared going to the bathroom wouldn't help. He'd told someone—hadn't he?—that he was cold, but although Dayna had draped a blanket over him, it didn't help. He couldn't stop shivering and his skin felt clammy.

Fear lapped at him, dulled his vision and hearing.

He hurt. Everywhere.

"Are you sure?" Kandi asked, her disembodied voice yanking him back. "If the trip does more damage…"

"We can't leave him the way he is." Beacan's tone was authoritative. "He could be bleeding internally."

"Do you think…?" Dayna said. Her voice fell away.

"What are you talking about?" Park managed after what seemed like a long, long time. He tried to focus on Beacan.

"About the best way to get you out of here." Beacan knelt on the floor beside him, leaning over and speaking slowly. "Do you think you can make it to my rig? I'll carry you, try not to hurt you any more than you already are."

"Where—where are we going?"

"To Crater headquarters. They've got to have some kind of a first aid station there."

"Di—Diamond's closer."

"Not really, Park," Dayna said. She stood behind Beacan, her arms folded tight across her middle maybe because she didn't want to touch him—but hadn't she just been holding his hand, or had that been hours ago? "There's no decent road between Wolf and Diamond, remember."

He couldn't put his mind to a damn road.

"Park." It was Beacan again. "None of us know enough about—about first aid—to take adequate care of you. You need a doctor. We don't dare wait for the storm to let up."

"I don't feel…"

Now the two women were talking, but they must be whispering because he caught only disjointed syllables. Finally his sister's words cut through the fog.

"Hell no!" he snapped, then clenched his teeth as pain ground into him.

"Park, what do you mean?" she asked.

"*You* can't leave. Me, yes, it's got to be done, but not you."

"But—"

"Damn it, you can't!" Something hot exploded inside him, and he was forced to breathe through it, scared and angry at the same time. No one broke the silence. Instead they waited, as they should because this was his show—his reality. At last he continued.

"What if we both bail and the pipes freeze before we can get back. The-the sale could be screwed." He had to stop and rest, his anger at his sister growing. "Damn it, I-I'd think you'd have thought of that."

She looked hurt, wounded even, but he didn't have time for that. "I'm no good the way I am, and I'd be a fool to put off hav-having a doctor look at me. I've got insurance, damn expensive insurance. You've got to drain—you know how to do that, don't you?" he demanded.

"Yes." Her mouth was tight. "Of course."

Panting a little, he settled against the couch. Something oozed out of him, not blood but a little of whatever emotion had gotten him through the confrontation with his sister. An unpleasant smell filled his nostrils, but before he could make sense of it, his belly knotted and with it came pain intense enough to close his eyes. Fear chewed at him.

"Park?" It was Dayna. "What is it?"

He couldn't speak. Didn't she know that?

"Oh God, what are we going to do?"

His sister had asked the damn stupid question. She was answered first by Beacan and then Kandi. He was drenched in sweat and would give anything to be somewhere else, somebody different. It was vital that he assess the damage. At the same time, he didn't want to know what was wrong with him.

"My neck," he whispered.

"What's wrong with it?"

"I-I'm getting a kink in it."

He thought it was Kandi who took hold of his shoulders and manipulated them so he no longer felt the strain down the side of his neck. She was a beautiful woman and if Beacan wasn't around and he didn't look and feel like a pile of garbage…

They were talking again, leaving him with his broken body and fear. He glared at them, but they didn't seem to notice.

"He's right," Kandi was saying, her tone rich and warm and he couldn't stay angry at her—maybe the others but not her. "We shouldn't all leave, at least not before doing the things we've been talking about. If we can't get back…"

"Then what the hell do you suggest?" This from Beacan.

"Don't swear at me!" Kandi shot back. "Getting pissed doesn't help."

Beacan didn't answer, but Park thought he could hear the other man breathing. Good, let Kandi and Beacan fight. She'd need—need…

"What I'm saying is," Kandi went on, "I don't know how to handle a four-wheel drive, and Dayna's the only one who knows what has to be done to the cabins."

"I…" Park started but couldn't remember what he'd been going to say.

His sister ran her hand over his forehead. "What is it?"

"No-thing."

"What's wrong with him?" She sounded close to panic.

"Shock probably," Beacan answered.

He wasn't dead, damn it. Why the hell were they talking as if he was?

* * * * *

Beacan thought Park might have passed out while he was carrying him to the Bronco. Both women had gone out with him, Dayna spreading a blanket over the passenger's seat and Kandi holding up a piece of cardboard to act as an umbrella. Fortunately the wind had let up and no longer dominated everything. With Park a deadweight in his arms, he'd been hard-pressed to think about anything except keeping his footing. He wasn't sure how long they'd been in the cabin while they tended as best they could to Park's injuries and made their decision—certainly not an hour.

Kandi had unsuccessfully tried to pick up a weather forecast on the radio. The snow hadn't let up. Damn it, this wasn't the way he'd wanted the weekend to go—not at all. Sitting beside a fire with a drink in his hand and a beautiful woman next to him while it snowed was one thing. Having to haul out an injured man while memories of his infant daughter's last moments gnawed at the protective layers was…

As a catcher, he controlled much of the action on the field, but this—hell, who knew what was the right or wrong thing to do? One thing and maybe only one thing was clear— Park wasn't going to get better sprawled on a couch in a remote cabin.

"Here's Park's phone," Dayna said after he'd positioned an ashen-faced Park on the seat. "Maybe after you've gone a few miles, you can make it work."

"Thanks." He straightened, feeling a pull in his back.

She hung by his side as she looked in at her brother. "Park?" She cleared her throat and tried again. "Park? You'll be all right."

"Dayna?" The injured man spoke in a near whisper.

"What?"

"If-if anything happens to me, make sure," he took a rattling breath, "make sure Scotty gets everything."

"Don't say that! You're going to be all right."

"Dayna…"

"Tell him," Beacon whispered.

She stared at him a moment, her mouth working. "I promise," she said.

"Thank… Thank you."

Although there was nothing to do except get behind the wheel, Beacan remained where he was. Kandi had loaded the Bronco with what little there was in the way of first aid equipment, made sure he and Park had gloves and stocking caps, even packed a couple of sandwiches and a thermos of hot chocolate. In all that time, she'd barely said a word to him.

She now stood beside Dayna, a slender arm around the other woman's shoulder. He couldn't make out much about either woman's features in the falling snow, and although only a few feet separated him from them, he felt isolated. He'd driven in thick night fog, this snowy downpour was as bad, maybe even worse.

"I'll be back," he told them in the tone he used on rattled pitchers. "Before dark."

"I'll hold you to that," Kandi said. Then she blinked and shook her head. "Look, I... Take care of yourself, all right?"

It occurred to him that the two women were dependent on him. Only he knew they were here without transportation.

"Tonight," he said. Not that long ago he'd been counting the hours until he could get Kandi out of his life. Now he wasn't sure how he felt about her. "I promise."

Dayna had closed the passenger door after her brother was inside. She continued to stare at it, and he touched her shoulder. He thought back to the last time he'd tried to offer comfort to another human being, the shared pain.

"He's going to be all right," he said. "If he was badly injured, it would have shown up by now."

"Do you think?"

"He's shaken up, a few cuts and bruises. This is just precaution."

"He looks so pale."

"It's shock. Look, I know you're worried for him, but there's no reason to be."

She glanced up at him. "I-I hardly know him."

* * * * *

Beacan had all he could do to find the so-called road that skirted the lake. He'd been here enough times that he knew how wide it was and that he'd have to go precariously close to the water. What concerned him most was whether enough of it remained visible because if it didn't—

"My tires will provide decent traction, and we probably don't really need to be in four-wheel drive," he said, hoping to calm any concerns Park might have. "But it could get a little rough."

He'd cranked the windshield wipers as high as they'd go, but his view of the world remained blurred. He wanted to look over at the injured man to see if Park was aware of the deplorable conditions but didn't dare take his eyes off where he was going. The single lane track to his cabin had been cut through the trees, the trees themselves giving him his bearings, but once he reached the more open area near the lake, most if not all bets were off.

"If you get to hurting too much, let me know, all right?"

Park sucked in a breath. "I…owe you."

"I don't have you out yet."

"But I owe you."

"We'll talk about that later." He was sitting as close to the steering wheel as his substantial body would allow but tried to hunch further even more. He couldn't see his proverbial hand in front of his face let alone the end of his hood. He'd turned on his lights, not that they did any good.

"You…don't have to do this."

"We'll talk about it later, all right? Right now…"

"What?"

The windshield wipers struggled back and forth, and his eyes wanted to follow them, maybe because the wipers were easier to make sense of than the veil of white that had become his world. He mentally pushed against the veil, not that it did any good.

A tree—shadow slid by on the right and then—where the hell were the landmarks?

The snow hadn't been coming down like this as they were getting ready to leave, but he must have done something to anger the weather gods and they were retaliating by trapping him and the man he was responsible for in this vortex.

"Can't see...a damn..."

He was vaguely aware of Park straightening. "Are we on the road?"

"Sure." *Maybe.*

Although he was barely going fast enough for the speedometer to register, he let up on the gas. His foot hovered over the brake, and he fought the urge to put an end to this insane journey through nothing.

"Can I do anything?"

He didn't bother to answer.

"The lake..."

I know the goddamn lake's out there.

"Beacan? Maybe we should wait 'til it lets up a bit."

"I'm doing fine. You take care of yourself, all right!"

The inside of the window was fogging up, but it was a few seconds before he let go of the steering wheel and flipped the dial to defrost. The heat on his face did nothing to lessen his sensory deprivation. He was blind or if not that, the next damn thing to it.

One of the things he liked about his chosen career—or the one that had chosen him—was that he went about it in the out-of-doors. He loved having space around him, which had a lot to do with why he'd wanted the cabin and also had a house large enough for a small army. He hated smoky bars and spent as little time as possible in locker rooms. He also didn't like having reporters or fans crowd around.

The Bronco dipped to the left, straightened, and then leaned in the opposite direction. He thought he'd already made the ninety-degree turn onto what passed for a thoroughfare here but couldn't swear to it. The lake was— wasn't he about to reach where the road came within spitting distance of it?

"Help me here," he said tersely. "How far do you think we've traveled?"

"Not far. We're barely moving."

Brilliant deduction. Why he hadn't waited out the blizzard, he couldn't say except that's what Park had suggested.

Was that mist from the lake? It was getting hard to breathe, probably because between them and the cranked-up-to-the-max defrost, they'd used up most of the air in the Bronco. He debated lowering the window but that would let in the snow, and as long as he kept a barrier between himself and it, he could almost believe it hadn't become everything. Swallowed everything.

At least the motor hummed. Oblivious to conditions, it did what it had been built to do. The wheels turned. And although he could tell when they went over half buried tree trunks, the vehicle's shocks prevented him and Park from being jostled about. Just because he couldn't see—

He knew the moment they began to slide. He just couldn't do a damn thing about it. Clutching the steering wheel, he thrust his chin forward, blinked repeatedly, and swore.

"Look out!" Park bellowed.

There was no time for Beacan to tell Park to shut the fuck up.

* * * * *

"What was that?" Kandi demanded.

Dayna, who hadn't been able to make herself go inside, heard it too. "Water," she said, surprised by how calm she sounded.

"It's more than that."

"Something hitting water."

They ran together. Snow clutched at Dayna, grabbed her boots and threatened to tear them off her feet. She could barely breathe for the frozen crystals packing in her nostrils. The same snow nearly blinded her, and she wondered if her eyelids would freeze.

"Where are they?" Kandi gasped.

By way of answer, Dayna grabbed Kandi's coat sleeve and dragged her with her down the path she'd trod so many times through the years. Although she saw nothing except the great white curtain, she knew the land angled down toward the lake before the bank dropped away. Roots and grasses growing there kept the dirt there from being ground into nothing, but the slope would be slick.

As she neared where memory told her land and water met, her left boot lost traction, and she nearly fell. Righting herself, she stared down. Something had sliced through the snow there and exposed the steeply pitched earth beneath.

"Oh God," Kandi hissed.

Then, although Dayna's mind refused to jumpstart itself, Kandi dropped to a crouch and peered into what existed of the lake. She heard water slam against grass and rocks and dirt and something else—something metallic.

"It isn't deep," she said. Her jaw didn't want to work. "Only a few feet this close to the shore."

"The vehicle wouldn't be submerged?"

"No." Joining Kandi, she scooted forward on her rapidly freezing rear end until her feet dangled over the edge. The lake was sound and movement, little else. In her mind, it existed forever, deep and deadly instead of the shallow basin logic knew it to be.

"Beacan! Park! Can you hear us?"

Ice crystals flung by an angry wind slammed into her exposed flesh. Despite the storm, she finally made out the dark outline of tree trunks and then the demarcation between air and water became clear. That wasn't all.

"I see it! The Bronco."

Kandi leaned forward. "Beacan! Beacan, are you all right?"

The wind laughed at the question, and the lake itself took up the joke, whistling and whining. Dayna fought to stop breathing so she could hear better, but her lungs cried out for air and she sucked in ice.

"Park!" she bellowed. "Park!"

A masculine voice cut through the gloom. "I can't move him. I think…he's stuck."

Weak with relief, she took another deep breath and propelled herself forward, gasping when her feet first hit water. She asked Beacan if he was all right, but he didn't answer.

Water only a couple of degrees above freezing killed her ability to concentrate. Beacan repeated that he couldn't move Park, and if nothing else, she knew she had to do what she could to try to save her brother.

With her pitiful excuse for eyesight and the numb tips of her fingers, she found answers. From what she could tell, the

Bronco's rear end had slid into the lake first. Beacan had forced open his door and shoved his way out. She guessed it had taken him a moment to orient himself and realize he was standing in water that barely came to his waist. By then, the Bronco had listed to the passenger's side, submerging that door.

"Is he alive?" she asked Beacan who shivered beside her.

"I don't know."

Oh God, oh God. Beacan grabbed her and tried to turn her toward him, stopped her thoughts.

"I *have,*" he sucked in a noisy breath. "We *have* to get him out of there."

"How?"

"By going after him."

That came from Kandi. While Beacan struggled to shove the vehicle into an upright position, Kandi held the driver's door open and Dayna scrambled inside. Visibility was better now that the snow couldn't reach her, making it possible for her to spot her brother. He slumped forward, a weary old man resting his heavy head on up-drawn knees.

"Park?" Her jaw clenched and she tried again. "Are you all right?"

His head came up maybe an inch. "What…happened?"

Alive! He was alive! Something hot stung her eyes.

"Dayna?"

"Yes, yes, it's me."

"What…happened?"

Not bothering to explain, she tugged on the blanket she'd draped around him, hoping he had the strength to follow her. He straightened, then wailed.

"What is it?" she demanded, feeling nothing from the waist down. "What hurts?"

"E-everything."

"Dayna." It was Beacan. Despite the glass and metal between them, she could hear him. "Don't let him move. I'll get him out."

How, she wanted to know. Instead, she waited with her moaning brother while Beacan leaned in. Beacan slid his arms under and over the older man and lifted him.

Park screamed. There was another sound, deep, full of barely contained pain. She thought it must have come from Beacan, but he was already backing away from the Bronco with Park clutched to his chest.

"Kandi!" Beacan called. "Help me."

Beacan had wanted Kandi to guide him to shore, but before she could come around the vehicle, Dayna scrambled after her brother. She positioned herself next to Beacan and wrapped her arms around his waist. Together they stumbled through the water, and then Kandi was on his other side and somehow the three of them wrestled their way up and onto shore.

Beacan dropped to his knees, still carrying Park whose whimpering made Dayna want to clamp her hand over his mouth.

"I can't..." Beacan sucked in a raspy breath. "I have to—rest."

Something in Beacan's voice snagged her attention. She leaned as close as she could and peered at him, shocked by the pain etched in his eyes.

"What's wrong?" she asked.

"Back spasm. I need—just a minute."

"Park." She spoke loudly, emphatically. "You have to walk. Do you understand? Beacan can't carry you anymore."

Park didn't say anything, only moaned and cried. When she'd first plunged into it, she'd been aware of how cold the water was, but it hadn't mattered while they were rescuing her brother. Now everything hurt.

Park slid away from Beacan, gasping as he landed in the snow. Dayna stood on feet she couldn't feel and grabbed her brother's arms because if they stayed where they were, they were all going to freeze.

Where Park got the strength to stand she didn't know, didn't care. His singsong moan continued. Wondering if the storm itself was responsible for the sound, asking herself what it could possibly matter, she steered her brother in the direction of the cabin.

At least with her lashes snow-caked, she hoped they were going the right way.

She thought Kandi had joined them, but when she looked where she'd last seen her, there was nothing. Turning on her stump legs, she saw that Kandi had remained with Beacan. And that Beacan was trying to stand.

"You have to keep going," she told her brother. "We don't dare stop."

"I…know."

For a moment, the storm seemed to let up and she could see the hint of a light. It was warm where the light was and if they could make it—if all of them could, they might survive.

"Kandi? Beacan? Are you coming?"

There was no answer.

Chapter Ten

❧

Stepping inside Dayna and Park's cabin, Kandi hurried to the woodstove. Fighting her unresponsive fingers, she opened the heavy door and added several more logs to the fire. Her coat was relatively dry, but her sodden jeans stuck to her legs, and she wondered if it might be easier to pull the Bronco out of the lake than untie her boot laces.

On numb feet, she stumbled into the bathroom and returned with a handful of towels. After giving several to Dayna, she approached Beacan. Other that closing the door behind him and stumbling over to the fire, he hadn't done anything. Something in his eyes snagged her attention, but when she opened her mouth to ask what he was thinking, he turned his back on her. Like her, Dayna had taken off her coat and was trying to get her brother, who'd collapsed into a chair, to do the same.

"Beacan." She kept her voice both soft and forceful, waited for him to face her again. "You're going to freeze like that."

He nodded but made no effort to take the towel she extended toward him.

"Your jacket," she prompted. "Take it off."

Again he nodded. The flesh around his eyes had lost color, but she wasn't sure the cold was wholly responsible. Fighting the instinct to walk away, she yanked on his jacket zipper. It fell open, and he stared down at what she'd done and then, like a sleepy child obeying a parent's command, pulled it off. A puddle of water was forming at his feet.

"What's wrong?" she asked.

His eyes flicked to her, then away again. "My rig…"

It's more than that. "Maybe you can get a wrecker in here later and have it pulled out."

"Maybe." He turned his attention to Dayna and Park. "I'm sorry," he muttered.

"It isn't your fault," Dayna told him. "You couldn't see."

"The ground gave way. I thought I was—all of a sudden, I couldn't control…"

"I should have warned you about the slope there," Dayna said.

"If the lake had been deeper…" Blinking, Beacan concentrated on the other man. "Park? How do you feel?"

"I-I don't know."

Kandi wanted to laugh at the stupid machismo of men, instead, she brought a straight-backed chair near the stove and ordered Beacan to sit down. When he did, slowly, she had no doubt that his back hurt. She also knew not to ask him about it.

After rubbing her hands vigorously, she knelt before Beacan and started working on his laces but only managed to tighten the knots. Standing again exhausted her, and she had to rest a moment before going into the kitchen for a knife. When she returned, Beacan stared at it but didn't say anything. The knife was better designed for preparing vegetables, but she kept after the water-swollen strips of leather until they gave way. She'd started to loosen the boot when she felt something settle over her head.

"Your hair's wet," Beacan whispered. "I'll dry it for you."

She didn't feel like crying. Damn it, she didn't! And if her emotions threatened to slip out of control, it was only because they'd come close to disaster and she had no idea how all of this was going to play out.

"That's enough," he said when she'd finished with the unlacing. "I don't need you waiting on me."

"I wasn't. I just—it's hard for you to bend over."

Silent, he stood and unzipped his jeans and rolled the sodden garment down over his legs. His thighs and calves were colorless, gooseflesh everywhere. For reasons she didn't want to explore, they endeared him to her.

"Get out of your things," he ordered, his words jarring her back to her surroundings. "Dayna, is there something dry in there? Something for all of us?"

She could have done that, Kandi thought as Beacan headed toward the bedroom. Still if his back had recovered enough that he was able to walk, she, who couldn't remember the last time she'd relied on anyone for anything, had no objection to remaining by the fire. Not caring whether Park or Dayna noticed, she too peeled off her jeans. Like Beacan's, her newly exposed flesh looked nearly lifeless.

"Oh my God."

Dayna's moan pulled Kandi out of herself. Park's side bled from what appeared to be a thumb-sized wound, but that was only part of the story. His flesh there was discolored and bumped up unnaturally.

"I think his rib is broken," she said, her tone as calm as she could make it. "It was probably like that before, but the thing with the Bronco may have made it worse." If one end of the break protruded outward, where was the rest of it?

To Kandi's surprise, the man who hadn't seemed to care about anything except exploring his newly redecorated cabin and getting laid, turned out to have a calming effect on Park. It was, she thought, as if Beacan had been through his own nightmare and knew what needed to be done to master certain emotions.

When he'd seen what was wrong with his side, Park had looked a heartbeat away from passing out, but then Beacan, who'd returned from the bedroom with an armload of clothing, had ordered him not to move. Park even allowed Beacan to run his fingers over his injury. She still didn't like the deliberate, almost delicate way Beacan moved, but people kept things to themselves. She knew that all too well.

"I'd like to tape it," Beacan said when he'd finished his exploration. "Wrap some cloth around you to hold everything in place. It should make you more comfortable."

"Are you sure?" Dayna asked.

"It worked on me a couple of years ago. Of course I also had x-rays. Damn it, man, I'm sorry."

If Park heard the latest apology, he gave no indication. Instead, he stared at his shivering sister, but whether he was after comfort or blamed her for what had happened, Kandi couldn't say. Dayna, too, had removed her wet jeans and when Beacan handed her a pair of sweats, she stepped away from her brother's side and pulled them on. Kandi did the same with the faded sweats Beacan gave her. He'd found some for himself, small for his muscular legs but better than nothing. No one said anything to Park about getting out of his pants, which had begun to steam from the blessed heat.

"What are we going to do now?" Dayna asked.

The question hung in the air, and Kandi wanted to turn her back on it. "We can't stay here," she said.

"No, we can't," Dayna agreed.

"Someone's going to have to walk out." Although the stove didn't need any more stoking, she opened the door and looked in. The flames were alive, feeding off the wood and reawakening her brain. "I'll do it."

"You?" This from Dayna.

"I'm not hurt."

"Neither am I," Dayna said.

"But if we go, you'll have to leave your brother."

Dayna paced over to the window, wiped at the condensation, stared out. "Damn this snow. Damn, damn, damn."

"Kandi's right, Dayna." Beacan's voice was barely above a whisper. "He'll do better if you stay with him."

"I'm not dead!" Park snapped. "Don't…talk like I am!"

Beacan ignored him. "Kandi, you and I'll go."

The better part of an hour passed before Beacan and Kandi were ready to leave. First, Beacan wrapped strips of sheeting around Park's middle. Then, after shoving his feet back into his sodden footwear, he and Kandi trudged over to his cabin where he had a winter coat, another pair of boots and wool socks. Kandi put on dry boots that had belonged to Park and Dayna's mother along with a snowsuit and a heavy, waterproof coat that nearly came to her knees. Dayna located several pairs of gloves and insisted Beacan and Kandi take them. She also filled their pockets with food they would need for energy.

Park said nothing during the preparations, and Dayna didn't encourage his participation. She'd been in her middle teens before the first seeds of rebellion against her father had taken root. Before that, she'd accepted that the man had a need to dominate her space, to all but tell her when and how and why to breathe. Even now, after nearly ten years of independence, it was easier to acquiesce if she had no choice and to walk away if she could. Whatever her brother going through was his to deal with. She wanted nothing to do with it.

"Well," Kandi said at length. "Beacan, if you're ready…"

The athlete glanced at the window where the rhythm of snow and wind appeared unchanged. "As ready as I'm ever going to be." He pulled his stocking cap down over his ears. "I don't know how long this is going to take. I hope to hell we don't have to spend the night out there, but if we do…"

"The night?" Dayna couldn't keep disbelief from her voice. "I…you think that might happen?"

He didn't answer, but why should he? Her question had been so pig stupid. It was already after noon with darkness coming in maybe five hours. "Wait," she prompted. "For tomorrow. It-it'll get so cold once the sun's down."

"We don't have the time, Dayna." This came from Kandi. "Your brother…"

"But if something happens to the two of you…" Feeling sick, she turned toward Park. "Park, tell them…they shouldn't…"

Her brother stared at nothing. He'd barely moved since they'd placed him on the couch and seemed to have shrunken into it. If he'd been her father, he would have already told her what needed to be done.

"It's all right," Kandi said. "Listen to me, it's all right. Look at the way we're dressed. Nanook of the North has nothing on us."

"You don't know…"

The other woman stepped toward her, padded arms extended. "Life's a risk. We're going to get through this." She indicated Beacan. "Because both of us are too damn stubborn not to."

Beacan might have nodded, but she wasn't sure.

"If something happens to either of you," she said, "I'd never forgive myself."

Kandi placed her gloved hands on Dayna's shoulder. "Nothing's going to. Believe me, I'm a long way from being ready to meet my Maker."

"I hate this! God, I hate this!"

"Keep Him out of this." Kandi didn't quite pull off a smile. "The Maker, if that's who He is, and I aren't on the best of terms. Besides, the way I look at it, we all go through this life on our own." Dayna thought Kandi squeezed her shoulder, but with all the layers of fabric, she couldn't be sure.

"Compared to some of the things I've done, a snowstorm's not even on the list," Kandi went on. "It'll take more than a little winter to make me cry uncle."

"Don't do it," she implored the athlete. Her head roared, and she'd started to shiver again. "I don't know why it took so long for me to realize the risks you'd be taking."

"If we don't, your brother might die," Beacan said.

"We don't know that! I couldn't stand it if something happened to you."

For a moment she thought Beacan was going to agree with her, but then he glanced at Kandi and something changed. He became harder, stood straighter. She sensed hatred swirling around him, but whom it was directed at she couldn't tell. Didn't want to know.

Why was Park acting like this, doing and saying nothing? Maybe he'd weighed his life against the others' and considered his more important.

If that was the case, she despised him.

When the door closed behind Beacan and Kandi, Dayna had felt numb. It wasn't until Park told her she needed to bring in more firewood that she forced herself to move. After putting on her tennis shoes—her boots were too wet—she wrapped a musty-smelling muffler around her neck, buttoned herself into a spare coat kept at the cabin, and stepped outside.

The air didn't feel as cold as it had earlier but maybe she was getting used to it. She forced herself to look into the snow and analyze it. The flakes were as swollen as earlier, but they'd turned from a swirling kaleidoscope into a white waterfall. It was beautiful. How could she not have seen that?

The wind still sang its own discordant tune, and even without trying, she made no sound as she walked. It was as if the birds and other wildlife—and the lake—had never existed. Her father had called her a daydreamer and ridiculed her whenever he caught her staring into space. She now knew that her ability, her need to project herself into her own world had been a survival mechanism, and although that hadn't been necessary in recent years, the habit had remained.

This moment in time she wasn't Dayna Curran, unemployed master gardener, the sister of a wounded man, perhaps dependent on two near strangers for her survival. She was now a pioneer, a member of a caravan of covered wagons heading west toward a new life. Spring, summer, and fall were behind her as were the Great Plains. She and her family—she wasn't specific on that—had staked out a claim in California or Oregon and had managed to build a cabin before winter. A member of her mythical family had been responsible for the many cords of firewood, and on this day that was no different from the others, her chores were simple. She'd help with the evening meal, and when it grew dark, she'd settle beside a fire with one of the many books she'd brought with her.

No, she amended as she brushed snow off the chest high stack of wood, maybe she'd been alone during her trek West. Yes, that was it. Her family was dead, victims of some deadly disease. She'd mourned their deaths, but because they'd been wealthy and she'd been born with an adventurous streak, she'd used her inheritance to forge a new life for herself in the wild land. Because her family had had a farm—yes, a prosperous one with fine healthy animals and a more than adequate garden growing from rich black earth—she'd been confident she could duplicate that once the journey was over.

She'd hired a man to help her drive her oxen team and then hired another to do the heavy work of erecting her cabin, but she no longer had a need for either of them. Other pioneering women had shaken their heads when they learned she intended to work her farm on her own, and she'd taken pride in knowing their skills and independence and courage couldn't equal hers.

As for the man in the cabin—

Picking up a piece of wood, she laid it in the crook of her arm. Then she reached for another.

The man in the cabin was an Indian who'd been leaving venison at her door. For a long time she'd known she was being watched, not by someone she needed to fear—fear was an alien emotion in today's fantasy—but by someone who'd been intrigued by her.

Why was he sitting beside her fire?

She'd loaded herself down with as much wood as she could handle before the answer came. Her brave had observed her for a long time, and she'd been content with that, but finally they'd both sensed a deeper need. One afternoon she'd heard a knock and when she'd opened her door, he'd been standing there. She'd invited him in and although they hadn't been able to communicate with words, that, too, was all right.

Because their bodies spoke the only language needed.

He'd been the perfect lover, his dark body covering hers and bringing her to life. He'd tasted of the wilderness. With him, she could be the woman she'd only dreamed of — wild and bold. Hungry.

They'd had sex that first time on a rag rug near the stove, but then she'd taken him into her bedroom and he'd slid on top of her and —

"You-you're all right?"

Reality returned with her brother's words, and she closed both the door and the fantasy behind her. She didn't try to wipe the wind-caused tears from her eyes.

"It just took awhile, that's all." She walked over to the wood box and dropped her load. The thud-thud made her head ring.

"I got worried."

Nothing concerned Park. He was oblivious to emotion. Wasn't he? "I think the wind's let up a bit. Maybe they'll be all right."

"I hate owing him."

The pioneer woman in her had been fearless. That's why the nameless warrior had wanted to bed her. "That's not the point, Park," she said firmly. "For once, money has nothing to do with it."

"Money is always part of it."

"For you, maybe. Not me." Here by the fire it was so warm that she felt trapped inside her heavy clothing, but the cracks around the door and window let in cold. She didn't know where to stand.

"That's for sure," he said sarcastically.

Earlier, she'd tried to convince herself that she was imagining how pale her brother was, but being away from him had cleared her mind. It amazed her that he was in an argumentative mood.

"And what do you mean by that?" she asked as her nose and lips tingled.

"I wasn't going to say anything because what the hell difference does it make, but you don't have a job, do you?"

"I—it's kind of..." No! A woman capable of walking alone across the country wouldn't be afraid to answer a question.

"No. I don't."

"That's what I figured. When you couldn't wait for me to put the cabin on the market, I guessed you must have a damn good reason for wanting the money. Otherwise, you wouldn't have cared whether it rotted."

"You wanted to be rid of it too."

When his eyes closed and his breath labored, she was afraid for both of them, but after a minute, he blinked and focused on her.

"What happened?" he asked.

"With my job? The company went out of business."

"I told you they would."

"What you said was that they were ripe for a takeover."

"Because the owners couldn't manage their way out of a paper bag. Don't tell me. You hung in there until the bitter end, didn't you?"

"They're good people. Haven't you ever heard of loyalty?"

"Loyalty?" He snorted, then his face contorted. "Let me guess. You didn't even go looking for another job until they locked the doors, did you?"

"It isn't your concern!"

"Isn't it? You're going to wind up on the street."

"It's my life, Park. Not yours."

"You're my responsibility."

Responsibility? Like a stray dog? Ignoring him, she walked over to the window and stared out. The sun hadn't yet started its downward journey, which meant the clouds were responsible for the lack of light. There weren't any shadows, only unrelenting gloom. Even a pioneer woman would feel dread.

"I hate this," she whispered. "Damn, I hate this."

Chapter Eleven

ဆ

Beacan led the way, not because he saw himself as some great white hunter, but his larger feet put him in a better position to cut trail. Other than agreeing that they needed to cover as much ground as possible as quickly as possible, Kandi hadn't said anything. If she'd asked if they were going to get through this in one piece, he would have known his role, reassured her that of course they'd come out of this rescue mission no worse for the wear.

However, she'd only wrapped her muffler around her neck and nodded. He had the sense she'd walk until her legs broke off.

Good, he tried to tell himself, but he was a summer person, played a summer game. He'd grown up in southern California where winter meant putting on long pants instead of shorts and had been an adult before he'd seen his first snow. His body wasn't made for this crap, not with his too thin blood and wrecked back.

"You don't have to do this." He spoke to Kandi without looking at her, trusting she could hear despite the erratic windblasts.

"Neither do you."

"Yeah, I do."

"Why?"

"Because…" The past lapped at him, sought to pull him back into that hospital room where all his new father dreams had died. "It doesn't matter."

"Doesn't it?" she challenged. "I'm supposed to buy that you're willing to risk your life for some man you can hardly stand?"

"I'm not doing any more than you."

She didn't say anything, not that her silence surprised him. His head pulsed and he could hear his heart beating. Once, not long enough ago, he'd prayed for his own death. "Do you ski?" he asked, seeking escape from the horror of that time.

"No."

"Me either."

"That's what we get from living where we do—not much snow there."

There wasn't enough snow on the ground that he had trouble staying on the road his Bronco had failed to navigate, and even if there'd been twice as much, it didn't take a rocket scientist to figure he should walk where there weren't any trees. He found it disconcerting to look into the forest and admit how easily a person could get lost in there. He'd heard about people who'd become so turned around that they'd never found their way out of the wilderness and had watched a TV show about a man whose camper had broken down on a logging road on his way to the Oregon coast. According to his diary, he'd slowly starved after becoming trapped by snow.

"You didn't answer my question," Kandi said. "Why are you doing this?"

"What would you prefer I do?"

"I don't know. But first you offered to drive him out and then when your car slid into the lake, you would have carried him into the cabin if you hadn't been half frozen."

"He couldn't do it on his own."

"Maybe. Beacan, what if I'd said I wasn't going to risk my neck? You wouldn't have gone out on your own, would you?"

"I don't know."

"Why not?"

"What are you getting at?"

"You tell me. Is he worth the risk we're taking?"

Because the wind had settled down, he no longer spent every moment wondering whether another tree was going to fall. Just the same, unless they turned around, it would be a long time before they saw any other human beings. A lot could happen during the hours they'd be forced to spend together — too much if he wasn't careful.

"What kind of name is Kandi?" he asked. "Did your folks really give you that one?"

When he concentrated, he heard her too big boots brush against snow, but mostly he was aware of the sounds he made. The endless crunch-crunch-crunch kept him company. But would it keep him in the present?

"What is it?" he pressed. "Don't you like your name?"

"I like it, and it isn't the one they gave me."

"Yeah? What did they — ?"

"It doesn't matter, all right."

* * * * *

It didn't hurt that much as long as he didn't move, but whenever he changed position or had to go to the bathroom — which came up too frequently — Park wondered if he might pass out.

"What are you doing?" he asked when Dayna came out of the bedroom. She'd been in there a long time it seemed to him, maybe hiding from him.

"Taking inventory of what clothing is here. Is there something you need?"

He needed out of the hell he'd gotten into, not that telling her that would make any difference. Today reminded him too much of the night, nearly five years ago, when his first wife and the mother of his only child had told him she was leaving him. She had a career, didn't she? A healthy child and a husband who'd hinted he was ready for another one. She had a nearly three thousand square foot house in a brand-new subdivision where the houses were almost the size of the lot, and a six-month-old Toyota.

But she'd wanted something more—a lot more—he'd found out that sweet-smelling summer night when it had all fallen apart. A husband.

Well, what the hell was that?

"No," he told his sister. "I don't need anything." Then because he'd been down the road that led to his divorce too many times, he asked his sister what she'd found in the drawers neither of them would have dared touch while they were growing up.

"Not much, at least not much in the way of Mother's things. It's almost—" Dayna pulled a rocker close to the stove and sat down, "—it's almost as if she knew she wasn't going to be back."

"Either that or nothing changed over the years and she still had nothing."

"Maybe." Dayna rubbed her hands together. "The heat doesn't reach the bedroom. If we wind up having to spend the night, I'd better set up beds in here for us. Do you think you'll be able to sleep?"

"How the hell would I know?"

Her eyes widened in that hurt way of hers, but instead of retreating into herself as she and their mother had always done, she stared at him.

"Park, I don't want you talking to me like that," she said. "I know you're hurting. I wish we knew how this is going to turn out, but our fighting won't help."

"You never were a fighter," he said, breathing shallow against the knives in his side.

"I know." She rocked back and forth several times. "I used…"

"You used to what?"

Her head came up and she again focused on him. "When he got after me, I'd stay awake half the night asking him in my mind why he was the way he was, trying to tell him that he made me feel worthless, and I couldn't love him because of it."

"But you didn't say anything to him, did you? Not even after you left home."

"No." She leaned back. "Giving in had been so ingrained in me. He was so quick verbally while I…I have to think things through, work them this way and that. I wish I was different."

"You too?"

"What do you mean? Look what you've accomplished."

Someone had turned on the kitchen light but nothing disturbed the gray that surrounded both of them in the adjacent living area. Shadow ate at reality, sucked him into darkness. "What have I accomplished?"

"You're wealthy. When-when you first left home, he said you'd never amount to anything, that you didn't have what it took to succeed."

"Did he?"

"But then you bought a house before you turned twenty-one and he stopped saying those things."

A log snapped inside the stove, the sound sharp and sudden, but he wasn't distracted from what was happening between his sister and himself. Even the knives weren't enough to pull him away.

"I told him I'd saved enough from my job for the down payment, but it was a lie," he said.

She waited for him to continue.

"It belonged to a man who worked at the same place I did. He had some financial problems—his wife had left him and was taking him to the cleaners." An image of that hollow-eyed man intruded, and he…he only half succeeded in pushing it away. "He said he was going to burn the house down so she couldn't get that too." One knife blade bit deep, and he sucked in an unwise breath. "I-I convinced him to sign it over to me. He was half drunk when we went to the title company." Sweat trickled down his armpits. "I-I wanted to refinance at a lower interest rate, but I didn't have enough of a credit history that any bank would touch me. Still, I got the place for less than half of what it was worth and then turned around and sold it two months later."

"Why didn't you tell him?"

It occurred to him that she hadn't called their old man Dad since the conversation had begun, but then neither had he. "Because he would have found something wrong with the way I handled things. You know he would have."

She got up, walked into the kitchen area where she grabbed several sections of paper towel and used that to wipe condensation off the living room windows. He envied her easy movements.

"I used to try to understand why he was like that, but it no longer matters," she said.

"I came to the same conclusion."

"Did you? For a long time I thought the two of you were alike."

"I was...never sure." *Stop hurting, just the hell stop hurting.* "All the time I was growing up, I believed he and I thought the same way, but if that was the case, why was I in such a hurry to get out on my own?"

"You were just seventeen."

"Yeah." Exhaustion closed his eyes but not his thoughts, his voice. "Same as you. I-I damn near starved at first. Probably would have if I hadn't been so determined to make it."

"Determined pretty much sums him up," she said with something that might have been a chuckle.

"It does," he admitted. "That's one thing I got from him that I don't regret. Maybe the only thing." The knives were digging, digging, eating at him from the inside. Maybe he was bleeding internally.

"When I was by myself—" He forced his eyes to open again. "I had a lot of time to think. Did you feel that way, that when you were around him you couldn't think?"

She was no longer trying to stay ahead of the condensation, simply stood there with the wet paper towel balled in her hand. "Yes."

"But it got better once you left, didn't it?"

"Not for a long time."

"I think it was different for me, kind of like going to bed drunk but waking up sober." He started to laugh but something slammed into him, stopping him and making him gasp.

"Park!"

"It-it's all right."

"No." Hurrying over, she knelt beside him and took his hands. "It isn't."

* * * * *

One step and then another. The good little soldier marching. Marching and breathing in air cold enough to keep the headache running at full speed. Stumbling sometimes because there was no way she could anticipate every bump or dip in the road.

Beacan's back as he led the way kept Kandi focused. If it wasn't for him, she might have lost herself to the snow. Not in it, she amended because the road showed them the way, but everything was either snow white or the dark gray of clouds and tree trunks. Her depth perception was shot to hell and forward movement was nearly impossible to judge for the not too simple reason that the snow kept coming at her, coming and coming and coming.

"Kandi?"

"What?"

"If you need to rest, let me know."

"I'm fine. I-I knew all that exercise was going to pay off some day."

"I hate it."

"What?" She shook her head, dislodging some of the snow clinging to her stocking cap. "You hate exercising?"

He stopped, turned toward her. The corner of his mouth twitched. "The sameness of it. The relentlessness."

"But you have no choice because of what you do, do you?"

"I sure as shit don't."

She'd walk away from him, what the hell did she need with someone who turned everything into an argument.

She'd tell him she was going on alone, and would have if it didn't take so much effort.

"I'm sorry," he said, surprising her. "You were just making conversation."

She wanted to start walking again, yet she needed his voice reminding her that she wasn't alone out here.

"Why?" he asked.

"Why what?"

His study of her went too deep. She positioned herself so her side was to him and looked at a long, gentle slope to her right. It seemed to go on forever and then fade into nothing.

"Why did you take me up on my invitation to come here?"

"I told you. I've never been to Crater."

"That's not it." His voice turned fierce, reminding her of the way the wind sounded as it slammed a tree to the ground. "And even if it was, was it worth the tradeoff?"

"What tradeoff?"

"Having to put up with being screwed."

"What are you talking about?"

"I'm not stupid, Kandi." He licked snowflakes off his upper lip. "I might be a dumb jock but even I know when a woman's body is lying to me."

* * * * *

Dayna had spent the last several minutes trying to get more than that one station to come in, anything that might give a weather report, but there was so much static that she'd given up. She wanted to concentrate on the sounds from the outside world, to be quieted and calmed by music, but she was too restless. Too unnerved by her brother's pain and hollowed-out eyes.

"I'm thinking," she said without looking at him. "Maybe I should drain the pipes at Beacan's place. That's the least I can do for them. But if you don't want to be left alone…"

By way of answer, he ordered her to first go out to their workshop for the wrenches she'd need. Then, his monologue slowed by his frequent need to concentrate on his breathing, he described how he believed the water system at the other cabin worked.

"I've got it," she interrupted when, for the third time, he warned her to release the pressure valve at the top of the water heater before attempting to empty it. "Park, it's not as if I haven't done this before."

His snort said he had his doubts. Forcing herself to remain calm, she reassured him that, yes, she'd dress warmly and, yes, she'd take along some Teflon tape and washers and, no, she wouldn't be gone long.

She'd forgotten how much bite there was to the wind, but thinking about it made her sick with concern for Kandi and Beacan so she concentrated on the task at hand. Park had told her so much about Beacan's cabin that once inside, she quickly oriented herself. Before tackling the hot water heater, she turned off the refrigerator, placed its contents in the ice chest Beacan had brought with him, and left the refrigerator door open so the interior would start to warm. Enough hot coals remained in the stove that she only had to add wood to get it going again.

The cabin's original metal pipes had all been replaced with plastic, which would greatly facilitate the task of removing the traps. After turning off the power to the well, she attached a hose to the hot water heater runoff valve and carried the other end outside so it could drain.

Her movements became automatic and she easily ticked off each step of the project, still she heard her father.

"Not this way, like I showed you." "It's got to be done right. Otherwise, don't do it at all." "Not so fast, missy. You think you're so damn smart. Well well, you're wrong. Wrong. Wrong."

Barely aware of what she was doing, she picked up a throw pillow and squeezed it.

"Do you hear me, you bastard!" she screamed. "All those years of believing I couldn't think without you and now you don't know enough to wipe your own ass!"

With that, she hurtled the pillow at the window. The glass rattled but didn't break. As the sound fell away, silence engulfed her. The cabin felt empty. As if no one would ever come here again.

* * * * *

Jace Penix scooped up a double handful of snow and began compressing it. Back in high school he'd been a fairly good quarterback and would have been tagged as the starter if a phenomenon, who went to college on a full athletic scholarship hadn't been the same age. It would feel good to release—

His palms stung, forcing him to look at what he was doing. It was cold, burn-the-flesh-cold, back up to a fire and stand for a long time kind of cold.

And it was still snowing.

Leaving the Forest Service truck he'd turned into a makeshift snowplow by attaching a blade to the front end, he walked back a few hundred feet and climbed onto the berm he'd created. From where he now stood, he could look down into a small valley—or at least he could have if trees and falling snow weren't in the way. He wasn't the only employee trying to keep the rim road clear this afternoon, and although he couldn't see or hear the other vehicles, communication was a simple matter of keying in the CB radio. Just the same, the storm isolated him.

Jace pressed the heel of his hand against his forehead. From the moment he'd seen the first snowflake, he'd known he'd have to stand face-to-face with last winter. Summer had been bearable because heat stood between him and the season of Cherokee's death. Even yesterday, the air had tasted like autumn, but that was gone now.

He'd thought he might go crazy when the march of time forced him back into winter, and yet he felt saner this afternoon than he had for days, weeks, months. After all the dread and fighting, he was back to where it had all begun. He kicked at an icy chunk and watched it tumble a few feet down the hill before losing sight of it. The tracks of its passing, like everything else, might not last until morning.

What had dying surrounded by snow and cold and loneliness been like? That was the question he'd tried to distance himself from all summer, the one he calmly accepted this afternoon. Was it possible to look death in the eye, to make one's peace with whatever time life had granted?

To start down death's road and not hate the one who'd let him go on it?

* * * * *

Beacan no longer walked as an athlete walked. Even with her eyelids and cheeks and most of all her nose frozen, Kandi knew that. She wanted to ask why, but if he told her, something would shift between them. Not that it hadn't already, she admitted, and wondered how he'd known she'd faked her orgasms. What forced her to mull it over when it would have been easier to simply walk was whether other men had known. Why her skill as an actress or lack of it mattered. Why she'd pretended.

Something was on the road ahead of Beacan. At first startled but now simply disbelieving, she watched a great black bird march one way and then the other, oblivious to what had caused all other creatures to head for cover. This symbol of nature was at home here. If it feared nothing, why should she?

"Crow," Beacan said as she drew beside him and pointed.

"Not a blackbird?"

"Hardly. It's much too big for that."

"Oh. I've never..." The crow lowered its head and pecked at the snow, then fixed its yellow-eyed gaze at her. "Do you know a lot about birds?"

"Some."

"Like what?"

"What does it matter?" He tucked his hands into his armpits.

"I was just...trying to learn more about you, I guess."

Judging by his expression, that was the last thing he expected her to say, but instead of taking the offered opening, he started walking again. When she held back so he could continue to break ground, he reached behind him, grabbed her gloved hand, and drew her to his side. He asked if she thought she could continue to keep pace, and she said yes. Despite her cold face, she wasn't shivering. That was a good sign, wasn't it?

"My mind hasn't been doing anything," he said. The crow watched their approach but showed no sign of alarm. "At least not beyond counting snowflakes."

Although she didn't believe him, she mentioned that she thought the storm had let up a little, and he agreed it was easier to see than it had been when they'd first taken off. By then they were passing the spot where the crow waited. It hopped to one side and squawked at them.

"Tell it to someone who cares," Beacan told the bird.

"Why isn't it flying away?" she asked. "It doesn't act afraid."

"It isn't, arrogant bastard. As for why it's staying on the ground, that's a lot of weight to get airborne."

"Then it's not so cold it can't?"

"My guess, it'll head for lower elevations before night."

If she and Beacan were birds, their journey would already be over. Although she risked stumbling, she continued to look over her shoulder until she could no longer see the solitary dark creature.

"I wonder if he's lonely," she said.

He didn't speak. "What about Dayna? If something happens to Park—"

"Don't think about them. We can't do anything except what we are."

"Life takes so many unexpected turns, doesn't it," she mused, not sure where she was going with the conversation. Although she couldn't feel Beacan's fingers through the layers of fabric, she was aware of bone and flesh and muscle, aware of him. "We think we're going to the grocery store for milk when we get hit by a bus and then—"

"You were hit by a bus?"

"No, but a drunk creamed me last year. I wound up with whiplash and couldn't work for nearly a month. He didn't have insurance or a driver's license."

"How'd it turn out?"

"My insurance came through, finally. Not before I hired a lawyer and threatened to sue though."

"You don't sound bitter."

"Bitter doesn't get me anywhere. It never has."

He looked down at his feet, then at her. "No, it doesn't."

Chapter Twelve

ဆ

At Beacan's prodding, Kandi presented sound bites of her background. She'd been born Catherine Alice, but when an older brother started calling her Kandi, the nickname had stuck. The brother was dead, the victim of a drive-by shooting shortly after he'd turned seventeen. She didn't mention him by name, neither did she give a name to her father.

Her mother, the original Alice, was still alive and living, Kandi thought, in San Jose although someone had told her she might have moved to Los Angeles. Winter before last, Kandi's Christmas card to her mother had been returned because there was no forwarding address. The phone number she had for her no longer existed, but even if Alice had tried to get in touch with her daughter, she probably couldn't since Kandi had changed residences more times than she could keep track of.

From what Kandi said, Beacan gathered she hadn't spent much of her childhood with her mother. He probed for details but didn't get any.

"If you ever need an example of a dysfunctional family," she said instead, her tone unemotional, "you don't need to look any further than mine."

"What about other siblings?" he asked over his shoulder. "You mentioned a sister."

"The last I heard, Holly was married to some guy who owns a bar. They had a couple of kids, maybe more."

"Then there was just your brother and Holly when you were growing up?"

"No," she answered after a short silence. Her voice, although tossed about by the wind, remained strong. "My mother had three more kids after me and some of the men in her life had kids of their own—you don't want to hear this."

"Yeah, I do." He sucked in frozen air.

"Well, I don't. I live in the present."

"You don't really believe that, do you?"

"Look, I'm sorry I started on this."

If he'd been a shrink, he would have known how to pull more out of her. Instead, because he didn't want to go down certain roads himself, he took the easy way out.

"When we get back," he told her, speaking loudly so his voice would carry, "I'm buying a snowmobile. That way, the next time we're in the wilderness, we won't have to hoof it."

"One with a heater?"

"Two of them. Black and powerful, two of the biggest, baddest machines out there. We're doing this in style."

"We?"

I don't know. First we have to get out of this.

* * * * *

Dayna didn't want to go back inside. If Park's condition had deteriorated while she was gone, she wasn't sure she had what it took to deal with the situation. However, to her relief, he'd actually put a kettle of water on the stove. When she mentioned it, he said he thought she'd like something warm to drink, and he sure as hell did. In an attempt to sidestep an interrogation about what she'd been able to accomplish next door, she told him what she'd done and that she didn't think there'd be a problem with residual water in the pipes.

"I hope so." He watched as she measured chocolate powder into a couple of mugs. "If you didn't put enough antifreeze in the toilet bowl, there's going to be hell to pay. The—"

"Park. Stop it."

"All I'm doing is—"

"I know what you're doing." Picking up the steaming kettle, she stared at it. Her fingers ached to send it hurtling toward her brother. To silence words identical to what she'd heard so many times from her father.

"You don't trust me," she continued. "Maybe you really don't know what you're doing, but I don't need it. I'm not incompetent."

"You're shaking."

He was right, but the cold seeping in through the old windows had nothing to do with the way she felt. "Trembling," she amended. "With anger."

"You never got mad. No matter what he said or did, you never did."

"And you did."

Suddenly exhausted, she concentrated on filling the cups with boiling water. After setting down the kettle, she carried one to her brother and placed it on the lamp stand near his elbow. The light was on, the shade so age-yellowed it did little to lessen the gloom. Park's coloring reminded her of old lemons.

"Why was he like that?" she asked, sitting down across from her brother. "Why did he have to control everything? He must have known how we hated it—at least he knew how you felt."

"He and I had our share of knockdown drag-outs all right."

"I don't understand. I never did, never will. Did dominating us make him happy? Maybe he liked seeing the fear in Mom's and my eyes."

"I don't know."

Park sounded tired. She should let him rest but—she first denied and then accepted the thought—they might never again have a chance to talk like this.

"I remember once," she went on. "I must have been ten or eleven—I'd gone to a Little League meeting and told the people there that I wanted to play softball. When I told Mom, she asked if he'd given permission. I said no, but all the other kids were signing up and I should be able to. She got that sick look on her face…"

"Like a trapped animal."

Like an animal with all fight stripped from it. "All she said was that I should know better than to do anything without first clearing it with him."

"He didn't let you play, did he?"

"No." Because she'd been holding onto her mug, her hands were now warm. She took a tentative sip and then continued. "It wasn't his idea and how dare I want to do anything on my own."

"But you became a runner."

"Yes."

"Why?"

"One of my teachers was the track coach. After watching me during P.E., he told me I had a natural ability and he wanted to help me make the most of it." Her eyes filled with unshed tears. Turning from her brother, she blinked several times.

"And the old man?"

"I was already on the team before he found out."

"How'd you manage that?"

"Not well. And not without sleepless nights," she admitted. "I knew what he'd say. It'd be the same as it had been with softball and going to school programs and babysitting and… It would have been easier to say no to the coach. I knew that."

"But…"

But I was dying. "I'd never had a compliment before. Not really. My grades—even with him monitoring my homework and helping me study for tests, I had all I could do to get Cs. I felt stupid. Stupid and ugly."

"You were never ugly."

Maybe. Maybe not. It didn't matter.

Park reached for his mug, stopped. His features contorted, and he rocked forward, hands over his belly.

"What's wrong?"

"I just didn't-didn't move right."

Sweat now coated his forehead, but she didn't know what to do for him. Feeling helpless, she watched as he settled back on the couch. Maybe it wasn't safe for him to have anything to drink or eat, but if she brought it up, he'd warn her not to do his thinking for him.

"You're not ugly and you're not dumb, Dayna."

"Then why did I do so poorly in school?"

"Because he had you tied in knots, made you doubt yourself."

"I—every time I took a test, I felt him looking over my shoulder. And if I had to speak in class, it was as if he'd become the teacher."

"Tell me about it. I felt the same pressure."

"He didn't see it that way. I'm sure he didn't. He thought he was helping. Being a good father."

"Fuck that."

Park had whispered, and yet his words were fire and ice.

"Living up to his responsibilities," she said. "Being the head of the house."

"And that's what you were running from."

"You think—"

"Don't do that, Dayna!" His eyes snapped shut and his breath became ragged. "Say what's in your gut."

Despite her fear for her brother, she turned her attention to what was taking place outside, maybe sought escape in it. Snow was cleansing, beautiful. It marked the passing of a season of growth and allowed nature to rest. She couldn't see her ruined car or the stumps of trees that hadn't survived her father's need to control his surroundings. All imperfections were gone, and those creatures that would spend the winter here were safe beneath the white blanket.

"Mark Kenneck was the track coach," she went on. "He had grandchildren and sometimes his kids would bring the little ones to school. He was so proud of them. Around his grandchildren, he didn't act like a teacher at all. He'd hug and kiss them and tease and let them tease him."

"A good man."

"One time—it was after the first race I won—he hugged me. Just grabbed me with everyone around and…" She couldn't go on.

"Back when a teacher could hug a student and no one turned it into something dirty."

"I-I guess."

"Did you love him?"

"It wasn't like—"

"Not that kind of love, Dayna." He fell silent, breathed. "Love as in this was someone you could trust."

"Someone I wanted to succeed for."

"No. The running was for yourself."

"You're right." She sighed. "But I wanted to live up to Mr. Kenneck's expectations. He believed in me."

"Accepted you for what you were."

Her throat closed. Nearly a minute passed before she could continue. "I'd never known what that was."

* * * * *

Being superintendent of a national park had its moments, but this wasn't one of them. In the four years he'd been here, Paul Soffin had seen and accepted the full gambit of human stupidity, but visitors' reaction to the early storm ranked high on the list. If he had a dollar — hell, a quarter — for every time he'd been asked how long the snow would continue, he could retire.

"Really?" had been the usual response to his warning that current conditions were expected to continue for at least two and probably more days.

"Really." He parroted the young couple who'd cornered him outside his office a few minutes ago.

"Then do you think we should leave?"

"If I was in your position I would."

"But we've only been married a month." The woman squeezed her husband's arm. "We couldn't get away for a honeymoon before and well…"

"We've paid for three more nights here," the man finished. "Do you think we can get our money back?"

"You'll have to ask the lodge management, but they've been checking people out all day."

"It's not fair." The woman reminded him of a four-year-old gearing up for a tantrum.

The weather was the weather. Fair or a rip-off didn't enter into the equation. "I can't order you to leave," he told them. "But if I didn't have the proper gear, I'd be packing."

"Honey!" the man started.

"No." The woman's second squeeze creased her husband's jacket sleeve. "I've got the rest of my life to sit in that damn apartment. Please, sweets. Please."

"But…"

"What's the matter?" she interrupted. "Maybe you don't want to be alone with me."

Leaving the couple to their argument, Paul started down the hill to the garage that housed most of the Service's official vehicles. His mind was still on which of them would win. Consequently, his feet were out from under him before he knew it was going to happen. The snowfall was everything poets said of it, but sitting here in slush and ice while flakes found their way down the back of his neck and exhaust fumes from departing vehicles clogged his nostrils didn't do much for his mood.

"You comfortable there or would you like help up?"

There was no mistaking Henri Lansky's bullhorn voice. "I think I've accomplished about all I care to down here," Paul said and extended his hand toward the large man.

"I take it you didn't do that willingly." Henri grinned.

"Not too likely," he admitted once he was on his feet. "I thought you were going to be near the north rim this afternoon."

"I was, but Jace said he'd take the plow and see what he could accomplish."

A nearby yellow sports car, the license plate obscured by snow, took that moment to slide off the road. It came to an inelegant stop against a snow berm.

"Damn fools," Paul muttered. "This wouldn't be a bad place to work if it wasn't for the idiots."

"I hear you. You don't have a problem with Jace replacing me, do you? I thought I'd better stick around here in case those engineers didn't have enough sense to hightail it home. Besides, Jace needed something to do."

"The first storm's going to be hard on him," he said. "Bring back a lot of bad memories for all of us."

Henri grunted agreement.

"How does he look?"

"How does he always look?"

That comment made Paul shake his head. He'd blamed himself for not being more aware of Cherokee's mental state last winter. The "if onlys" played endlessly through him, so much so that his first attempt at an incident report had run ten pages and left him emotionally spent. It had also proven cathartic. He'd tried to get Jace to write down everything he felt, but as far as he knew, the younger man hadn't taken him up on it.

"I'm not sure it's good for him to be alone," he told Henri.

"Me either, but we can't wet-nurse him. Those demons— only he can decide whether he's going to spend the rest of his life living with them."

"If he does, it's going to be a long, hard life."

* * * * *

"Close your eyes. Give the aspirin time to work."

"That's what you said the last time."

"And it helped, didn't it?"

"Yeah. A little."

A little wasn't what Dayna wanted to hear, especially when the only thing she had to offer her brother were pills that might not be good on his stomach. She'd argued against his drinking liquor, but when his voice took on the "I'm boss" tone that had been an integral part of her father, she'd given in. He'd taken his whiskey straight and could barely breathe or swallow, but now his cheeks had color they hadn't had before.

"Go ahead," he said. "You might as well read."

Desperate for some way to take his mind off his injuries and hers off the too short daylight hours and unrelenting snow and how Beacan and Kandi were doing and how long the storm might last, she'd gone through a stack of old outdoor magazines and had chosen the story of a couple of men who, in the 1950s, had decided to drive the Alcan Highway of Alaska in the winter. Why she wanted to read about something that in many ways paralleled their experience puzzled her. Maybe because obviously at least one of the adventurers had survived to write about it.

The beginning had been innocent enough, young optimists with a nearly new car and time on their hands. Back then the Alcan hadn't been paved and a sheet of ice peppered with a thin layer of gravel laid down by the highway department made for less than reliable traction.

"'It was already dark, but we were determined to make another twenty miles to a roadhouse where we could spend the night,'" she read. "'It was snowing ice and the wind kept coming at us, slowing us to a crawl. I was driving, and I didn't want to tell Carl I was scared because I couldn't see. The windshield wipers were working all right, but there was ice on the glass and it was getting thicker.'"

Shivering, she glanced up. Park's head rested against the back of the couch, and his eyes were closed. Outside, the whiteness increased.

"'The moment the tire blew, I knew we were in trouble.'"

Trouble didn't adequately describe what happened after that. The two had gotten out and tried to change tires, but the wind cut through them and the jack kept slipping off the snow-slicked vehicle. Giving up, they'd crawled back inside and cranked up the heater until they'd thawed, then turned off the engine to conserve gasoline.

The night had seemed to take forever, but that hadn't been the end of the nightmare. Wise in the way of storms, the few truckers who were the only ones to travel the highway in winter had holed up for the duration. Unable to travel, cold, hungry, and scared, the two had been forced to spend close to eighty hours together. Only the narrator had survived.

"'I kept thinking about how one stupid decision can affect a person's entire life,'" she read. "'After Carl died, I asked myself how I was going to tell his parents and the girl he'd been dating. Then I thought about my family, not knowing whether I'd see them again. My sister hadn't been married long and was expecting her first child. I wanted to be an uncle. I wanted to become a father, a husband. But maybe none of those things were going to happen.'"

A sharp sound pulled her out of the frozen world those simple words had created. Park's mouth was open and he was snoring. Telling herself he must be feeling better if he could sleep, she started to lay down the magazine. Instead, she continued reading.

The narrator didn't spend much time wallowing in self-pity. When the storm finally let up, he'd been forced to decide between trying to walk to that roadhouse or waiting for help. He'd opted for waiting because he wasn't adequately dressed for a long trek, especially if it started snowing again.

"I couldn't remember how long we'd gone since seeing any other vehicles," he'd written. "That was probably good because if I'd known, I might have despaired. I did despair. No matter how many times I warned myself that I'd go crazy if I went on thinking the way I was, I couldn't help it."

A wind gust slammed into the cabin, rattling the windows and threatening to push open the door. Dayna tucked her feet up under her, shivered, and then stared at the stove with its life-giving heat.

Chapter Thirteen

ȿ०

He was alone. The wind, coming from everywhere, cut into him. Even if he had the presence of mind to do more than place one foot in front of another, he couldn't do anything to decrease the punishment to his mind and body.

Alone?

Beacan repeated the word, only slowly and inexactly making sense of it. It seemed impossible that he could feel so isolated while the storm moved around and through and inside him, but it must be so because he couldn't—

"Kandi?"

A blast of air tore the word apart. Scared, he repeated her name. A force more powerful than any he'd encountered in thirty-one years of life shredded each letter. He stopped, something he'd wanted to do for so long he'd barely been able to think beyond it, and turned around. His world was a fluffy white blanket but without a blanket's warmth.

"Kandi."

Whatever devil god had taken control of his world laughed at his pathetic attempt to make himself heard. His fingers fisted, and he imagined clamping them around the devil god's throat and squeezing until...

Reaching inside himself, he summoned the strength that had gotten him through eight games in six days, including a twenty-one-inning affair that hadn't ended until after midnight followed by another starting early the next afternoon. Back then he'd put on his chest protector, shin guards, mask, and mitt because that was what he did for a living. Now he began retracing his steps because the life of the woman who was both his lover and a stranger might depend on it.

Going back the way he'd come felt wrong. Progress was so hard-fought and this felt like retreat, and after he'd found her—there could be no other alternative—he'd only have to go forward again. They both would.

Trees surrounded him. Although the evergreens were now trapped under snow, he sensed their awesome strength and age. Kandi might have accidentally veered off the road and then quickly become disoriented. If that was the case, or if she'd been blinded by ice shards, he might never—

"Kandi! Kandi, where are you!"

The wind laughed at him, sucker-punched the side of his head. He'd relaxed his fingers, but with the blow, they again became fists. Holding them up to his cheeks, he pressed, both in an attempt to regain some semblance of feeling to his face and because, maybe, his fists would give him strength.

"Kandi! Please!"

He wanted to hold his head up so he could better search for her, but if he didn't watch his footing, he might lose sight of where he was going, might get too close to the carnivorous trees.

If they had hold of her…

"Kandi!"

"Beacan?"

Relief so great it nearly stripped his muscles of all strength, stopped him. He again unfisted his fingers and cupped them around his eyes, an inadequate shield against the relentless flakes. The day had a forever quality about it, might go on and on until it exhausted him. He had no idea how long they'd been traveling or how many miles they'd covered.

Shaking his mind alert, he searched for her, finally locating her down on her knees by the side of the narrow road — at least he guessed she was at the road's edge. Trudging over to her, he started to offer her a hand up, but she waved him off.

"What's wrong?" he demanded after he'd positioned himself as a barrier between her and the worst of the wind. "Did you hurt...?"

"This is alone."

"What?"

"This is what it really is to be alone." Her voice was so low he could barely hear her. "I thought I knew what it felt like, but I was wrong."

"I couldn't find you. Damn it, I thought something had happened to you."

"It won't."

"How do you know? Damn it, Kandi!"

"Don't talk. Listen."

He did as she ordered because he was quite frankly afraid of her. The storm continued to mimic a train's engine. His mind refused to acknowledge anything more or less than that.

"It's incredible," she said.

"Incredible?"

"Nature's power. I'm humbled by it."

Nature could also kill. Didn't she know that?

"We live in cities," she continued, "where we're insulated from so much of what this planet of ours is really about. We think we understand the weather because we study and talk about it, but that's not the real thing."

"You're saying this is?"

"You don't agree?" she asked and stood, the gesture so effortless that she put him in mind of an ice dancer.

"Sure it is." He thought he'd gotten over his fear for her, but having her close and real brought it back again. He had to fight not to embrace her. "It's a fucking thrill a minute."

"Don't swear."

"You want me to send up a twenty-one gun salute because I'm stuck in the middle of a blizzard?"

"Don't be sarcastic."

So much snow had settled on her stocking cap that it was almost as if she wore a beehive hairdo. She'd pulled the cap down to her eyebrows and her coat collar was buttoned to her chin, making her all eyes, nose, and mouth. Her lips were blue.

"You're cold," he said.

"True. You?"

He embraced the cold as numb silenced his back. To avoid an explanation, he nodded.

"I don't mind," she said. "At first it hurt, but I've gotten used to it. It keeps me on the move."

"Frostbite?"

"I don't think so. At least not yet."

The word "yet" hammered at him. "We have to get going," he told her. "You can commune with nature while you're walking."

"I guess." She'd gone back to her near-whisper way of talking, forcing him to work at distinguishing her from her surroundings. "But I might never do something like this again, might never feel this kind of challenge and…"

"I should hope to hell not."

"And I don't want to forget it."

* * * * *

"I've been thinking," Dayna said to the unmoving, blanket-covered lump that was her brother. "I think I should bring in all the wood I can."

"Not a bad idea."

"It means I'm going to be opening and closing the door a lot. That's not going to bother you?"

"Why should it?"

"The cold?"

"I'm fine, Sis."

Intent on putting back on her coat, she was slow to make sense of what her brother had just called her. "You're not just saying that?" she asked. "I don't want to make things any harder for you than they already are."

"I'm weak." He closed his eyes, breathed, opened them again. "This soft old body of mine has taken a hell of a beating, but it's not like I'm going to die."

She forced a laugh. "You better not. I'll never forgive you."

He chuckled, the sound fading into a cough. "I wish I was of more help."

His nap—she'd told herself that was what he'd been doing—must have revived him. She picked up her gloves that, thanks to the wood heat, were once again dry and started to put them on. Then, before giving herself time to question what she was doing, she walked over to her brother and kissed him on the forehead.

He looked up at her with old, old eyes. "You've never done that before."

"I know," she said instead of pointing out the obvious, that they seldom saw each other.

He was silent for several moments. Then, "I was going to ask why, but I don't have to, do I?"

She shook her head. "Because of him."

"Yeah, because of him. How one man can fuck up so — Look, the electricity might not last much longer. If it goes, the water in the hot water heater is — "

"I know. Park, I'm glad we're having this time together."

"So am I," he said when she was both certain and afraid he'd tell her she was crazy.

She'd forgotten how hard it was to make progress in the storm, either that or the wind had gained strength without telling her. After bringing in two armloads of wood while she inhaled countless flakes and nearly froze her nose, she took a short break by asking Park if he wanted anything to eat.

"Not now." He hadn't moved from his spot on the couch. "Maybe if I rest a little longer I'll whip up something for dinner."

"You cook?"

"Between wives I learned how to keep from starving." He patted his stomach. "Come to think of it, maybe I don't need a wife after all."

"I can't advise you on that." She tried to wipe snow off her shoulder, but the flakes had sealed themselves to the fabric.

"A wife's more trouble than I ever thought one would be — at least that's the way it's been for me."

"I'm sorry."

"You know what I wish? That you'd never feel the need to say that word again."

"What?"

"Apologizing. He ingrained that so deeply inside you that—"

"I like this," she interrupted. "We can blame him for everything."

"Sounds good to me." His smile bloomed, then died. "I think—look, Sis, you'd better finish before the snow gets any deeper."

* * * * *

He shouldn't have pushed her, Park thought as his sister left for what, her fifth trip to the woodpile. Neither of them had brought up the reason behind her effort, not that they needed to because storm sounds said everything. Even if Beacan and Kandi walked all night—which sounded impossible but might be necessary so they wouldn't freeze— they'd be lucky to reach the rim road by morning. His and Dayna's rescue could come about sometime tomorrow, but only if the weather cooperated. And if the storm continued, they could be here much longer than that.

The questions of what "much longer" meant, and if the other two had known what they were in for when they volunteered to go after help, pushed at him until he struggled to his feet in an ill-advised effort to escape them. The last two times he'd gone to the bathroom there'd been blood in his urine. He hadn't told Dayna about it just as he hadn't said anything about how much breathing hurt. Although he hadn't particularly wanted to, he'd stayed by Scott's mother's side throughout her labor and delivery. On a scale of one to ten, he figured what he felt wasn't even on the same chart, but he wished to hell he knew what he'd done to himself.

One thing, the pain, particularly in his belly, had receded. He would have taken that as a good sign if his belly didn't feel as if he'd eaten an entire Thanksgiving dinner.

Making the trek from living room to bathroom took a long time, not just because he was weak but also because he had no intention of risking a fall. He pulled down his sweats, careful not to look at or touch his distended belly and aimed at what he hoped was the toilet. It didn't hurt to pee, and when he stepped back, he was relieved to see he'd pissed yellow, not red.

Scott's potty training had begun just after his second birthday because Rachael had decreed that the time had come. After a week of Scott showing absolutely no interest in the project, Park had told Rachael to back off, but she'd pointed out that he spent so little time with his family that he had no right to have an opinion about anything.

"I'm sorry, son," he whispered. "I sucked as a father, didn't I?"

He still did, he reminded himself before his reflection in the bathroom mirror distracted him. He hadn't shaved this morning and his lower face looked dirty. What there was of his hair lay plastered to his skull, shrinking his head and making the rest of him look too big. At least he'd recently applied hair dye and was spared being reminded of the unwanted gray.

When he heard the door open, he fought the need to remain where he was—to let the small room's smells and memories take him back to his childhood. But if he did, the memories would be bad.

"You *are* feeling better," Dayna observed as, shuffling, he joined her in the larger room. "I think I can get about three more loads, but that's going to pretty much deplete our supply."

Walking back to the couch, he lowered himself onto it. He felt nauseated and barely alert enough to keep up with his end of the conversation. His sister had blurred around the edges.

"...keeps playing," Dayna was saying.

"What keeps playing?"

"The old tapes." When she'd first started bringing in wood, she'd wiped debris from her arms, but she hadn't bothered this time. "The ones he planted inside me."

"What are they saying?" He wasn't sure his eyes were still open.

"That only a fool allows himself to run out of wood. I should have noticed the stack was getting low and done something about it. That..."

"That what?"

"That I'm stupid."

"I told you, he was wrong."

A song ended on the radio she'd finally gotten to work, and a commercial he didn't try to concentrate on began. He heard his sister's ragged breathing.

"Do you really believe that?" she asked.

There she was, still misty around the edges, her eyes so big they belonged on a deer and not a human being.

"With all my heart."

Dayna walked outside and closed the door behind her, but although she wanted to finish her task before nature's fury—an apt phrase if she'd ever heard one—overwhelmed her, she leaned against the side of the cabin and stared into what had nearly become a white waterfall.

Park, her brother, had acknowledged that she had a brain. Given the fact that she could beat him up if he said anything different, maybe she shouldn't give much credit to his compliment.

Yes, she should. Could. Would.

"Thank you," she whispered. A tear stung her eye and was lost in the cold. "Thank you for understanding."

She'd loaded herself down with eight or nine pieces of wood and was nearly back to the house before asking herself what she'd meant. Park, who'd lived in his own world, hadn't understood her when they were growing up. Maybe when she was too young to remember, she'd run to him for comfort, but something had taught her that he couldn't give her what she'd never gotten from their parents. Still, he'd acknowledged her intellect, and she'd never been given a compliment that meant more.

"Park," she said as she maneuvered herself and her burden inside. "I want to thank—"

The sight of his twitching arms and legs silenced her.

* * * * *

Kandi had been eighteen months old the first time her mother left her. She didn't remember anything about time she'd spent with her chain-smoking grandparents and wouldn't have known she'd wound up in the hospital with an asthma attack if someone—she couldn't remember who—hadn't told her about it.

Her mother had been beautiful once. She had the pictures as proof. Now, however, the woman could probably pass for sixty although she was nearly twenty years younger. The last time Kandi had seen her, her hair had been nearly white.

White like her surroundings.

Her too big boots kept rubbing her heels, and blisters would have formed if it hadn't been for the three pairs of socks. Trying to distract herself from the weights clamped around her feet, she took a mental tour of her closet, but although men liked to gift her and she didn't refuse them, material possessions had never meant that much to her.

It was easier to ask herself why she hadn't told her supervisor she didn't know when she'd be back inside walls with too few windows and small, crowded elevators, a desk the size of a card table, no view, and the heating/air conditioning system going all the time.

Mountain air was wonderful! Virginal. Even with snow making capturing enough oxygen difficult, the difference between what she was breathing now and what she was forced to take in on the job was incredible.

"Beacan?" They'd been walking side by side, their hands frequently touching, because he hadn't wanted her to fall behind again. "What are you going to do when you're no longer playing baseball?"

He gave no indication he'd heard.

"Maybe coach?" she prompted.

Still nothing.

"Can you hear me?" she asked, tapping his glove.

"I'm not deaf."

"Don't tell me you haven't thought about it."

"Of course I have."

"Then?"

"Why are you wasting your energy talking?" he demanded. "In case it hasn't occurred to you, we might have to walk all night."

"I know. I simply asked—"

He grabbed her arms and spun her around, making her face him. Her legs, trapped by snow, hadn't kept up with the rest of her, and she was forced to lean against him to keep from falling.

"I thought you were in love with silence," he rebuked. "What the hell are you babbling for?"

"Babbling?" She'd been manhandled in the past, more than manhandled as a child, which was why she'd taken a self-defense class and could run as if the dogs of hell were after her. However, under these conditions, neither of those skills would get her very far. "Why don't you want to talk about it?"

"Because right now it isn't important."

"But when this is over you—"

"*If* this gets over."

"All right. *If.*" The storm had rubbed her raw. As a consequence, he was going to get raw. "You'll have all kinds of money. Maybe you won't have to work."

"Maybe I won't."

"Aren't you lucky." She wrenched free, not because she'd suddenly received superhuman strength but because he obviously no longer wanted anything to do with her. "A life of leisure."

"Maybe you want a piece of the action."

"What do you mean by that?"

"You wouldn't be the first gold-digger to get her claws into a man. Is that why you're doing this, so I'll feel beholden to you?"

"Fuck you."

"Now there's an idea."

She opened her mouth for a retort when the insanity of the argument hit her, and she laughed.

"What's your problem?" he demanded.

"No problem. Look at where we are." Despite her bulky clothing, she did a fair job of encompassing their surroundings in a broad sweep of her arms. "God knows where, maybe writing the next chapter in the Donner party story. And we're fighting. About what?"

"About what I'm going to do with the rest of my life." He trapped his too pale lower lip between his teeth, nodding slightly.

"Spend your money," she suggested.

"Yeah. Right."

"That's not what you want to do?"

"No."

"Then—"

"All right! I don't have an idea in hell what's going to happen after I hang up my cleats."

Chapter Fourteen

୫୬

The wood Dayna had been holding clattered to the floor. After a heartbeat, she stepped over and around the pile, nearly losing her footing when her boot slipped on a log.

"Park! My God—" She tried to take his hand, but it jerked away. Feeling rebuffed, she cast around as if the room itself might provide answers.

"Can you hear me?" she asked. "What happened? My God, you were…"

Blood-tinged foam ran down both corners of his mouth. He lay half on, half off the couch, his heels banging against the floor. The less than brilliant deduction that he was having a seizure froze her in indecision.

"How?" She sounded no more than four. "You were doing fine."

His eyes had rolled back in his head and he looked almost inhuman, insane and helpless. Angry with herself, she clamped down on the instinct to run. Her brother needed help, her help. There was no one else. But she'd never taken a first aid class and had only a vague understanding of what her role should be in an emergency—this emergency.

Propelled by his uncontrollable body, he was in danger of sliding the rest of the way off the couch. She started to run her hands under his armpits when it occurred to her that he might be safer on the floor. After shoving aside a log that had rolled close, she knelt before him and carefully drew him down to her. Supporting his lolling head, she ignored the bloody spittle now on her arm.

He continued to jerk and make harsh, animal sounds. As she cradled his head in her lap, she pushed his sweat-soaked hair off his forehead.

"I'm here, Park. You're going to be all right. I'll take care of you. Do you understand? You aren't alone."

But *she* was.

"What happened?" she asked stupidly. "You were doing all right. You said you were."

Trying to replay their last conversation, she concentrated on the curtain rod over the living room window. She hadn't noticed the spider web there before and made a mental note to remove it.

"What am I supposed to do?" she asked. "I—Park, please. What am I supposed to do?"

It was both hot and cold down here on the floor. There were several throw rugs throughout the room, but she sat on hardwood, her rear end rapidly cooling. By contrast, she'd broken out in a sweat—either that or she was absorbing her brother's body temperature.

His contortions went on and on, turning what she'd believed about his poor physical condition into a lie. The back of his head pounded against her thighs and pelvis and he became heavy—so heavy. Trapped her. He seemed to relax slightly when she stroked his forehead so she did that. *This can't be happening*, repeated endlessly inside her.

"It's going to be over soon." Using the hem of her coat, she wiped spittle off his mouth. "This can't go on much longer and then…" *And then what?*

Seconds became minutes. Although she hated touching his stiff, hot limbs, she tried to straighten his arms and legs.

"You're fine. Fine. I won't leave you. Park. Park? Can you hear me?"

More blood dribbled from between his clenched teeth and she wiped that away. Concerned he might be biting his tongue she pulled back his lips. Revulsion washed through her.

"It's all right. Your tongue's safe, I think. It's all right. All right. I won't…"

Won't leave him although every muscle and blood vessel in her body screamed with the need to do just that.

"I love you. Do you hear me? I love you. I won't let—won't let anything happen to you."

But it already had.

Her right thigh had gone to sleep. With less care than she'd exhibited the first time, she repositioned him.

"It's still snowing. I wish it would quit. I keep thinking about Beacan and Kandi, worrying about them."

Park wouldn't care about the others, not with what he was experiencing.

"It's a seizure." *I think.* "That's all. Lots of people have them." *Do they?* "It's going to be over soon and then…" Red-tinged foam continued to spill from his mouth. If he'd had serious internal damage and that was causing his body to…

"Look at me, Park. Please. I don't know where you are, but I need you to come back to me. They say…they say that people in comas can still hear." *At least some of them can, maybe.* "I know you can hear me. Feel my hand on your forehead. Does that help? I think…I think it does. Oh God, I hope—"

Her right calf tightened, warning of a cramp. Pointing her toes, she contracted her muscles in an attempt to ward it off, but she'd soon be in pain if she didn't change position. Still, her brother—

"I'm going to move a little. I'm not going anywhere. I'd never…"

With his head cradled in her hands, she got to her knees. There was a throw pillow on the couch, and she managed to reach out and grab it. Placing it under his head, she settled him down again.

"Is that all right?" She went back to stroking his sweat-slicked forehead. "I'm still here. Still here."

His muscles were giving out, either that or—please—he was getting over his seizure. No longer trying to say anything, she concentrated on his legs. His heels had been beating against the floor for so long that surely he'd bruised himself. If they were too badly injured, he might not be able to put back on his boots, let alone make the journey out.

No. They didn't have to walk. Beacan and Kandi were doing that for them.

* * * * *

Wasn't there a fairy tale about a snow princess? Kandi wondered. Maybe she'd turned into that creature, magically transformed from the shell of a human she'd always thought herself to be. That was fine, fine. A snow princess—a snow princess what?

Beacan was just ahead and if she concentrated, she could distinguish him from the snow, but she'd been doing that for so long there wasn't anything wrong with letting go just a little. Nothing wrong at all.

Snow princess. Or maybe ice maiden. No, a person could live in the snow if they worked at it. On the other hand, ice...

Polar bears thrived in climates far harsher than this. Seals too and foxes, maybe. She wasn't too sure about the foxes. Walrus, yes! Walruses didn't freeze, swam under sheets of ice, sunned themselves on glaciers. Proud of herself for coming up with three and perhaps four living creatures that embraced temperatures beyond her comprehension and experience, she opened her mouth to tell Beacan. What stopped her was cold on her teeth that caused an instant headache. That and the memory of how he'd snapped at her the last time they'd spoken.

Fine. Let him have his hang-ups, and his bad back. She'd walk him into the ground, prove that his damn muscular body was no match for her determination. Even if her numb feet and not much better hands and constant shivering were signs of frostbite, she wouldn't give up. In the end—

She lifted her left leg, prepared, once again, to swing it over the ever-deepening snow, realized it hadn't come free. Trapped, she lost her balance, chest and chin plowing into powder. Cursing, she struggled to right herself.

"Beacan! Wait."

He gave no indication he'd heard, but although that alarmed her, getting free was more important. By settling her upper body weight over her hips, she managed to bring herself to an erect position. Freeing her legs without the aid of forward movement took a great deal of effort, but she finally got herself going again. Not only that, the exertion had pumped enough blood through her system that her shivers decreased.

The snow had become so deep that it was nearly up to her knees. It was less under the trees, but if they tried to walk there, they risked losing sight of the road.

Forget the snow princess business. If she was destined to be royalty, she wanted a tropical island kingdom. Intrigued by the idea, she tried to conjure up an image of her, in a bikini of course, tanning on a white-sand beach, but she'd never been in a humid climate let alone the tropics, had no idea how one went about ruling subjects.

"Beacan?"

He stopped so quickly that she wondered if he'd been waiting for the excuse. He'd become a polar bear, his human features all but obliterated by his snow-coating. There were even flakes on his brows and lashes. His nose was red, the rest of his features pale. He stood with his hands on his hips, breathing deeply. Not for the first time, she asked herself if they were going to get out of this alive.

Instead of turning the question over to him, she forced herself to walk up to him and asked if he'd ever been to the tropics. He shook his head. Obviously, he thought she'd lost her mind, but then maybe she had. So what?

"I'm just trying to think of something other than what we're doing," she explained, keeping her arms down by her sides, or at least as close as possible given her bulky clothing. Flakes fell like dandruff around them. "You've played Florida teams, haven't you?"

"Yes." He looked up at the sky, blinked and shook his head again. "We don't have time for this. If I tell you there's so much humidity there that sweat never evaporates and your lungs fight to reject the hot air, will you let it go?"

"You didn't like it?"

"My chest protector stuck to my uniform, and I thought I'd never get it off, and I passed out once in the middle of an afternoon game so, no, I didn't like it."

On the verge of asking what it felt like to pass out, she remained silent. At first she thought she was simply tired and thus unable to concentrate fully, but that wasn't it. Something or someone was out here with them.

"Kandi?"

"What?"

"Are you all right?"

"Yes, of course." Crazy, that was it. They were alone. Alone. "I was… It sounds as if there's a lot of things you don't like about what you do for a living."

"Where did you get an idea like that?"

She'd hit one of his hot buttons. "You could have shined me on about passing out or not mentioned it. Why didn't you?"

"I'm not interested in shining you on."

Why not, she started to ask, then let silence do the job.

"Maybe when this is over, you'll sell your story to the tabloids," he said. Frowning, he glanced over his shoulder. "Jock crumbles in life or death struggle, something like that. I guess I'll have to take the chance."

He wasn't shivering, not this polar bear man. "Maybe the publishers will be talking to you, not me," she told him.

"I don't think so."

"Why not?"

"Because you're a survivor."

"You don't know anything about me so how can you say that?"

He smiled, almost. Looked around again. "Kandi, it's my job to read other people. If I'm good at communicating to a pitcher or know when a batter is likely to make a mistake, it's because I know how to get into their heads."

"All right. What am I thinking about?"

He covered his nose and mouth with his glove and breathed into it. "We don't have time for that. Maybe later but—I'm sorry."

"For what?"

"For jumping on you earlier." His surroundings again distracted him. "It's not your fault that I don't know what I'm going to do with the rest of my life."

Jace stalked to the front of the four-wheel drive he'd converted into a snowplow, but although he needed to raise the blade a few inches, his attention slid off the task and into the forest.

This was a storm. Not a tease or one of those fierce things that thrilled and briefly challenged but blew itself out before it had done any damage or left any imprint, but a beast with staying power. Crater Lake and the surrounding area would be changed by it. Taken from fall into the heart of winter.

He pulled his collar up around his neck, but he hadn't bothered with a hat, and his head was rapidly cooling off. He couldn't stay out here long, should—

Cherokee was about to begin his second winter in the wilderness, not separate from what was larger than trees and mountains, part of that vastness, forever locked in it.

What was that like?

* * * * *

The stove wasn't giving out as much heat as it had earlier, but Dayna didn't leave her brother's side. She didn't know how long his fit had lasted and couldn't say when she'd realized he was coming out of it. She'd begun to feel hopeful when she no longer saw only white in his eyes and kissed him when he focused on her. He'd looked puzzled and a little frightened and then, his words disjoined, he'd asked what they were doing on the floor. He didn't have the strength to get back on the couch and weighed too much for her to be able to do the work for him, but she managed to make him more comfortable.

As she was tucking a second blanket around him, he told her he felt like throwing up. She hurried for a bowl but didn't get back with it in time. Fortunately he didn't throw up much and she wiped it off his chin and shirt, trying to keep his attention off how much blood it contained.

"I don't remember," he said as she cleaned his face with a damp washcloth.

"What don't you remember?"

"I had a seizure, right? That's what you said, didn't you? You'd think I would have felt it coming on, but I didn't. I was thinking…thinking maybe I could do something to help you, but after…"

"Don't worry about it." The back of his neck felt clammy.

"I can't help it, Sis. It scares—"

"I like it when you call me Sis. Did you when I was little?"

"Sometimes. He didn't approve."

"Damn him. I need to stoke the stove. Are you going to be all right?"

He nodded yes, but she could tell the gesture wore him out. She'd positioned him so his back was propped against the couch and had placed a pillow behind him. When his head lolled back, it didn't go far. She hurried to complete her task, but afterward, instead of returning to him, she stood with her back to the stove, warming herself.

His color was all wrong, gray and yellow and his fingers still trembled. She hated his loud breathing, but what the hell did that matter when he might be—

"You started to say something about-about being scared," she said, desperate for the sound of his voice. "Do you want to talk about it?"

He straightened and then let his head fall back. He spoke to the ceiling. "I don't know what-what's wrong with me. I wish my phone worked. Most of all I wish to hell it would stop snowing. It isn't letting up, is it?"

She glanced at the window, but condensation coated it and made it impossible for her to see out. Still, she knew. "No. I'm sorry."

"Stop apologizing. You don't have anything to do with the weather."

From where she stood, she could see at least a half dozen spider webs, but she no longer had any interest in removing them. If spiders could live here year-round, they had more right to make the cabin their home than she and her family ever had. "I think it's ingrained in me."

"He can't get to you — to us — anymore. Let it go, Dayna."

"How?"

Instead of answering, he placed his hand over his belly.

"What is it?" she asked. "Where do you hurt?"

"It doesn't…matter. Dayna, I don't…don't like who I am. The kind of father I've been… Scotty…"

"What about Scott?"

His reply was lost in the harsh snap of the radio signaling that the electricity had again gone off. She waited the better part of a minute, and then lit the candles she'd placed on the kitchen table. She half expected her brother to rebuke her for wasting them while it was still light, but he didn't. Neither did he comment on the loss of electricity.

"You were saying something about Scott," she prompted.

"He — Dayna, if I…"

"If you what?" She knelt near her brother, stared at him.

"He-he's going to be tall, taller than me. He has more hair than I ever did, thank goodness."

"Does he have your mind for math?"

"His mother says he's good at it. I see his grades, eventually, but they don't tell me enough."

"But you talk to him—"

"He's always in a hurry. You know how it is, kids wanting to be with their friends or on the computer or—sometimes I feel as if I'm talking to a stranger." His eyes were open but unfocused. "I never wanted it like that. When he was born…"

"I remember," she supplied. "You were off on a business trip when Rachael went into labor."

A tear leaked out of Park's right eye and slid toward his nose. "But I got home in time for the birth. After he was born, I kept looking at him, trying to make sense of him. He-he was so perfect and he was part of me. I'd helped make him and yet he was so much more."

The storm she'd closed outside tapped at the windows. She didn't feel intimidated by it and yet its presence made concentrating on her brother difficult.

"I'd hold him—I was afraid I wasn't doing it right—I'd hold him and pray I'd be everything he needed in a father."

"You? Prayed?"

Park's attention flickered to the nearest window and then returned to whatever private place he'd found. "I never knew—when Rachael got pregnant, I saw it as a reason to make more money. She had her mother and sister and friends and didn't need me so…"

There were three of them involved in this conversation, Park, her, and the weather.

"I had no idea having a child would change me the way it did."

He'd spoken so softly that she barely caught his words, and it took a moment for the weight and honesty of them to register.

"I-I want to be a mother," she said. It was a confession, honesty traded for honesty. "But I'm afraid I don't know how."

"It's different for women." His colorless lips barely moved and his lids slid down over his eyes, locking him within himself. "They give birth. If there's divorce or-or… The children are expected to stay with their mother. Fathers…fathers have to fight for…"

His fingers began twitching again, first clawing for something on the wooden floor and then tightening around one of his shirt buttons. Alarmed, she scrabbled toward him. The shadows, the damnable shadows, made reading him difficult.

"Park?"

"I'm… I don't feel… I think I'm going—"

She finished the sentence for him, reached for the recently cleaned bowl and shoved it close to his mouth. He jerked forward and his eyes popped open. They were huge, the irises more pink than white.

"Scott," he mouthed when he'd finished vomiting. "Scott."

"He isn't here, Park. It's just you and me."

"But he—" Park clamped his hand over his mouth, spoke from behind his fingers. "I love—tell him I love him."

"You tell him," she started but although she wanted to scream at him not to scare her this way, she didn't have time.

Park jerked again, broken at the waist, his neck like cooked spaghetti. This time he made no attempt to aim his vomit at the bowl. Instead it surged from him, a waterfall of red liquid. The blood filled the bowl and ran over onto both their legs.

"Park!"

Chapter Fifteen

 හ

Park died sprawled in his blood with his sister's arms around him. Dayna hated the feel, the smell and yes, the taste of her brother's blood, but she wouldn't let him die alone. She remembered, vaguely, thinking it was all right to continue to kneel where she was because nothing she did or tried to do would change what was happening to him. She remembered, vaguely, saying goodbye as his breathing became less and less tortured.

Mostly she was aware of hammering wind and snow, of smoke being forced back down the chimney and leaking out around the stove seams, of lights and radio and refrigerator repeatedly trying to start before sighing into silence. Finally when all those things had imprinted themselves on her, pain stabbed at her knees.

When she changed position, Park slid out of her grasp and landed on the wet floor with a plopping, squishing sound. His pathetic excuse for hair was soaked in blood, but at least his eyes looked at the ceiling, unaware of what had happened to him at the end.

She had to reach for the couch twice before she managed enough of a grip that she got to her feet. She wanted to strip off her clothes and step into the shower and not think about using up what might be the last of the hot water, but if she walked out of this hollow room, Park would be left alone, and she might not be able to force herself to come back. Besides, how could she think about leaving such a mess?

The mess of her brother's dying.

A low moan escaped her dry lips. Appalled and horrified by what she was seeing, she backed away, not stopping until she collided with the front door. Along with everything else that had happened since she'd last come inside, she'd removed her coat and put it somewhere, and if she went out the way she was, she'd be unable to stay long — might freeze if she walked more than a few feet.

"No. No, no, no," she chanted, only a little comforted because she managed to keep from screaming. If only the radio would stay on, she'd crank it as high as it would go, throw a blanket over her brother's body and —

She couldn't stay here!

Not thinking, she reached for the only jacket within sight and wrapped herself into it. It was Park's, smelling of him, and reminding her too much of his contours. The door resisted her attempt to open it, forcing her to put her thoughts and muscles to the task. As she pushed it out and into the wind, icy shards stung her lids and cheeks and she cried out.

What time was it? The mix of gray and white both stole the day and held it suspended. From where she stood on the porch, she couldn't see the lake and wasn't sure whether the mounds to her right were what was left of her car and the uprooted tree or something else. Her bulky boots would hinder and perhaps harm her if she decided to head for Crater and yet —

Walk out?

Frowning, she debated whether she'd asked the question or if someone else was responsible. If the decision was hers alone she'd, she'd what?

What are you thinking? Help will be here tomorrow, and it'll be all right. Someone — someone will tell you what caused Park's death and then you can — oh God, you can tell Scott he doesn't have a father anymore.

She started crying, her tears small and nearly silent, impossible to contain. Thinking to protect her hands, she tucked them into her—Park's—pockets.

He'd accomplished so much in his life, much more materially than she ever would. He loved his son and worried about being a good father and…and what?

Her tears kept falling, first cooling and then freezing on her cheeks. She wanted to howl, to tell someone that her brother was dead and she needed to mourn him although she barely knew him. Most of all she wanted to run and keep on running until she'd found that someone, or died trying.

Winter flexed its muscles, delighted in its strength. The storm had brought the season to life and filled it with energy, and it increased its grip on the landscape. The mountains and trees and rocks had been created to withstand such punishment. Winter, working as one with the storm, attacked the year's soft, pale new pine needles, ferns and grasses, burying the earthbound life under freezing layers.

The creatures—and there were too many—who'd been caught unaware by the season's first storm, hurried to protect themselves. The lucky ones had taken refuge in underground homes, not caring what took place on the surface. The unlucky huddled behind boulders or against tree trunks, backs to the wind. Some, like the rutting buck and just-impregnated doe, knew in a way that was ageless and all instinct, that they'd waited too long to leave the high country. They hadn't given up the battle for survival and wouldn't as long as their hearts beat. Still, standing side by side for warmth, they trembled and not just from the cold.

The fish were better equipped for the quick change in seasons. As the lake's temperature dropped, instinct sent them deep and their systems began to slow. No longer darting after food, they rocked with the water, accepted.

Above, wind and snow played with the lake's surface. Caught in the storm's grip, water became thin ice sheets only to be repeatedly shattered, forced into angry but helpless whitecaps. The lake knew neither exhaustion nor strength, only that it obeyed its master.

That master was the storm.

*   *   *   *   *

Two feet but on its way to becoming three, in places the snow had already piled up so that Jace didn't try to attack the white mounds with his makeshift snowplow. He'd cranked the cab's heater as high as it would go and would be sweating if the snow weren't packing on the roof or being pushed in around the doors.

At times the wind slammed into the cab with such strength that he feared the glass would break. Between that sound, the heater fan, and engine noise, he could barely make out what came to him via the CB.

The windshield wipers, whipping at top speed and still not doing their job made him slightly dizzy. If he dared take his hands off the steering wheel, he'd have pressed his hand to his stomach, but he didn't because the steering wheel was his link to strength.

"Jace." It was park superintendent Paul Soffin, his voice cracking and snapping as it reached him across the miles. "Can you hear me?"

"Barely."

"What's it like where you are?"

"Snowing."

"Don't be a smart-ass. A few minutes ago I thought things were calming down a little, but the way things are blowing right now, I don't know if it's ever going to end."

"What's the weather report?"

"Not good. Look, I'm going to call you in. You're not making any headway anyway, are you?"

Jace started to shake his head, and then remembered to yell "no".

"All we're doing is wasting gas and maybe risking injury. Give it up."

"I'm almost to the road to Wolf. If there are hikers out there, they're—"

"Everyone who signed out is accounted for."

"That doesn't mean—"

"I know, I know. There could still be fools out there, but we don't know that and I'm not taking chances with you or the other rangers' safety. There's hot coffee here."

The thought of warmth spreading through his stomach was a powerful incentive. Still, the spur road he was heading toward was a popular jumping off spot. "Give me ten minutes," he compromised. "If things haven't let up by then, I'll turn around."

"Ten minutes. No more."

After Paul signed off, Jace leaned forward, straining to see out, but it was like driving into feathers. The sense of disorientation isolated him and stripped away the world.

The snow had been coming down like this the night of Cherokee's death. It had been late afternoon by the time Jace and Kailee had finished making love and he'd pulled his mind together enough to ask himself why his friend wasn't back.

If only he'd organized a search party while it was still light. If only he'd ordered Cherokee to stay with him instead of skiing off on his own. If only…

This truck cab with its cold plastic seats, dirty dashboard, and glove compartment filled with pliers, screwdrivers, and maps was everything. Crater Lake and the forest around it no longer existed, victims to Mother Nature on a rampage. The storm had become a vortex, holding him prisoner, sucking him down, down... Cherokee had always been "out there" just out of sight, scared and lost, angry and accusing, but now he was in the cab, taking up too much room and oxygen, staring, reaching—

Something pulled Jace out of himself. For a moment he didn't know what it was but then, as he inched the truck closer, he realized he'd come upon another vehicle. Trapped under snow, he couldn't tell the make or model but was fairly sure it was a sedan. He maneuvered as close as he dared given the weapon the snow blade represented and then considered his options—not that he had any. After putting the truck in park, he put on his stocking cap and buttoned his coat. He had to lean his weight into the door in order to open it, and the blast of snow-filled air blurred his vision and made breathing difficult.

One hand over his nose and mouth, he slogged to the vehicle. The top layers of snow were powdery, making the job of wiping it away relatively easy, but ice had encrusted the windows. As he'd expected, the car was locked. After circling it in a vain attempt to see in, he returned to his truck for his ice scraper. Finally, he removed the last of the barrier and peered in. From what he could tell, the interior was empty, and immaculate. He'd never been particularly interested in vehicles but knew this one was expensive. It was built low to the ground, a drawback for traveling over uneven roads, hardly the kind someone addicted to hiking into the middle of nowhere would choose.

A memory tapped at him, then scuttled away. He peered in again, this time noticing a CD player. The cigarette lighter had been removed but nothing was plugged into the receptacle, making him think it might have been used to charge a cellular phone. There was no sign of the phone, but the owner could have put it in the trunk for safekeeping or taken it with him. After wiping off the rapidly accumulating condensation, he noticed that the driver's side floor was clean. No. This was no hiker's vehicle.

All right. So the owner hadn't gone off to commune with nature. The vehicle was on the turnoff to Lake Wolf, which meant—

The thought that had escaped him a minute ago returned, solidified. Yesterday he'd talked to a young woman who'd told him that she and her brother were going to Lake Wolf. If they'd ridden in together, they might have left one of their vehicles here.

"I hope you know what you're doing," he muttered as he plodded back to his truck. "And I hope you've been listening to the weather reports."

He stopped with his hand on the doorknob. He had no reason to worry, nothing except the memory of what had happened last year and the eyes of a woman with the power to see beneath his surface.

Be careful. Please.

* * * * *

The weather now reminded Beacan of a roller coaster ride. He could handle the chugging up to the top and even hanging at the peak wasn't so bad but once the downward plunge began—

When the wind roared and snow seemed endless and inescapable—

Stopping, he waited for Kandi's familiar presence. He'd lost track of the number of times he'd asked if she needed to rest, and the answer had always been the same. She was doing fine, damn her.

"What is it?" she asked as she caught up with him. Her voice was hollow, part of the scream that made up his world.

"What are you?" he demanded. "Superwoman? Don't you ever get tired?"

"Of course I do."

"Then why —? No, you don't."

She said something but he didn't catch the words. He used his club hands to pull her closer. Under all those layers, she was shivering.

"You're cold. Why the hell didn't you tell me?"

Instead of answering, she looked around, but why he didn't understand because it all looked the same and maybe there was no getting out of this hell.

"Why didn't you tell me?" he demanded.

"It doesn't matter. We have to keep going."

She was right, but that wasn't the point. The women who'd been in his life since his divorce—whether he'd invited them in or they'd invited themselves—had looked to him for many things, sex and money being chief among them, but Kandi hadn't asked for either.

Although he wasn't sure he was shivering any less than her, he pulled her into the circle of his arms and let her breathe into his chest.

"Are you all right?" she asked.

I've been better. "You're so damn strong. I know I've said that before." Hadn't he? "It's a compliment. Take it as one."

"I will," she said, her response coming on the tail of a puff of warm air.

"You'd make a good catcher."

"Or an offensive lineman."

"You're not big enough."

"But I wouldn't give way. I'd dig in and —"

"The way you're digging in against the storm?"

He felt her nod and accepted that they were in this together as he'd never been in anything before in life—his daughter's death and the subsequence collapse of his youthful marriage, the drive toward the World Series hadn't come close.

"I'm glad, if we have to do this," he told her when he hadn't known the words were waiting to be spoken, "that it's you here with me and not…"

"And not some other woman?"

"Yeah."

"Beacan?"

"What?" he asked when she didn't go on.

"I don't have any claim to you. I-I never—I don't want one."

"Just some good times?" he asked with a forced laugh and shadows all around.

"That's-that's not what I had in mind."

Then what did you have in mind, he wanted to ask, but he hadn't let a woman get close to him in years. With his mind sluggish and the shadows making their impact and yet needing to find a way through her layers, he asked what she thought about while they walked.

"You call this walking?" she asked.

She still hadn't backed away from him and he took it as a sign of something—maybe more than just her need for warmth.

"I'm not trying to be technical here," he pointed out. "So, what do you think about?"

"Florida."

"I thought you said you'd never been there."

"I haven't but, when you're no longer playing ball, where are you going to live?"

"I don't know," he told her although he'd thought about it, a lot. "What about you? If you could live anywhere, where would it be?"

"It doesn't matter." She shrugged. "I've never—a lot of people want to live where it's warm year-round, but to me weather is just that, weather."

"What about friends you want to stay near?"

There was her silence again, heavy, impenetrable like thick fog or this near blizzard.

"No friends?" he pushed.

"Not many."

"What about your siblings?"

"No."

Not enough, Kandi. Not enough by far. "Don't they mean anything to you?"

Her answer came in the form of hands pressed against his chest and a quick twisting of her body as she broke free. "We're wasting time," she said.

He grabbed her wrist, his fingers awkward but strong. "What about your brothers and sisters, Kandi?"

"They don't give a damn about me."

"Why not?"

"Fuck you."

"Why not?" Then, not sure why, he told her that his father had worked two jobs all the time he was growing up so he could concentrate on baseball.

"Every summer from the time I was twelve, my folks sent me to baseball camps. I learned from the best, ex-pro players who charged plenty. It's always bothered me that my folks sacrificed so much for my sister and myself. She's had asthma all her life. She's been in and out of hospitals, nearly died a couple of times," he went on while the elements tried to steal his words. "They wanted her to have as normal a childhood as possible so between giving me the chance to see where my skills might take me and her needs they—do you know what I'm getting at?"

"No."

He didn't believe her. "You don't have to ask how scared my folks were that my sister wasn't going to live because I'll tell you. My mother didn't work so she could be there all the time to take care of her. I'll give you that. And more." *Not everything but more.* "But you have to give me something in return."

"I don't owe you anything."

He'd never been as angry as he had that August night two years ago when an opposing catcher came home with his spikes aimed at his unprotected forearm. He'd put on the tag and then, his blood streaming into the dirt from the punctures, he'd pummeled the bastard until the umpire and his own pitcher had pulled him off. This afternoon with the storm part of him, that anger returned.

"Don't you?" he demanded. "You let me fuck you. Let me break trail. Let me warm you just a minute ago. We might die out here. Die! Damn it, I deserve more!"

How she'd gotten free he couldn't say, maybe because he'd been so focused on what he was trying to say that he'd let her go, maybe because she'd become stronger than him. But although she could have distanced herself from him, she didn't.

She kept her head high and spoke into the wind. Defied it. "My family didn't want me, Beacan. They threw me away."

They threw me away. It hadn't been quite like that, but what did it matter?

After yet another futile attempt to make his cell phone work, Beacan had started walking again and although it would have been easier, safer, to fall a few feet behind, she matched his stride and broke her own trail. Her well-conditioned legs were so tired she wasn't sure how much longer she could order them to fight the cold, white quicksand that was their world, and she tried to send her thoughts to that place called Florida, but they wouldn't go there now.

She hated Beacan, hated her vulnerability around him. At the same time, she wouldn't be where she was without him and had to give him credit for keeping them on track.

Only, were they still on the road?

Focusing, she took in her surroundings. Everything looked the same. There was no distinguishing one tree from another and although the road dipped and rose, went around a curve or even straight for a short while, left and right turns blurred in her mind.

She'd allowed Beacan to break trail most of the way while she concentrated on trying to stay warm, following him like a bloodhound only her sense of smell, like her other senses, had frozen. She could still see, but when everything was white…

Something scraped her right cheek, and if she hadn't screamed her last scream while still a small child, she would have done so now. Before she could put her mind to determining what had struck her, she collided with a low, snow-laden branch and was stopped by it.

Caught between anger and dumb acceptance, she tried to push it aside, but there was so much to the branch. It went on forever, constituted everything.

"Beacan."

Surprised by her tone, she fell silent. If he heard her hesitancy, her almost fear, he might no longer think her strong.

Backing up, she freed herself from her prickly prison. She needed to tell Beacan there hadn't been any trees on the road on the way in which meant they'd—

There he was. Standing with his head down the way she did at the end of a marathon and a hand pressed against the small of his back. He was too much outline and shadow, nearly swallowed by white. A barrage of flakes swirled around him. In the past, he'd stood separate from the storm as if in defiance of it. Now his body accepted.

Either that or it had surrendered.

"Beacan." She put effort behind the word. "What are you doing?"

Giving up, she thought he said but that couldn't be. She meant to tap his elbow but wound up covering his gloved hand with hers. Beneath the layers of fabric, she felt corded tension.

"Your back's hurting, isn't it," she said.

"Some."

"Do you want to rest?"

"No."

"Then—"

"I don't know where we are."

"I-I, ah…"

"I'm sorry," he said. He turned his wrist so he was holding onto her hand.

The trees were everywhere, everything. Reaching into the clouds but whether in defiance or acceptance of a greater power, she didn't know. "It isn't your fault."

"Yeah, it is." He still hadn't looked at her.

Fear was an emotion from her childhood. She'd buried it along with the memories of that time, but now it clawed at her. "I never asked you to take care of me."

He didn't answer, but there was no silence because the swaying, sometimes buckling trees sang their own tune. "I can't remember—" she started and then had to stop and battle what might become panic if she let it. "Where we left the road."

"All I thought about was not stopping," he said. "Going. Just going."

"And your back."

"And my back."

"What's wrong with it?"

'Disintegrating disks."

"Oh. I didn't know."

The heat and power of his gaze reached her through layer upon layer of white. "Not many people do. I don't say much to the press...about anything."

"Then why did you tell me?" she asked even though she was sure he wouldn't answer. It wasn't dark yet. She had to think about that, hold the night at bay and find the road again because without it...

"There are things I never talk about," he said. "Things I keep..."

Yes, there are, Beacan. You think I don't know that?

"I hate this storm," she told him when that wasn't what she wanted to say at all.

"Maybe—" He looked behind him. "Maybe we can retrace our steps."

"Maybe."

Chapter Sixteen

❧

"—forecast is for more of the same, a lot more. The present system hasn't reached full strength, and, folks, it's going to be cold tonight."

Dayna held her breath and willed the roaring in her ears to end.

"So far all we've gotten in the city is rain, not that I need to tell anyone that," the radio announcer continued. "However, as temperatures drop, it should turn into snow, maybe not on the valley floor, but folks living on hills need to factor in scraping snow off their vehicles in the morning."

The announcer sounded as if he was in his late teens or early twenties, his voice cheerful and upbeat. Dayna felt a hundred years old.

"Tune into KKSS, your favorite country and western station in the morning for updates about possible school closures. If the buses can't run, the kiddies will have the day off. Back when I was in school and trudging five miles through snow and ice, we never thought of—all kidding aside folks, meteorologists are saying it's mighty unusual for a storm with this much punch to come so early in the season."

Dayna tried to stand. Her legs weren't ready.

"My cousin lives in Prospect," the announcer continued. "I just got off the phone with him and he's going to bring in his marijuana plants for safekeeping."

Puddles of water from the snow she'd tracked in during her last trip outside had collected around Dayna's feet. If he'd been here, her father would have ordered her to lap it up.

"Chains are required from Prospect on, and the folks at Crater Lake announced they've closed the north entrance. My advice, stay away or they'll have you shoveling snow."

The too young man prattled on, but Dayna couldn't concentrate. The cabin was cooling off, but the ability to deal with that, like her ability to listen to the disembodied voice, had been spent.

No one should have to squat on hand and knees, face to the floor as they swallowed and swallowed and swallowed, but she wouldn't have had any choice just as she'd had to spend the night in the attic after she'd protested being sent up there once to clean out cobwebs and bat droppings. In her father's world, children did as they were ordered.

Her good-as-dead father.

Something so weightless it barely registered touched her wrist. On the verge of flicking off the tiny spider, she sank back in the chair and watched it crawl along her flesh. Maybe she and her spider were the only living things in here.

Both horrified and comforted by the thought, she marveled at the strength and tenacity of her almost microscopic visitor. If she found herself surrounded by a forest of giant hairs, she'd stop where she was, paralyzed by indecision.

"Don't be afraid," she whispered. "I could never hurt anything. Except for him. I used to dream about doing something to him. Running over him with a car or shooting him or forcing him off a cliff or…"

The radio station snapped and became little more than static. She ignored it. "My mother never raised her hand against a soul," she continued. "Maybe he beat everything out of her, left her afraid to breathe. Fire. I always thought setting fire to him would be best of all."

She looked over at Park, seeking agreement, but her brother only stared at the ceiling.

"I used to imagine tying him up and pouring gasoline over him and lighting a match and throwing it at him and standing there watching him burn to death." Her breath caught and then came in a rush. "That's what I wanted."

Her spider was inexhaustible. He could climb up and over and down hairs for as long as he lived. He would never—

Kandi and Beacan were out there, and the storm was still gaining strength. The north side of Crater Lake, which was where they were heading, had been closed!

The spider and murder thoughts forgotten, Dayna surged to her feet and hurried to the window. She heard the wind scream its way down the chimney and the clink, clink, clink of ice crystals against brittle old windowpanes and the awful creaking the trees made as they struggled to stay upright.

"What am I going to do?" she asked and was immediately ashamed because she'd put her own concerns before the two people who'd gone after help, help her brother didn't need anymore and they might not be able to reach. "If something happens to them, no one is going to know…"

Know she was here.

Know Beacan and Kandi were in trouble!

Her stomach cramped. Cold sweat broke out all over her and ran down the small of her back. She paced to the stove and threw in more wood without first turning the damper. Smoke billowed into the room and she coughed—coughed the way her father would have if she'd turned her murderous fantasy into reality.

She couldn't tell how much snow was on the ground or remember whether the wind had let up at all today. She tried to tell herself that Kandi and Beacan were warmly dressed and strong and had had no qualms about what they were doing, but those assurances did nothing to blunt her fear.

Fear.

That was what she felt each time her father walked into the room and it was eating a hole through her this afternoon.

What raged outside wasn't a call to adventure, pristine and beautiful, peace in a white blanket. It was death for two decent people.

* * * * *

Jace had only been back in his rig a few minutes when he felt compelled to return to the stranded vehicle. Once again he approached the half buried one, this time with a wrench dangling from his fingers.

Although he knew it was useless, he again tried the doors and even pressed against the wing windows hoping one of them had been left open. They hadn't which meant—

He should tell his boss what he'd found and ask for advice. He didn't because he knew what Paul would say.

What was he thinking of? He couldn't break into a vehicle that cost more than he made in a year. The owner would probably sue him, would have every right to. He could get fired over this. Could—

Halfway through the process of turning away, he stopped. Last year he'd argued down his sense of responsibility and Cherokee had died.

After sucking in a deep breath, Jace gripped the wrench in both hands and swung the tool-weapon at the driver's window. The glass sagged inward and became a spider web of cracks but didn't splinter. Again and again he swung and connected, eventually proving himself more powerful than the glass which still hadn't shattered but had separated enough that he could hook the wrench around the slits and pull. Snow pushed through the jagged opening, landing on leather and the few glass shards there. After making sure his wrist was protected, he reached in and fumbled around until he found and depressed the power door release.

Now sitting behind the wheel, he tried to look out, but there was no seeing past the packed snow. A registration card was attached to the sun visor, the plastic encasing so misted over he couldn't read it, and if he tried to pull out the paper inside, his wet gloves might ruin it.

After a couple of awkward attempts, he got the glove compartment door to drop down. The interior was empty except for an owner's manual and a stamped and addressed envelope. The letter was hand addressed to one Scott Curran from Park Curran.

Jace sat weighing his options for several minutes, then removed his gloves and ripped open the envelope.

"Dear Scott," the letter began. "I'm writing this while waiting to talk to one of the doctors involved with your grandfather's care. I don't know if he's going to tell me anything I don't already know, but one thing you'll learn as you get older—you can't allow people to think they've put one over on you. Having your grandfather in this home is costing me a lot of money. I have every right to know whether that money's being properly used."

So far Jace hadn't learned anything except the writer had a son. He read the next paragraph.

"I'm sorry you couldn't come with me. I'm certain your mother has told you that you needed to stay in school and I respect her decision, but I wanted you to see the cabin just once. Aunt Dayna and I plan on being there no more than two nights. I hope I can take some pictures so I'll at least have that to show you. I have to be back in the office by Thursday so will try to call you Wednesday night. Maybe we can firm up those plans to take in a Seahawks game. I can get tickets and would like nothing better than to go to one with you. Love, Dad."

Park Curran planned to leave the cabin no later than Wednesday, tomorrow. Was still there? He and his sister Dayna.

* * * * *

Sometimes, for weeks on end, KYGH meteorologist Homer Harkins was hard-pressed to find anything compelling to say about the weather, but tonight there was nothing artificial about his somber expression.

"This isn't going to last forever," he said after giving a wrap-up of the day's developments. "And we aren't moving into another ice age, but if you went by a snapshot of what developed in Alaska and then moved our way, you might think so. Fortunately, the front is sagging a bit so temperatures should moderate. However, I stand by my earlier prediction that before this is over, the mountains are going to get enough snow off this one system that it could measure a typical winter's snowpack."

He glanced over at the serious but too young anchors. Their attention, as they'd been coached, was riveted on him.

"I've been on the phone to folks at both Crater and Diamond Lakes. As of about fifteen minutes ago, there's twenty-three inches of snow at Diamond and nearly twenty-six at Crater. It's a dry snow and with the wind gusts, there's a lot of shifting around. Both places have plows going, but they'll have to shut down when it gets dark so they're not sure they're accomplishing anything. They're still trying to make sure no one's in the wilderness."

"Do you think that's possible?" the female anchor asked.

"I have no way of knowing. Unfortunately, no one does."

* * * * *

"We have to think. Stop walking and think."

Kandi nodded. She stood leaning forward as if the upper half of her body was too heavy to support, putting Beacan in mind of a boxer at the end of the fifteenth round. The long hair she'd tucked under her cap had worked free and hung around her face. Between that and her snow-packed coat and the swirling flakes she didn't bother to wipe from her face, he wasn't sure how much longer she'd remain separate from her surroundings.

He felt the same way, not as human as he'd been at the beginning. This not much more than hundred pound woman refused to give up, and neither the hell would he, but maybe he was too cold and tired to care. The wind—the damnable wind—one moment he was barely aware of its impact and then the next, he wanted to curl up in a ball and surrender.

"We don't know where we're going," he said. "Where we are."

She worked at freeing first one leg and then the other, plodding closer to him until his numb flesh acknowledged her presence. "No, we don't."

"If we panic—"

"I won't," she countered. "And neither will you."

"You think you know me that well?"

Her attention drifted off into the trees, then returned to him. Her eyes spoke of acceptance and concern but not fear, not surrender. "You've had plenty of time to if you were going to," she told him.

"So did you."

She smiled. "Maybe we just don't understand the situation."

"I keep telling myself I should have a plan," he admitted.

"Why?"

"Because I'm a man." It was his turn to laugh. "Because men are supposed to know how to get out of situations like this."

"I don't expect anything of you."

He shivered, no colder or warmer than he'd been since they'd taken off, only dragged down by the pain in his back. "You don't expect anything of anyone, do you?"

"No." Her gaze remained steady.

"Why not?"

"We're supposed to be coming up with a plan."

"Why not?"

"Can't you figure that out?"

"Yeah." He didn't hurry the word. "Your parents deserted you, and that taught you not to trust anyone."

She continued to stare at him.

"I don't blame you," he said. He wished he knew what words would help and whether anything he said might distance her from him. "If it had happened to me, I'd feel the same way."

"It didn't."

"No." He paused, and then let it out. "But I can listen if you feel like talking. I'm sure as hell not going anywhere."

She tried to laugh. "Maybe I will—but not now. Not until this is over."

This. The word slammed into him, gripped his aching back and sent another shiver through him. "We have to—damn this wind!"

"Maybe-maybe we should wait until it lets up a little, until the snow slacks off. Right now we can hardly see."

"You think we should curl up under the nearest tree? Surrender like—"

"No! Not surrender!"

"Wrong word?"

"Wrong fucking word." Her anger hadn't abated. "I keep thinking…" She'd been holding her hands tucked under her armpits but now slid them into her coat pockets. The longer she stood there, the more snow piled on her.

"What are you thinking?"

"That we're the only ones who can get ourselves out of this."

* * * * *

Park hadn't taken his wallet off the dresser this morning. Dayna found it, not because she was looking for money, but her restless energy had taken her into the bedroom. She stared at the finely tooled leather for a long time before picking it up, feeling the weight and identity of it. It carried no memory of her brother's heat.

She carried it into the living room and sat down at the couch that backed up to the lakeside window because from here she couldn't see her brother's body. Cold seeped in around the window, and yet that wasn't what made her shudder.

Park's wallet wasn't as fat as their father's had been, but when she opened it, she discovered it held three hundred dollar bills as well as a half-dozen twenties. There was nothing smaller. He had Discover, VISA, and MasterCard as well as several from exclusive clothing stores. He was a member of the local country club, carried his stock broker's business card as well as his doctor's phone number. He didn't have a library card. The only item of a truly personal nature was a posed and smiling picture of Scott.

What would she say to her nephew? What words would she use to try to blunt the shock of his father's death? Park and Scott didn't—hadn't—spent that much time together, so maybe Scott's grief wouldn't carve a deep wound inside the boy but she, who had little experience with love, couldn't answer that.

Although it didn't matter, she returned the cards and money to their proper places. He'd tucked a gasoline receipt in with the money, making her wonder who would be responsible for dealing with Park's final affairs. She had no idea whether he had a will although surely someone worth as much as he was would have seen to that. His beneficiary wouldn't be either of his ex-wives and certainly not their parents.

He hadn't asked if she'd act as his executor or whatever it was called, probably because he knew she didn't have the expertise or knack or inclination for the task, but wouldn't one sibling talk to another about his wishes for his only child if he weren't around to see him to adulthood?

"What kind of a funeral do you want? Did-did you want to be an organ donor? What about flowers, a charity people can give to? Park, I don't know any of that."

The window shuddered as it had many times before. She should have taken down the screens and fastened the shutters in place, but if she'd done that, she would be sitting in darkness and the storm, no matter how much she hated it, was better than that.

She'd started to close the wallet when her gaze again fell on Scott's picture, and she traced the outline of his eyes, nose, and mouth with her fingernail. Had her father ever carried a picture of her or Park?

Jerking upright, she looked around for whoever had asked the impossible question, but there was no one—except for Park and he'd never speak again.

The window rattled again. The sound propelled her to her feet and she stood in the middle of the room, trapped. After too much indecision, she walked over to the radio and unsuccessfully tried to tune it in again. Because she didn't own a watch and hadn't bothered to reset the cabin's clocks after the electricity went off the last time and couldn't bring herself to check Park's watch, she had no idea what time it was. The day had gone on forever but would eventually end.

And then what?

And then she'd spend an endless, sleepless night alone and in the morning…

In the morning, Kandi and Beacan might be dead.

A moan escaped her lips, but although she whirled one way and then the other in an attempt to escape the thought, it clung to her. The white she'd so recently thought of as beautiful was cruel, a silent, frozen death. A storm had killed Cherokee, a young, healthy man comfortable with the wilderness. Neither Beacan with his athlete's strength or Kandi with her runner's legs were as well-equipped for survival.

Where was her spider? She needed to talk to it, needed—

Why had she allowed Beacan and Kandi to leave? Yes, she'd been afraid for her brother, but that gave her no right to allow two other people to risk their lives.

Realizing she was rocking back and forth, she forced herself to stop. Then she pressed the heels of her hands against her eye sockets with such strength that when she released the pressure, for too long she couldn't see.

If only she could remember what she'd said when the decision to stay or leave was being made but she had—

No! She'd been about to say she had no memory of her involvement, but even if the details remained vague, she knew certain things about herself. Her entire life had been one of wrapping her hatred and murderous thoughts deep inside her, tiptoeing, not making waves, having no opinions. Surely she'd acted true-to-form today and as a result, two good people might not live to see tomorrow.

Three people dead. Only her still alive.

"No! Fuck it, no!"

Bellowing helped. Cursing felt wonderful. And when her gaze settled on her brother, she knew what she had to do.

Chapter Seventeen

࿐

"Beacan? Are you awake?"

The athlete responded sluggishly, one muscle at a time. For the past half hour, they'd been sitting at the base of a forked evergreen. They'd chosen the spot because they hoped the branches would catch most of the falling snow. The laden branches also served as protection from the wind.

At first, the lessening of punishment to her body felt strange, as if she wasn't done doing penance, but gradually Kandi had regained her equilibrium.

"I'm awake," he answered.

"I thought maybe you'd fallen asleep."

"No. I was…resting."

Either that or taking himself to somewhere quiet and safe. She must have had a reason for speaking but couldn't remember what it was. Despite the relative protection, her teeth still ached and her mind felt sluggish. Still, fear wasn't a complex emotion. The word was synonymous with dark alleys, a truck barreling at you with the smell of burning rubber staining the air, waking up alone and hearing a sound that didn't belong. Even she who put little stock in her continued existence knew that.

"Did you?" Beacan asked.

"Did I what?"

"Fall asleep."

"No. I was thinking of Florida, again." *Maybe.*

"Good idea. Kandi?"

"What?"

He turned toward her and she felt his breath on her cheek. "There's really no one waiting for you when this is over?"

"What does that have to do with today?"

"Don't," he warned. "Damn it, stop shoving me away."

"If you're asking if I have a boyfriend, the answer is no. I don't play that game."

He tried to straighten his leg, but there wasn't enough room so he tucked it against himself again. She felt his shoulder against hers and fixed on the one spot on her body that was warm.

"I don't care about a boyfriend," he told her. "I'm talking about family."

She closed her eyes, not that that made the world, which was nothing and everything, go away. "I know you are."

"Then…"

She didn't know how far they'd gone or how many more miles they'd have to travel before they reached civilization — whatever that was. Most of all, she hated facing the fact that they'd have to spend the night here, and that by morning one or both of them might be dead.

"I don't remember my parents, not really." She spoke softly yet strong. "Someone gave me a picture of them, but I burned it one night when I was drunk."

This was easy. She could regurgitate her past and get it over with. "It wasn't much, a newspaper clipping of a dance with them all over each other. I was told my mother was fifteen when I was born and that my father dropped out of school and took a job on a fishing boat out of Alaska soon after he learned she was pregnant. Some agency tried to contact him to get him to pay child support — maybe he died."

"Maybe."

Talking exposed her teeth to the cold, but she kept going. "No one ever adopted me because my mother moved in and out of my life.. It's like that for a lot of kids. They're bounced from one foster home to another while their parents try to get their acts together. Try to decide whether they want to be parents."

Beacan wrapped his arm around her and pulled her close. She rested her hand on his thigh.

"There were so many foster homes. I was in one for nearly three years, from the time I started kindergarten until second grade." *Don't feel. Just talk and then be done with it.* "They're the ones I have the strongest memories of."

"What about before that?"

"I don't remember anything before kindergarten." Her eyes, worn out from the wind's assault, felt dry.

"Do you try?"

"No." Her throat closed down and she had to wait before going on. "Someone must have taught me my numbers because I could already count when I entered kindergarten. And colors. I knew them."

"What about friends?"

She couldn't say she was warm everywhere their bodies touched, but it was better than before. As long as she didn't look at him, the words might continue to come.

"I liked the swing best. That and running."

"Even back then."

"Yeah. I didn't need anyone else to do those things."

"What about birthday parties? Do you remember going to any?"

She thought. "One. I was older then, eight or nine." Colors and voices flashed through her mind, made it easier to stay in the past. "The people had a finished basement and it was full of girls. They giggled—I didn't understand why everything they said came out as a giggle. I wanted to leave, but I'd just changed homes and I didn't know the phone number of the people I was living with. I, ah, I can't stand places without windows so I went outside. I remember—it had been raining and the grass was wet and when I knelt to feel the moisture, my pants got soaked. When my foster father came to get me, that pissed him."

"Damn him."

"You can't really want to hear this."

"Yes, I do."

The telling didn't get any easier but by concentrating on the flash shots that were her past, she gave him what he wanted, what, to her surprise, she needed to tell him. Despite her splintered living conditions, she'd spent her childhood in and around San Francisco, and there'd been a continuity of sorts with her social workers. One, a tall, long-wristed man who smelled of pipe smoke, had been there from her earliest memories until he retired when she was thirteen. He'd encouraged her to call him whenever she needed to talk. She hadn't thought she ever would, but then she'd learned he could figure sales tax in his head and asked if he could help her get into an accelerated math class and by the end of the week, he had. He'd taken her clothes shopping when she started junior high. She wasn't sure how he'd learned she'd outgrown nearly everything she owned and that the elderly couple she was living with hadn't bought her anything.

Shortly before his retirement, he'd introduced her to his replacement, a young woman just out of college who spoke too much and spent their time together staring at her engagement ring and filling out forms. She'd left the agency in less than a year and after that came another woman who spoke to her maybe twice before turning her over to someone else. After that the faces and voices all blurred together.

The parade of social workers was easier to talk about than other things and yet the storm knifed into her, found her secrets, pushed them out. She must have once been a virgin, but that had been stolen from her when she was too young to fully realize what was happening. The first time — at least she thought it was — had been with a foster mother's younger brother. He'd twisted her arm behind her and pushed her face into a pillow and pulled down her jeans and panties and forced himself into her. Beacan didn't ask for more details, which was good because she might have told him to go to hell.

"I bled afterward, and it hurt so much to go to the bathroom that I screamed, but they didn't take me to a doctor," she said. "It happened again the next time he came to the house."

"The bastard."

Had he been? Back then she'd had no way of knowing because there hadn't been anyone to talk to — any way of knowing whether what had been done to her was wrong or right. Another man had molested her before she became old and strong enough to say "no" and mean it. Her past was one of dark passages and great holes, she told Beacan. She had no intention of trying to turn on any more lights.

At sixteen she'd walked out of her last foster home because they wanted her to go to church three times a week. She'd gotten a job at a pizza parlor, which, after going to school, left her with time for maybe five hours of sleep a night but enough money for a studio apartment. She'd lied about her age on the job application and had stolen the five hundred dollars she'd needed for a deposit. Her furnishings came from Goodwill.

"You got through high school," he said. "That wasn't easy."

"Getting decent grades has never been hard. I have a brain."

"Yeah, you do." He stared out at their world. "Our upbringing was so different," he said softly. "Mine secure and filled with love, yours… Everything you and I have done up until this point—it's almost as if we didn't live on the same planet. What brought us together…?"

She wanted to be swallowed by nothing, wanted back the blanket she wore around her emotions. But more than that, she'd needed someone to know who she was.

* * * * *

Dayna had found ski pants in her parents' dresser and although she hated that it smelled of her father, she'd put them on over her mother's thermals and her own jeans. When Beacan and Kandi had taken off, there hadn't been enough snow for them to consider trying the journey on skis and besides, there was only her father's pair. She wore his shoes because they fit the bindings. She also had on two sweatshirts and a parka he'd probably paid several hundred dollars for. Her pockets were stuffed with the granola bars that hadn't gone with Kandi and Beacan, the flashlight from her glove compartment, and Park's pistol.

Now as she closed the cabin door behind her, her mind settled on the pistol. She'd found it in his coat pocket, the cold weight first causing her to recoil and then drawing her to its strength and power. Her father had insisted his daughter learn how to handle a rifle so it wasn't the thought of carrying a weapon that disturbed her—just that her brother had believed he'd need one out here.

Her attention was drawn to what remained of her vehicle, and she laughed. There was no way it could be repaired. She'd have to contact her insurance company and file a claim—something she'd never done but now filled her with a sense of purpose. At least once she returned to civilization, she'd have more to do than just deal with her brother's death.

As her route took her past Beacan's rig, she saw that snow had turned it into a vaguely defined mound, but unlike hers, it hadn't been ruined, simply half-buried in water. She supposed that if it spent the winter there, it wouldn't be salvageable, but she preferred to think there wouldn't be much difficulty in making it serviceable again.

In making her trips to and from the woodpile, she'd worn a path in the snow but it didn't matter that there wasn't any here because the skis kept her on top. Her father had insisted she learn how to ski, but she hadn't stayed with the sport after leaving home, and the necessary movements didn't come easily. Fortunately, after about a half mile, she settled into a workable rhythm.

The heavy sky pressed down on her. When the sun set, the temperature would drop and a crust would form over the snow. She could deal with the crust, find a way to make it work for her, ease her passage. As for the cold—she was well-dressed and determined. And sleepless nights were nothing new to her.

Then there was the darkness.

"It's letting up."

Beacan nodded but was slow to join Kandi who'd stood and was holding up her hand as if trying to stop the snow.

"We have to take advantage of this lull," she continued. "Find our way back to the road."

"I know." His back hummed and danced like a live electrical wire.

"Are you—do you need help up?"

No, he wanted to tell her. *No, I don't need your goddamned help.* "I don't know."

She returned to him, a slight, strong figure buried under the layers of clothing that kept her alive. Instead of telling him how to handle the body part only he could possibly understand, only he feared, she waited, her eyes not probing too deep. Still, he hated exposing his weakness to her. He told himself that cold had made things worse and maybe he'd wrenched his back in the accident, and for the most part, he believed himself. Yet, the time was coming when he could no longer move.

Jaw clenched and eyes stinging from pain-spawned tears, he managed to get to his knees but his spine was old rubber, which left him hanging there like an arthritic. Still not saying anything, she stepped behind him and wrapped her arms around his chest. Her legs were widespread and slightly bent as she worked for and with him, providing muscle. He did what he had to, the accompanying moan filling his throat and nearly choking him. Finally though, he was on his feet.

"I have to know," she said. "Can you do it?"

"I don't have a choice."

"That's not what I asked."

"Yeah, I can do it."

"All right." He couldn't tell whether she believed him or not. "I'll try to keep us on level ground."

"Do you know where the hell you're going?"

"Out of here," she said.

Then, without waiting for him, she half scrambled, half swam out of the depression they'd been in and he followed her with his screaming back and determination. She was right. The snow had all but stopped which had the effect of holding late afternoon suspended. The wind continued its maddening work, blowing the top layer of flakes over the forest floor. There was beauty in the movement, proof of how dry the snow was, looking like morning mists over a lake. The wind would soon obliterate their tracks.

She must have known that because she didn't stop to rest but continued to stare at the ground searching, ever searching for some sign of where they'd come from. It was there but illusive, and they had to be careful not to anger the mist gods. If they did, those faint but precious indentations might disappear.

A dozen, no, a hundred times he nearly told her he couldn't match her pace. Instead, he fixed his gaze on her small rear end and pumping legs. He imagined he could feel the heat of her thigh muscles, her hard and competent ass, and her runner's determination. He no longer cared that she had full breasts, only that the lungs beneath them were equal to the task she'd set for herself.

Their world was beautiful, wild and savage, deadly and perfect. Who could hate something so immaculate even if it had the power to kill? He believed in God and yet there'd been a time when he'd cursed that God. Today he could only stand in awe of what the Creator was capable of. If he was destined to die here, so be it.

And yet as long as Kandi lived, so would he.

Maybe.

* * * * *

Thank goodness the snow had let up, Dayna thought as she left Lake Wolf behind. Just the same, it was already so deep she couldn't see last year's seedlings. The air was cleaner out here than in the cabin, not tainted by smoke and blood stench and memories. She was grateful that skiing took so much concentration it left little room for thinking — barely enough to question her wisdom in taking off so late in the day. The decision might not be perfect, but it was better, far better than sitting in a chair near her brother while she waited for help that might not come, while she worried about Kandi and Beacan.

One sliding step, two. One and two. Over and over again. Legs no longer burning. Gratitude for all the years of running that maybe had been in preparation for today.

God wasn't part of the equations. How and when she'd come to that conclusion she couldn't say. What she knew was that if there was a God and He'd believed she should grow up afraid, she wanted no part of Him. This thing she was doing today was for her, by her. Her alone.

Enough! There had to be something else she could think about. Her brother, not the inert body she'd left behind but the living man everyone else still believed him to be was important, influential. He marched to the tune of cell phones, the Internet, wheels and deals. His life was measured and planned, and he had appointments waiting for him. When he failed to keep those appointments, the alarm would be raised and a search launched. He hadn't planned on staying at the cabin more than two nights which meant that by tomorrow late someone would —

Tomorrow evening was a lifetime away, perhaps beyond the end of her life.

A weight slammed into her chest and she stopped and placed her hands on her hips, fighting to breathe. Her gloves slid off the waterproof fabric of her father's coat and she let her arms dangle. She wasn't sure how long she'd been skiing — time kept caving in upon itself — but it didn't matter because her surroundings were so incredibly beautiful. Virgin.

Deadly.

* * * * *

"Jace. Jace? Can you hear me?"

Jace turned off the windshield wipers and leaned toward the CB. "Barely."

"I tried information," Henri told him. "There's about a half dozen Currans in the Portland area but none at the address you gave me. The kid's mother might have an unlisted number or she could have remarried."

"What about Park Curran?"

"I was getting to that." Henri sounded irritated. "Look, I agree. Those people probably are at Wolf, but that doesn't make it a crisis. If they've got the brains they were born with, they'll hole up until this is over."

"He told his son—"

"I know what he told his son. There's a number for your Park Curran, but when I called, I didn't get an answer. According to the machine, there's a business number he can also be reached at. And so you don't have to ask, I tried that one too. Turns out it's for a cell phone."

"Can't you get the police to—?"

"If I called the cops and asked them to run down this Park character, they'd tell me they have more important things to do and what the hell was a ranger doing breaking into his car anyway. Look, you said that from what you understood, the brother and sister practically grew up around Wolf. They know the weather here."

"But you couldn't reach him through his cell phone."

"Not because he and it are in the bottom of the lake or Big Foot got them. Because the storm's messed up reception. I'm telling you and I hope to hell you'll listen—this isn't Cherokee all over again."

He knew that, he tried to tell himself so anyway. When Henri told him that according to the forecasters the worst of the storm wasn't over, he said he understood and, yes, he'd start back before it got dark. Then Henri signed off and he was left alone with the sound of the powerful motor and laboring heater.

Needing something to do, he turned the wipers back on. Once he could see out again, he leaned forward and stared at the car he'd vandalized. If and when he had to face Park Curran, it might make more of an impact if he followed up his confession with an explanation of the efforts he'd gone to assure himself that Park and Dayna were safe. He wasn't sure what...

Someone was walking toward him, no not someone. *Something.* It appeared both part of and separate from its surroundings, darker, lean, eyes like...

Eyes he knew.

Barely aware of what he was doing, Jace reached for the door handle and stepped out. He had to concentrate on keeping his balance in the snow but didn't take his gaze off the shimmering figure.

"Cherokee."

The man-creature gave no indication it heard and with night lapping at its edges, Jace was less sure of its existence than he'd been when he was in the truck. A year ago he would have told himself he was drunk or letting his imagination get away from him, but the past year had been hell and he no longer knew anything.

Doubted anything.

"Cherokee."

Perhaps the sound of his voice startled the man-creature. Either that or like a soap bubble it hadn't been strong enough to withstand—withstand what? Whatever it was, Jace was now alone. He felt lightheaded and the back of his neck prickled. It was hard to breathe.

The wind had begun to pick up again and the flakes fell faster, blurring the line between reality and illusion. He felt himself being sucked into the energy, seduced and challenged. His mother had told him that the first time she saw him, he'd taken hold of her heart and she'd known without reservation or regret that she would die for him.

This wilderness had the same grip on him. It was part of him. Or maybe he'd become part of it.

He'd failed Cherokee and Cherokee ceased to exist because the wilderness had absorbed him. In some respects, he envied his friend because Cherokee's battle to keep himself separate from his surroundings was over, because— he prayed—he'd found peace and a place to spend eternity.

Alone.

Jace's mind clamped down and no more thoughts came. On legs that knew what they needed to do, he returned to the truck and reached behind the seat for the snowshoes he'd put there a few days ago, a compass, headlamp, and an extra coat.

Then he contacted Henri. He was leaving for Wolf, he told the big man. He'd be back when he'd done what he had to.

Chapter Eighteen

ℬ

So much snow swirled around her that Kandi couldn't be sure. Leaving Beacan, she made her way onto the flat, treeless stretch. The snow didn't support her weight any better here than it had elsewhere, but she was beyond caring.

In her mind's eye, she saw herself sitting behind the wheel of the old Jeep that was her pride and joy as she followed a meandering road to wherever it wanted to take her. The day she was creating in her mind was warm with the sun softening tree pitch so its heady scent coated the air. Sturdy trees would reach unchallenged into a blue sky. Maybe thunderheads would roll over the horizon in late afternoon and the bright sunset would be reflected in them, but for now—because it was the way she wanted it—nothing broke the clear heavens.

She'd have taken the top off the Jeep, plugged a Native American tape into the player and crank it up so the haunting flute notes became everything. Her hair would stream out behind her, a willing prisoner of the wind. She might sing, or she might lock herself in her own silence.

Maybe she'd never leave that gentle and all-embracing forest.

"Kandi?"

Startled, she tried to turn around, but it took too much effort so she simply waited for Beacan to join her. Her eyes felt hot, almost as if she'd been crying.

"I think this is it," she said. She kept emotion out of her voice. "The road."

They stood side by side for a long time, hunched against the weather. Then she said, "It's going to be dark before much longer."

"I know."

"We aren't going to reach Crater today."

"No, we aren't."

We'll have to spend the night out here, she told him but only in her mind.

"We were wrong," he said, his voice rough. "Wrong to think we could do this in one day."

"Yes, we were."

"I'm sorry."

"It's no more your fault than it is mine."

"You wouldn't have done it any other way?"

Her growing up had been what it had been. It was the same now and she told him so.

"Maybe I need your outlook," he said. When he shifted position, his shoulder brushed hers. She didn't try to draw away. "I've been holding you back."

He had but that, like everything else, wouldn't be altered by words. Still, she didn't know whether to love or hate him for bringing up what had to be faced.

"I tried." The wind tore at his words, and she could only guess she'd heard him right. "Sucked it up and pushed, but— I've reached the end."

Night waited in the trees, a panther biding his time to hunt.

"Kandi?" His voice tailed off and she heard him breathing, felt something hot and hollow pour out of him. "If you're going to get through this alive, you'll have to go on without me."

"I know."

"Do you?"

"Yes," she told him. "If I go your pace, it's going...it might prove fatal. I've been trying to decide whether we should stay together until morning, but it can't be that much further to the rim road. The sooner I get there—"

"And if you don't reach it before it gets dark?"

"Then I'll keep on going."

She waited for him to tell her she was crazy, that she risked getting lost with only a flashlight to guide her, but he didn't and she chose to believe that he'd decided there wasn't anything she couldn't accomplish.

The hot, hollow sensation continued to swirl around him, distracting her from what had to be said. "I want to play the macho male," he told her. "But I can't."

"I never asked you to."

"No, you didn't."

The night's panther breathed, the sound rumbling, echoing, maybe never-ending.

He touched a thumb to her cheek. "Maybe you can't do it."

"What?"

"Is that why you haven't said anything? Because you're exhausted."

A panther senses its victim's weakness and attacks that weakness. "No."

"Then—"

She turned into him, not smooth or graceful, but it didn't matter. She had to stretch to reach his lips, and when she laid hers on them, she couldn't feel anything. "I don't know enough about you," she told this man she might never see again. "Not the important things."

"What?"

"You kept after me until I told you everything, but you won't do the same thing."

"This is hardly the time to—"

"When? After we're both dead?"

His lips parted, and he mouthed the word "no". She waited, but he said nothing, only stood there with his eyes dark with pain and the something else she'd been unable to tap.

"I've stood naked before you, emotionally naked." She pressed. "I just wish to hell—forget it!"

Instead of giving him time to respond, if he was going to, she backed away. She needed to tell him she'd be back, but what if—

"How did you know?" he asked.

"Know what? That you're this rich, handsome young man who doesn't have a care in the world, except for his back. Your sister's health isn't the best and your parents sacrificed for their kids. Other than that, life's been easy street for you—or has it?"

"Kandi, this isn't the time…"

"No, it isn't. I'm supposed to risk my life for you, for this stranger I've been screwing. You might die and I'll never— God, forget it!" She looked over her shoulder at the waiting wilderness, fear and determination raged within her. Most of all she wished she'd never met Beacan Jarrard. "I have to go now," she said.

"Be careful, all right?"

"What choice do I have?" she asked. "You too, all right?"

"I will." He rocked back on his heels, the gesture giving her the freedom to leave. Then, as she started to turn away, he said, "Wait. I want you to have something." Using his teeth, he pulled off his right glove, removed his World Series ring and handed it to her.

"What—?"

"If— Give it to my parents, please."

* * * * *

One moment Dayna was lost in the swish-swish sound her skis made. The next, she felt herself being wrenched to a stop, her right leg continuing on as if unconcerned with what had happened to its companion.

In a move designed to save her from further injury, she executed something approaching a swan dive. Still, she wound up doing the splits, which resulted in a burning sensation along her inner right thigh.

When she tried to breathe, she sucked in snow. After the resultant coughing fit was over, she righted herself and took inventory. A ski was supposed to withstand a brief encounter with a rock or tree, wasn't it, but she didn't know how old her father's skis were or whether years of temperature extremes had undermined them in some way.

It didn't matter.

She tried to release the bindings without taking off her gloves, but when that didn't work, she pulled off the left one and attacked what held her prisoner to a useless appendage. For several minutes afterward, she ran her hand over the sleek surface. Then, angry, she stood and threw it spear-like as far as she could.

After a moment, she absorbed the wilderness and made her peace with it because during the worst of her childhood, she'd always had the forest to turn to. She might not be able to walk or run into it, but it had been there, patient and understanding.

Since removing the skis, she'd sunk nearly to her knees in the snow, but she felt no burning need to free herself. Instead, she drew a granola bar out of her pocket and ate, savoring each crunch. When she could no longer taste anything, she fingered her flashlight.

She didn't need it yet, but the time would soon come when the beam was all that kept the wilderness at bay. Whether she'd be able to continue to walk once it became dark was a question she couldn't yet answer. What mattered was the precautions she'd take to make sure she didn't let the flashlight slip out of her grip because...

Night in the wilderness was total. While skiing, she'd taken the trees for granted, but now that her pace had slowed, their impact played on her nerves. Trees represented life and once it was dark, she wouldn't be able to distinguish between what was real and what existed only in her mind.

* * * * *

Beacan remained standing until he could no longer see Kandi. Then he tried to put one foot in front of another, but he'd been motionless too long, and his back seized. Like a pregnant woman trying to ease the strain caused by her distended belly, he pressed his fingers into his spine. He'd kept his gaze on Kandi, imprinting his last image of her in his mind, but now he turned inward. Kandi might not approve of or want to hear about his hunting trips, but at least he knew what to expect from a wilderness night. The difference this time was that he was alone with the knowledge that all his money couldn't get him through it alive. It did no good to dwell on the backroads rigs he and his companions had used to get to the remote areas they'd chosen because the only one he had access to was buried in a lake.

Not having a weapon with him made him feel, not vulnerable really because he'd already made his peace with that emotion, but no longer set apart from his surroundings. If it weren't for what he wore and the artificial light that might fail him before morning, he would be an animal.

An animal without the skills or resources to survive, dependent on a woman who might or might not return. Who might not live until morning.

Lifting his head, he gave the unseen flakes access to the exposed parts of his face. The cold revived him, and he slowly, cautiously began twisting one way and then the other. His back had become the old Chevy his father had driven long after it should have been put out of its misery, the one that hated morning cold. His father had known the engine's ways and had patiently coaxed it to life. Tonight the son could be patient, could smile as his back's halfhearted fits and starts gradually became a serviceable hum or if not a hum, at least a plodding acceptance of what was being required of it.

He would walk. Somehow.

And if that weren't enough, he'd join his daughter.

* * * * *

Back on the road, Kandi tried to tell herself that because she was moving at a sloth's pace, she wouldn't make the mistake of losing her bearings again, but the storm was a whirlpool capable of forcing her into endless circles if she wasn't careful. She couldn't fight it. Hell, she knew that. She'd survived childhood rape by accepting what was, and was prepared to do that again, but rape took only a few minutes and then she had her body and personal space back again. This was everything.

She was hungry, suddenly, ferociously hungry. Why she'd gone so long and put out so much energy without wanting to gnaw nails before now she couldn't say. Turning her back to the wind as she'd done so many times today, she pulled a granola bar out of an inner pocket where she'd put Beacan's ring, tore off the wrapping and finished in three quick bites. A chunk stuck in her throat, and she swallowed repeatedly until she'd dislodged it. She couldn't remember how many bars she had with her, not that it mattered because one wasn't close to enough. At least, she thought with a small measure of pride, she hadn't inhaled the second one like some half-starved dog.

After polishing off a third, her head felt clearer and a small current of warmth ran up the middle of her body. She started to berate herself for waiting so long to restock, and then decided not to waste energy on something that didn't matter. She and Beacan had talked about how to conserve their flashlight batteries, but she was unsure whether it was better to leave the light on or subject it to repeated on/offs. She'd have to play that by ear.

She was tired, so tired. The snow carpet put a long shag rug to shame and the effort of sucking one boot out of the frozen fibers and plunging the other into it would leave her more sore than any workout or marathon ever had.

Marathon!

Forget a ten-K. This was the ironman event and she the only participant from the United States. If she failed, her country would be shamed, her financial backers disillusioned and maybe wanting her head on a platter.

One thing about being dead, she thought as she left her paper litter behind, she wouldn't have to face a critical press.

How had Beacan made it through over a hundred plus games with a back that needed replacing?

* * * * *

Jace had never felt comfortable wearing a headlamp, but it was easier to keep his balance with his hands free. The rhythm of his legs was everything. They'd become the proverbial well-oiled pistons, and as long as he kept going, they would last forever—at least that's what he told himself and when another voice called him a fool, he roughly silenced it.

The snow and wind didn't bother him, in part because he had on goggles designed to remain condensation free. When he'd found Cherokee's goggles among his belongings, he'd been unable to touch them. Cherokee had been missing nearly a week before his mind raked through the coals of his final memory of his friend, and he'd recalled that Cherokee had been wearing sunglasses, which could be nearly worthless in the snow and might have contributed to his death.

Tonight he wouldn't make the same mistake.

And if he made one of his own…

Not good. Not good. Tonight was about two people trapped in their cabin.

Although his snowshoes were designed for making his trek as easy as possible, he had to concentrate on every move because the snowpack was uneven and the light strapped to his head less than trustworthy. Still, he made decent time, and if the weather didn't deteriorate dramatically, he'd reach the cabin by dawn.

Night was a blanket, dense and heavy, so cold that even with the balaclava that protected everything except his eyes and nose, he risked frostbite, but this was about atoning for the greatest failure of his life, and so he pushed his thoughts toward Dayna Curran and her brother. There was every possibility they'd call him forty kinds of a fool and point out their well-conceived plan for dealing with this minor setback in their plans. If that happened, he'd beat what he hoped would be a dignified retreat and they'd never understand why he'd…

He had sentenced Cherokee to an eternity here. If there were such things as souls and his friend's might find a measure of peace because of his actions that was why…

Time came and went, touched him with its presence and then faded off into nothing. He skied, breathed, shifted the weight on his back, tried to follow in the wake of the light his headgear cast, came to accept that night had a weight and presence of its own. Because the park had been his home for as long as it had, his mind's eye carried a map of its plains and valleys, rocks, trees, creeks, and wildlife. Nature's creatures accepted winter on its own terms, but he wasn't so sure about man. Man, it seemed to him, had stepped beyond natural boundaries and thus the old laws and orders might no longer exist. Man, with his so-called prodigious brain, had developed ways to hold death at bay, to cure the incurable and give life to those who once would have never been created. Man had cheated the grim reaper, and in the process filled the earth with his kind. Uncounted species of other forms of life had ceased to exist because man impacted everything.

The only element still not under man's yoke and control, Jace thought tonight, was the weather. Maybe the time would come when sun and clouds and wind saw what had been done to the earth and flex their collective muscles. They'd either deprive mankind of warmth and rain or, like tonight, scream in white rage.

It didn't matter to him.

* * * * *

Until nearly midnight, the snow and wind remained at a steady pace. The temperature fell somewhat but the cloud cover prevented things from dropping much below freezing. As a consequence, the four isolated humans believed they would live to see the morning.

But as the need for sleep became something to be fought, the wind took a deep breath and exhaled in a long, unending breath. Individual flakes became a curtain of ice crystals and took over the air, making it nearly impossible for the humans to breathe. Beacan, exhausted from fighting pain, was the first to embrace shelter. He chose a tree near the road because he was determined not to become lost again. Like a dog curling before a fire, he screwed himself as close as possible to the trunk and pulled his knees up against his belly. He might not be able to move in the morning, but surviving this moment and the next was all he could concentrate on.

Kandi's fight lasted longer. She told the storm she wouldn't stop because she'd told Beacan she wouldn't and she still had a little strength and strength was a terrible thing to lose, but her temples throbbed. Her legs and arms became lifeless sticks and yet her muscles remembered how movement was done.

Only when she nearly passed out because she couldn't get enough air in her lungs did she plod into the nearest thicket. She didn't want to think about Beacan, refused to acknowledge that he too was out there, exposed and helpless. When she ran into branches, she dropped to her hands and knees and burrowed into a snow mound pushed and shaped by the wind. She tried to dig out more space for herself, but her club hands had become useless. At least the storm couldn't reach her down here.

She ate her last granola bar. Although she was thirsty, she knew better than to further lower her body temperature by trying to melt snow in her mouth. Her mind closed down, tunneled into nearly nothing. Awake and yet not, she held onto her image of the way Beacan had looked as they drove to Lake Wolf.

Dayna had less control over how she wound up spending the night. She became a sheep driven by a massive blizzard-dog with biting teeth and no warmth in its breath. In her rush to escape the snapping teeth, she paid little heed to where she was going and didn't try to keep the flashlight beam aimed ahead of her. As a result, she lost her footing and tumbled down, and down until she landed against what might be a boulder. After getting herself upright again, she swam-scrabbled around to the other side of the mound and found — glory be — that little snow had reached this small spot. Laughing, she drank some of the hot chocolate in her thermos. It didn't matter that the chocolate was barely tepid. She was alive.

Unlike her brother.

* * * * *

When he could no longer go on, when the storm became a monster with great hands pressed against his chest, Jace lifted his face to the wind and howled.

Chapter Nineteen

෨

It was June, school out, the stands filled with children. Beacan loved the high, enthusiastic voices, bright-eyed kids shoving papers or balls at him to be autographed. He'd joined with several of his teammates in buying tickets for low-income children and made a point of acknowledging them with a grin and a thumbs-up.

The days were long and warm, the evenings stretching on and on. The team had jelled, accepting and understanding each other, and either the team was in a hunt for the pennant or reporters left them alone and he could concentrate on his skills, his knowledge. Crouched behind home plate, he might think of ice cream or beer or maybe both, strangely not whether he'd find a woman to spend the night with. June was young, promise, freedom, an adolescent.

He came awake slowly. In his mind was the knowledge that something wasn't right, but he put off facing that something until he tried to straighten his legs and the beast took hold of his back and gnawed down to his spinal column.

He couldn't move.

Amend that, he said ten pain-heated minutes later. Because no one was there to hear or watch, he'd screamed and cursed and didn't care that he looked like a paraplegic fighting to turn useless lumps into functioning limbs. Once he was on his feet, an effort that drenched him in sweat and made him oblivious to the bone-deep cold and still falling snow—he zipped down his pants and aimed. The steaming yellow hole fascinated him because he hadn't thought that much heat remained in him. Morning was still trying to make up its mind whether to stay, but there was enough light that he could see the road — or rather what remained of it.

Maybe three more inches had fallen during the night, and it had a shine to it, proof that the top layer had crusted over. The heavy lumps that were his feet concerned him, but he'd slept with his hands tucked under him, and once circulation had been restored there, they worked relatively easily. Thankfully he hadn't lost his stocking cap and his coat had turned out to be as waterproof as the manufacturer's claim. Maybe once all this was over, he'd tell them and they'd hire him to promote their product.

He hadn't frozen to death after all, had breathed his way from one end of the dark to the other. Eyes open because otherwise his back might claim him, he muttered a prayer of thanks, then made a bargain with his Maker. If God would allow his back to function today, only today, he'd never ask for another thing.

* * * * *

Child fear had been footsteps in the night and the creak of an opening door, a man's heavy presence, a hand over her mouth, a hot "don't say a word" slamming into her ear, fingers wrapping around the hem of her nightgown and her legs, hips, belly, waist, budding breasts being exposed. She'd breathed her way through the rape — rapes — and then stumbled into the bathroom and cleaned herself up and thought her helpless thoughts of revenge.

This morning, fear shoved its sharp edge past the web of nothing Kandi had become during the night and forced her to face it. She responded, not by cowering as the child she'd once been had, but with a low, determined snarl.

Every inch of her body hurt. What she remembered of the night existed as fragments of trying to find a comfortable position, struggling not to think, seeking some small flicker of warmth, being more alone than she'd ever been in a life of aloneness. Night's thick and inescapable blanket covered her.

It was gone, eaten by what passed for morning in a storm. The wind had rested somewhat during those too long hours when she was trying to restore herself, but it was awake now, full of challenge.

She made herself stand, crying out as circulation returned to her legs. Fascinated, she followed her blood's path throughout her body and was deeply, deeply grateful that she could feel her feet and toes. She credited that to her ski outfit, the several pairs of wool socks, and the years of running. Running had been essential, something she had control over and could take pride in. While she ran, she thought of what her body was accomplishing, her surroundings, nothing else.

This morning she needed to run, as she never had run before. Instead, with the damnable snow gripping her like quicksand, and her eyes already weary of the effort to focus, she could only manage one labored step at a time. Her mind filled with thoughts of death—not her own because she still felt relatively alive and strong—but Beacan's.

* * * * *

The storm was her father. If she could remember how it was done, Dayna might have laughed at that analogy, but it was true. He'd been overbearing and controlling, a great and all present force that demanded and demanded.

Created a spineless wimp who cowered her way through life.

"No!" She screamed at the storm/father that was everything this morning. She would not, would *not* cower! Instead, she'd dig herself out of her snowcave and plant her unfeeling feet on the road and do what had to be done.

If she existed separate from her newfound determination, Dayna wasn't aware of it as she squatted and relieved herself. Unscrewing the lid to her thermos and drinking the last of the cold chocolate sludge and throwing away the no longer needed weight took incredible energy, but then sugar hit her bloodstream and brain and she clenched her teeth and walked into the monster.

Her mind flickered to what she'd left back at the cabin, but she pulled free because thinking about her dead brother took too much energy. She felt the same way when she pondered how Kandi and Beacan had spent the night. Instead, she blinked her world into focus and took in the snow-laden trees, the long—too long—white-carpeted road, lacy flakes being blown in what she thought was a southerly direction and accepted it as beautiful.

The wind whispered and laughed and sometimes argued with itself. Although she occasionally caught the sound of her breathing and the beat-beat in her temples, the wind dominated. She could, she understood in a deeply primitive way, fight that power or accept it. She chose to accept, or perhaps the truth was that the storm had acknowledged and approved of her efforts at self-preservation and was rewarding her by letting her become part of its world.

She had to struggle to make any progress and occasionally deluded herself by thinking that the faint, irregular indentations on the road had been made by snowshoes, but she was with the storm, of the storm, fed by it and feeding off it.

She had a skill. Plants understood her and she understood them. She knew what each needed to grow and thrive. They blossomed under her care and rewarded her in ways she couldn't articulate. She was jobless because her employer had gone out of business, but was that her fault?

No. She could, would, take her skills and present them to another…

No, not just another nursery. There was a particular one that catered to the landscape trade and dealt in volume. She'd been afraid to approach them because the business was run by a couple of men whose size and energy intimidated her, but they dealt with a vast array of living things and were just now venturing into water gardens, not particularly successfully from what she could tell. After seeing one of their artificial ponds at a home show, she'd researched what thrived in a watery environment.

When this—this hell was over and she'd told Scott that his father was dead and done what she needed to for her father—she'd approach the men and ask—no, convince them—that she was the right one to make that aspect of their business succeed.

Despite her vow not to let it happen, her mind bounced back to what she was doing and once there fastened itself in place. She tried to judge the wind's strength and whether the snowfall was picking up, but she'd been part of this greatness for so long that she couldn't assess its moods.

Were Kandi and Beacan still alive?

I'm sorry. Sorry. Sorry. Sorry.

My fault. I shouldn't have let —

But it was their decision to —

Wasn't it?

Sorry. Sorry. Please forgive…

Please, please, please be alive.

Fear returned, chewed into her, left bleeding holes and weakened her and if she allowed that to continue—

She'd opened her mouth and let the moan, the howl escape before she'd known it was inside her. Instead of being swallowed by the storm, the howl eddied around her, energy and essence.

Maybe her monster surroundings were making her less human. In truth, she didn't mind that because becoming something primitive might increase her chances of survival. No one was here to judge her performance, no one determined to mold her one way or the other.

No one…

He stood to her left, a shadowy substance covered in a lacy white veil. He didn't move. No puffs of moisture came from his nostrils and yet his eyes were alive. He was a mountain man, ancient Indian, fantasy and illusion.

Maybe.

* * * * *

Swish sigh. Swish sigh. Lulled by his snowshoes' sounds, Jace found momentary respite from the internal critic. His gloves and face covering were made of polyester fleece with a Teflon finish, rendering them waterproof and warm. Under his GoreTex and polyester fleece parka he wore both a thermal and a turtleneck. His trail boots were a miracle of waterproof nubuck, polyurethane, and some insulation he didn't remember.

As such, he existed inside himself and became whatever he wanted to be, controlled and contoured his experiences. His journey would take forever and minutes. Although he hadn't brought anything to eat, his belly made no demands on him and he denied his fatigued muscles. His world was this whiteness, this freedom, air beyond virginal and the heavens so close he felt himself being drawn upward.

Poets waxed about winter storms. Mountain climbers and skiers accepted the challenge and although some became victims of the furious strength, that didn't lessen the appeal.

Today he understood that appeal and willingly became part of something greater than himself. He sang with the wind, moaned when the trees did, felt flakes on, around, and inside him and knew nothing else.

Most of the time.

Whenever he let his guard down, the voice returned to ask questions and demand answers, called him stupid.

He'd taken off too late in the day and had been forced to spend the night in the open. Not completely a fool, he'd keyed in his PTT and told Henri where he was and that his plans were to continue onto Wolf in the morning. Henri had cursed him but in the end had agreed to hold off spreading the news that would mean the end to Jace's career.

"I'm scared for you," Henri had said. "You might not make it."

"Yes, I will," he'd told him and then documented what he was wearing and that he knew enough to take shelter within a grove of trees so the wind couldn't tear into him. Henri had called several times during the night, waking him from something that wasn't a sleep and demanding reassurance that he could still feel his extremities.

At dawn, Jace had told Henri he was taking off. Sounding sleep-deprived himself, Henri had informed him that Paul wanted to know where the hell he was and Henri had told their supervisor he wasn't his brother's keeper.

"This ain't right," Henri had insisted. "If something happens to you, my career's down the tubes so you'd better — look, turn your ass around and we'll break out the snowmobiles and do this right."

Snowmobiles. The perfect solution.

Or they would have been if Cherokee hadn't gotten to him.

* * * * *

Why couldn't she feel Beacan, sense him?

Kandi had never seen herself as intuitive. Like an unwanted animal, she'd learned to rely on herself and no one else. That hard-won lesson had gotten her to where she was and she was content with circumstances, thank you very much.

But damn it, the least Beacan could do was let her know if he was still alive.

If he was dead—there, she'd said it, thought it, thrown the word into the air and caught it when it came down— things would change. Her priorities—

She'd still be in the middle of this impossible blizzard with the flesh on her ankles rubbed raw and the tip of her nose feeling as if it might crack off and her nostrils sometimes bleeding and her fingers curled tight against her palms in a vain attempt to keep them warm and—

Are you alive, Beacan? I am but I'm on the move, which is keeping me warm, or at least warmer than I'd be if I had to sit. Has the cold sucked everything out of you? Have you given up?

Don't, damn it! You're too young, too strong, too rich!

The thought of all that newly earned money waiting for Beacan to spend or send off to the IRS snagged her attention. What if he didn't show up to claim it? Probably lawyers would get the whole bagful, which was a shame because he'd sacrificed his back to earn it and he wanted a portion to go to his parents and sister.

Beacan's family. The shadow images that went with those words stopped her, which allowed the wind to slice into her and nearly escape with a chunk of her resolve. Angry at it and her inattention, she straightened and sucked in air.

Don't you die on me, damn it! I'm doing the doing. It's your job to keep the light lit! I'm not going to tell your mother you croaked, not me! Got it!

She started walking again, the effort ratcheting her internal furnace up a few degrees and clearing her head. She wanted back her anger at Beacan, but it refused to surface.

He wasn't just a roll in the hay, a notch on her gun belt, something to brag about. The man, that pinnacle of physical success, was a living, breathing, caring human being with dark places of his own deep inside him—places she had a right to.

One who had parents and a sister who might have to go through the rest of their lives with the reality of his death.

A reality only she could give them, and only if she got through this herself.

* * * * *

Dayna's thigh muscles burned from the effort of putting one foot ahead of the other and then yanking free. Despite her vow not to, she'd finished off the granola bars. She'd tried to savor the experience of eating, but the concoctions had become soggy and she'd chewed mechanically, briefly debating whether she'd get any nutritional benefit from eating the wrapping.

She couldn't think in any clear or easily defined way. Several times a minute, she had to order herself to keep going. Even as she did, the marker Jace had erected in Cherokee's memory haunted her, and the absolutely insane and unshakable thought that Cherokee was nearby flooded through her.

It had to be her faulty vision. Her eyes lacked the energy to separate the trees from their frozen blanket, that was all, wasn't it? Only, the thing—the thing that stood with its arms at its sides, head up, legs apart as if balancing itself against the wind—illusion. Fantasy.

Sometimes she talked to it—him—whatever.

Told the Cherokee image that she'd never been so cold or this tired or tasted so much fear.

When she did, he'd nod and she knew, knew as she never had anything before in life, that he understood.

If she survived, she'd find Jace and tell him what had happened. The man wouldn't laugh at her. Instead, he'd nod and hold her in his arms and tell her he understood.

* * * * *

This was insane. Not the storm so much because its pace had remained steady for however long he'd been traveling this morning, and he'd factored in its existence so it was simply part of the picture, but his depth perception was shot, and with every step, Jace felt himself sliding off into nothingness. Maybe it was no more than the endless forest and its impact on his senses, but maybe he hadn't existed before today. The images that occasionally filtered through him were no more than part of some past life regression or a dream. When the here and now, the cold and wind noise threatened to become everything, he struggled to conjure up something, anything from the world beyond this place, but nothing came. Nothing.

The relentless movement was responsible, a world of white upon white and nothing that even whispered of civilization.

Civilization.

Whispers.

Shaken, he cast around for a tree to put between him and the wind. Once he'd positioned himself behind the semi-shelter, he pulled the PTT out from under the folds of his clothing and activated it. It squawked and hissed as he spoke into it, and when he was finished, he waited for Henri's response, but it didn't come.

"Henri," he tried again. "I don't know if you're out there. Maybe you can hear me, but I can't hear back. Is that it?"

The hissing became louder.

"Shit." He stopped and started again, yelling this time. "Henri, it's me! I'm all right and making pretty good time, I think."

How do you know, something mocked. Uneasy, he looked around.

"I'll try reaching you again in a few minutes." He considered saying something about his physical condition, but that would only be for him. "So far I haven't seen..." Seen what? Park Curran and his sister waiting for a bus?

There was only him, he thought as he put the PTT away. No world beyond this one, no other beating hearts. After a moment devoted to finding the shattered pieces of himself and reassembling them in some kind of order, he stepped out from behind the tree and again offered himself up to the elements.

As he did, he felt—not a presence and yet not nothing.

"Cherokee?"

Heart pounding, he let his legs take him where they wanted. Perhaps two minutes later, he found himself standing in front of one of the countless lodgepoles. It was no taller than most, nothing remarkable about it. And yet—

Still feeling as if he had no control over his actions, Jace crouched and reached out with the hand that had made a futile attempt at reaching the world beyond him. Some three feet of snow had stacked up around the tree's base, and there was no reason to want to dig down to the earth, and yet that was what he was doing, scratching like a dog.

His heart continued to hammer, and he had to fight to breathe, but finally he finished his task and, surrounded by displaced snow, he touched the top layer of pine needles. He started to wiggle his finger to enlarge the hole and then stopped.

Bones. A human skeleton. Stripped of everything that gave it character and definition, life and vitality. Propped against the trunk with the skull flung back and eye sockets staring at the sky.

He didn't know who he was or who'd taken control of him and understood that the bones existed only in his demented brain, but the message behind them needed no interpretation.

Death was at this place, in these mountains he'd once loved.

Maybe the siblings he'd come looking for. Maybe his.

Maybe Cherokee's.

Chapter Twenty

Was the sun overhead?

The question pulled Kandi out of the padded place she'd put herself into for safekeeping. When she looked up, the soft waterfall of flakes coated her face and forced her to close her eyes. She couldn't be sure, but it seemed as if the gray curtain was slightly less thick directly overhead. If that was the case, it was at least noon, wasn't it?

She was hungry, tired, cold, so cold.

Thinking that wouldn't get her anywhere, just as tears hadn't gotten her through her childhood. The lesson was deeply ingrained, and she suckled from it and renewed herself.

What were the pluses? Her thigh and calf muscles burned and trembled, but she'd keep moving, end of discussion.

Her stomach rumbled, and occasionally the hunger monsters tried to gnaw their way out, but this was a hell of a crash diet and if she didn't drop at least five pounds, she'd demand to know why.

The temperature was hard to get a clear handle on, but if it was freezing, it wasn't much below that. Tonight would tell a different story, one that sent another kind of monster clawing through her, but she had no intention of still being out here by then.

What do you think, she asked herself. *Making what, a mile an hour, maybe?*

If you're lucky.

So sue me. I'm doing the best I can.

I'm just making an observation.

Well, don't. I don't need a wiseass.

Her legs working, always working at the Herculean effort of walking, she waited for a response, but it didn't come. Good. Eyes closed to slits and her forehead feeling as if it might burst, she struggled to stay on what passed for the damn road and deny the fear, but it didn't work because the question and muscle stripping emotion slammed back into her. Someone had taken up residence inside her overworked brain, but she didn't know whom, or if she did, she wasn't ready to face that.

There's no one here. Just you. Park and Dayna are safe and dry. Beacan — Beacan…

You aren't a quitter. Never have been. It's kept you alive and sane. It will now. It will!

She'd started to go back into the mental cocoon she'd created for herself a thousand years ago when she realized that something had changed about her surroundings. At first, little registered except that there were fewer trees here. Lowering her head, she concentrated. Even when she and Beacan had made the nearly fatal mistake of losing their bearings, the dirt track had waited for them to return to it, but maybe-maybe what?

Only minimally surprised by her inability to order her thoughts, she planted herself. In the distance, the ground lifted slightly but what held her attention was that she'd reached something resembling a runway. If she'd stumbled upon a plane landing strip —

The thought died when she spotted a red pole sticking out of the ground. It was so thin that snow hadn't clung to it, and from here it appeared to be metal. Metal. Manmade. Her mind alternatively bunching and breaking apart, she approached and then touched it. It held no warmth, and yet she easily imagined a workman standing on a ladder as he hammered it into the ground. But why?

Angry because the object refused to give up its secrets, she pulled on it, but it had been firmly planted. Being out of the trees made her feel exposed, and she fought the drifting flakes by shaking her head, willing them to tell her something, anything. She was nearly certain there was another thin, red stick some fifty or sixty feet away.

Snow pole. You idiot, these are snow poles.

She shuddered, not the cold shivers that were a necessary part of staying alive, but something deeper. No one had bothered to mark the gravel road between Crater and Wolf, but obviously she'd come to something more important.

"The Crater rim road," she told the wind. "I've found it!"

That's good, isn't it?

Of course it is. Someone will come along soon.

How?

What do you mean, how?

The road hasn't been scraped clean.

Nooooo.

Because you're at the north end of Crater and they don't keep that road open in the winter.

"Not open?" Her little-girl whimper shocked her, and then the wind caught the question and bore it off into the wilderness, maybe shredded it.

How far was it to the Crater lodge?

She dug into her mind for the answer, found it, tried to reject it, finally accepted. At least ten miles.

She didn't have ten miles in her.

"Goddamn you!" she howled. If she had the strength, she would have attacked the storm that was killing her and might have already killed Beacan.

"Damn you, God!"

* * * * *

There was a vehicle in Lake Wolf.

Frowning, Jace stared down at the snow-blunted mound. The vehicle had been left backed into the water with the front tires clinging to the bank. He couldn't be sure of the make, just that it didn't appear to be a passenger car, which was what Dayna had been driving, and yet he was in the vicinity of the cluster of summer cabins which meant — what?

Turning his back on the lake, he worked at getting his bearings, no easy task since the storm had eradicated many of the landmarks. When he first reached the lake, he'd believed that once he spotted a boat dock, most of his work would have been done, but that hadn't been the case. He'd found a dock all right and after a couple of false starts, had made his way to the accompanying cabin. He'd gone all the way around the building before he'd determined that there was no sign anyone had been there recently. He'd gone through the same process twice more and begun to ask himself if this hadn't been a fool's mission from the beginning and Park and Dayna Curran were figments of his imagination. Deep down, he knew that wasn't true, but these were ghost cabins, and Cherokee had been walking beside him for hours.

Had someone been in the probably ruined rig? The thought turned him around and headed him back toward the vehicle, but he made himself stop before reaching it. If the driver hadn't gotten out within a few minutes of the accident, he or she was dead.

Dead. Beyond his help.

Although he'd already repeatedly tried to reach Henri, Jace again brought the PTT to his mouth and spoke into it. He couldn't be sure, but it seemed that the hissing squawk had decreased in volume, probably because the battery was nearly depleted. Standing here wouldn't accomplish anything.

As he started walking again, he tried to recall how the cabins were situated, but he seldom came out here. According to his watch, it was nearing two o'clock. His trip in had taken longer than he'd expected, and there was no way he could reach the Currans and get them out before nightfall. If they were all right, the three of them would wait until morning. Of course by then, Henri would have reported him as missing.

The wind coming off the lake had sharp teeth, and the lacy flakes that had accompanied him most of the way were being replaced by ice shards. Earlier, he'd been able to ignore the weight of his pack, but now it claimed more and more of his attention. Seeking distraction, he again pondered the disabled rig. The logical explanation was that the Currans weren't the only people at Wolf and someone had misjudged the road's width and had gotten so close to the lake that the vehicle had slid into the water. The storm could have muffled sounds but if Dayna and Park had heard and come to help—

Although he studied his surroundings, so much snow had fallen that whatever tracks might have once existed no longer did. Still, it wasn't difficult to imagine a small group of people taking refuge in one or more of the cabins, as they pondered their options—not that there were many. There was no way Dayna's vehicle could have made it out if it had been snowing awhile. They'd have to wait to be rescued, plain and simple.

By a ranger who'd gone off half-cocked with no way of getting in touch with his co-workers.

For a moment, Jace deliberated turning around and going back the way he'd come, beat feet back to his rig before dark. If Henri hadn't said anything, he might be able to cover his tracks. No one would be the wiser. He'd still have a job and the people here might not make it out alive. He'd never have the opportunity to ask Dayna why he hadn't been able shake off the impact of their brief conversation.

* * * * *

Dayna had long been fascinated by polar bears. That they thrived in harsh climates was only part of the appeal. She was also drawn to their strength and self confidence, the loving way the adults nurtured their young and the cubs' playfulness. Of course what she knew about them was limited to what she'd read or seen on TV when she would have given a great deal to watch them in their natural setting.

Would have. She no longer did.

Living alone had been important to her. Closed within the walls of the small house she rented, she was responsible to no one and did what she wanted when she wanted. No matter what the weather, she didn't miss a day in her garden and small greenhouse. The act of weeding and planting or simply checking a plant's progress centered her. It didn't matter that other people seldom saw what she created because the flowers she chose to bloom throughout the year were for her, nourished her. Were her children.

Head down, the collar of her father's coat pulled tight around her neck, she trudged. When she'd started out, she'd been able to judge the storm's moods, but it all ran together in her mind now. Whether the storm died or became a blizzard wasn't the issue because she had to keep going.

With winter coming on, it was time to plant bulbs, remove the bedraggled annuals, and trim back the perennials. She understood nature's need for rest and to some degree adopted the same standard by retreating to her living room with a stack of books, but even as she read the last pages of a fast-paced mystery, some part of her remembered the sun's kiss and a spring breeze's seductive touch.

Her parents had only been to her place once, her mother's eyes questioning as Dayna cut several roses and handed the flowers to her, her father asking how much she paid for rent and did she have a retirement plan. Although she would have loved to have her mother back, the woman never went anywhere alone and it had taken weeks for the taint of her father's presence to fade.

Pins and needles stabbed her forearms and pulled her back into the storm. She sniffed the wind and fought to make her eyes focus. It came to her that letting her arms hang at her side had resulted in a loss of circulation, and she tried to fold them across her chest, but they'd become too heavy for that. Finally she stuck them into pockets that had been set at just below waist level. Her left hand slid in easily, but the right was blocked by something.

No, not something, this was where she'd put Park's gun.

With her mind sliding into hibernation, the question of what to do with it was nearly impossible to answer. She'd taken it because—because it represented power she supposed, but what had she thought she'd do with that power—shoot the storm?

Firing it would create a sound, maybe enough of one that it could be heard above the sometimes raging wind, but despite the misty, mysterious presence she sometimes felt, she was more alone than she'd ever been and had no need to hear that sharp blast.

Useless then. And yet she couldn't bring herself to throw it away.

* * * * *

There was no shutter over the door and those designed to protect the windows remained hinged in the open position. For several minutes, Jace simply stared at the cabin while falling snow covered his snowshoes. As a result of the curtain of white between him and his destination, he couldn't tell whether any lights were on inside, and he saw no signs of a vehicle although Dayna Curran's car could be parked somewhere out of sight.

It wasn't until he'd forced himself to start walking again that it dawned on him that he didn't see any smoke coming from the chimney. If he couldn't be sure of the existence of an interior light, smoke wouldn't be any easier to spot. Still—

Finally, wondering if he was insane to feel like a racer approaching the finish line, he stood on the step leading to the door. There wasn't as much snow there as elsewhere, which was proof that someone had cleaned it off after the storm began. He saw no footprints.

Where had that someone gone, and why hadn't they finished what they'd come here to accomplish—prepare the cabin for winter?

He rapped on the door, his gloves making a dull thudding sound, and then repeated the gesture. The door remained closed and when, after telling himself he'd come too damn far and worked too hard to leave, he tried to turn the knob, he found it locked. Frustration and confusion backed him off the step and took him to the window to his left. The drapes had been left open. Snow had slid off the metal roof and added to what was packed around the cabin, bringing the depth nearly to the window ledge.

Dropping to his knees, Jace wiped the glass and pressed his face against the cold surface. A couch had been placed against the wall where the window was, its back low enough that it didn't hamper his view. On the opposite side of the room was a table. The interior walls had been covered with dark paneling, and another couch and two easy chairs were grouped around a cast iron stove. The living room flowed into a small kitchen. He couldn't tell whether anyone had left boots on the floor near the stove, not that wet boots would dry if a fire hadn't been lit. Still, their presence might tell him something.

It took some awkward moving around but finally he positioned himself so he could see the floor. Once again, he cleaned off the window, and then held his breath so condensation wouldn't cloud his view. His mind had started to record the fact that the living room contained area rugs when he saw the body.

Uncomprehending, he reared back, and then took another look. The body, a man's, lay on its left side with one leg curled up and the other outstretched. From what he could tell, the left arm was under the body. The right had flopped back almost as if he'd been trying to scratch his butt.

There was a great deal of blood.

No more than two minutes later, Jace was inside. He hadn't been sure what he should do, but when he spotted the shovel propped against the corner of the cabin, he'd used it to break the window glass. After clearing away the shards, he'd stepped inside.

The interior was no warmer than the outside and the blood around the body had coagulated. Jace stared at the two closed doors he assumed led to bedrooms and asked himself if the man's killer could be in there. Rationally, the thought made no sense, but then someone shouldn't have bled to death within a few feet of a woodstove.

Indecision still gripping him, Jace took in his surroundings. The refrigerator door was open and its interior had been stuffed with newspapers, a common practice when it came to winterizing a refrigerator. Someone had left a cooler on the nearby counter. There was a partial loaf of bread near it and dishes in the sink.

His hand went to the coat pocket that held his damnable useless PTT. Just the same, its weight reassured him, and with it now gripped in his fingers, he approached the nearest closed door. Although no one had responded to the sound of his breaking in, his heart slammed against his chest wall, and he watched with a kind of fascinated detachment as his free hand reached out.

In less than two minutes, he had his answer. He and the dead man were the only ones in the cabin. Dayna was gone.

If anyone asked him why he'd lit a fire before turning his attention to the body, he wouldn't have been able to say. It had a little to do with the fact that heat mimicked life, but mostly he was stalling.

The body was stiff and cold. The man looked to be in his forties but enough of his face was pressed against the carpet that Jace couldn't be certain. His hairline was—had been receding and his nails were professionally manicured.

Fury whipped through Jace, and it was all he could do not to kick the corpse. All this work, a night spent huddling in the dark while snow threatened to bury him, and the object of his search was dead—had been dead the whole time!

Only his anger didn't stem from that, the reality hitting Jace as he stood looking at the discarded ruin of a human being. This man—he wouldn't think of him as a corpse again—had at least died indoors with a cooler probably full of food nearby and most likely the woodstove providing adequate heat while Cherokee had had to do his dying in the uncaring wilderness.

Jace wasn't a cop, but he became an investigator now. Whoever this was had been wearing boots and work clothes, and in addition to the blood he'd obviously vomited, he'd sustained some kind of injury in the chest or ribs area.

As he was looking around for something to tell him whom the cabin belonged to, Jace's gaze fell on a table next to one of the easy chairs and the wallet that had been left there. When he picked it up, he was struck by its bulk but forgot that when he pulled out the driver's license and saw a fair resemblance to the dead man.

So this was Park Curran.

Where then was his sister?

Was she still alive?

Chapter Twenty-One

೫

The white tunnel surrounded Kandi. At times the snow let up enough that she dared hope she'd come to its end, but again and again the walls closed down, trapping her. Her thoughts remained within the walls, splintered glass fragments that went no further than determination and fear.

Something snapped at her with icy teeth but whether the storm was wholly responsible she couldn't say. The teeth wounded her, caused her to wince and moan, yet she didn't bleed. She was grateful for the wider, nearly level road she'd stumbled onto and tried not to think about its great length or her lack of progress because if she did, despair and resignation lapped at her.

What had happened to the crow she'd seen yesterday? Beacan had assured her that the bird was well-equipped for its environment and yet she couldn't help worrying about it. If one of nature's creatures couldn't survive this storm, what made her think that—?

Without warning, her right knee buckled and she pitched forward. Instead of immediately righting herself, she lay with her right leg caught under her and the other stretched out as if reluctant to have anything to do with the rest of her. Her head weighed a thousand pounds, and every breath hurt. If she remained where she was…

Look at me.

Feeling dumb and logy, a beached whale beyond caring whether it ever returned to the sea, she nevertheless raised her head and tried to focus.

Look at me.

Ahead of her, deep in the tunnel that was her world stood — what? By ordering each muscle in turn, she managed to stagger to her feet, but once she was there, she couldn't think what, if anything, she should do next. All she knew was that if she didn't move, the voice or whatever it was might find her again. Might take over. Her knee still felt weak so she sent her will to it. It responded with a sloth-like step and half-walking, half-dragging herself, she once again headed into the tunnel.

Look at me.

"Go away."

I can't. This is the only place I am.

"Go the fuck away." Her words had faded into nothing when she spotted a whisper of movement ahead of her. If it had been yesterday, she would have struggled to focus, but her eyes were as exhausted as the rest of her. Still, if she'd found —

The whisper movement blurred, became clearer, faded again, but her mind held onto the image and made sense of it. Waiting for her, surrounded by snow and winter, stood a human shape. Fear thudded through her, and she wanted to stop but maybe she'd never get going again if she did. A human? Help? Maybe Beacan but that couldn't be because he was behind her, a prisoner of his back.

"Who are you?" she whispered. "What-what are you doing here?"

Waiting.

"For what?"

No answer. She wasn't sure how she felt about that, both relieved and lonely perhaps. With what she could control of her mind, she counted her steps and locked her nearly useless gaze on the shadow. It turned from gray to blues and browns and became much more than delusion. Her knees threatened to buckle but not from weariness this time.

"Who are you?" she asked.

Cherokee.

"I-I don't understand."

No response, either that or not enough of her brain remained to process what was happening. Whatever it was lifted an arm in something approximating a wave and then she saw a face—hollow-eyed with concave cheeks and incredible sadness.

"What-what is it? Why are you crying?"

The question seemed to startle "him" and he began to break apart and become part of his surroundings. Terrified of being alone again, she lurched forward, counting steps and begging—begging what?

After a long—too long—time, she stood where the shadow had been. It hadn't reappeared and yet there was— Someone had left a heavy-duty pickup by the side of the road. Both the vehicle and the snow blade on the front caked with a thick layer of snow and more snow packed all around like a prison. The doors were locked, and the bed was filled with portable road barriers and shovels. Grabbing a shovel, she tried to break a window with it but only succeeded in exhausting herself. Someone would come for it, eventually. She couldn't wait that long.

After acknowledging that this abandoned truck had become as useless as the two vehicles at Wolf, Kandi came back to herself, back to reality. She had two choices, either sink to her knees on this empty road and die or struggle on.

Since starting out this morning the storm had risen and fallen, backed off only to slam into her again and again. When that happened, she turned her back to the worst of it and waited it out. Occasionally despair had raked her, but even when the emotion drew blood, she found a way to repel the attack. What she couldn't answer was how much longer she'd have enough strength.

Not long ago, she'd found reservoirs of warmth between her breasts and legs and in the small of her back, but now only her crotch retained any heat. Her body temperature had fallen and was affecting her ability to think, but that was all right because fear had a sharp edge she didn't want to feel today.

Crater Lake was to her left, somewhere. She didn't have the energy to make her way over to the rim, and even if she did, she wasn't sure she'd want to—maybe proof of how sluggish her brain had become, maybe because she was one small and miserable human being while the lake—the lake represented power.

Her knee again threatened to seize. It might be nothing more than an overstressed muscle but if she'd done something to the cartilage...

The thought caused her to chuckle. *Admit it, old girl, you're in more damn trouble than you've ever been. A blown knee's the least of your problems.*

Why was she doing this? No way could she reach civilization under her own power today and she'd never survive another night like the last one. She was dying. Imagining the unimaginable, still walking, still occasionally laughing and worrying about having her toes amputated and permanent damage to her knee and searing loneliness but dying.

Would it be easy, falling asleep and everything shutting down or would she fight and rage until the end?

She hadn't thought about Beacan in a while—at least she didn't think she had—but he came back to her now with his big, powerful hands and wonderfully fashioned body and bad back and the piss-poor amount he'd been willing to share about himself.

Maybe he'd frozen to death last night—or today and what she'd imagined she'd seen had been his ghost. Perhaps they'd meet in the afterworld she didn't believe in, link hands and skip—

The image of Beacan dead and stiff became a knife in her chest. Gasping, she stopped and leaned forward with her club hands propped on her knees. She had to get going again, but if Beacan was dead what was she doing this for?

Park and Dayna?

Herself?

* * * * *

Dayna had been able to pay this month's utility and rent bills, but if she didn't soon find a job, she wouldn't have the money for next month's indebtedness. She'd wanted to tell Park she needed her share of the proceeds from the cabin sale, but that money, he'd maintained, must go into an investment fund earmarked to help cover the cost of warehousing their father. As for the money the old man had amassed over his lifetime—well, Park was—had been—working at having that switched over to their names. She'd signed some papers to that effect, but in the meantime, she didn't know how she was going to pay her electric bill.

Like an electric bill mattered?

The storm's ability to keep on reinventing itself once again captured Dayna's thoughts. The need to stop and rest washed over her and threatened to suck her into its depths. That she was able to resist, that she knew how important movement was, gave her a sense of pride, but it didn't negate the fact that fleeing the sight of Park's body had probably killed her.

You're a coward. A damn, stupid, sniveling coward.

Well, maybe not sniveling, she admitted, her legs pumping, pumping but not accomplishing enough. She'd cried back at the cabin but hadn't since then. Throughout the lonely, dark, monster night, she'd worked with her fears and fought cold and come out the other side with her sanity intact.

She wasn't sure whether that was true because despite her best efforts, the storm monster had bitten off huge chunks of her. Even if it stopped snowing and the sun came out, it would be dark in too few hours.

She felt little, only continued to walk.

* * * * *

Jace shoved a log to the rear of the woodstove and watched it catch fire. It had taken him at least a half hour to put enough pieces of the puzzle together so that he understood, or believed he understood what had happened here. When he'd gone outside, he'd spotted a faint glow through the trees and had followed it to another cabin where a light had been left on. The front door was unlocked, and although the recently remodeled structure had been empty, he'd determined that two people had been staying there, a man and a woman from the looks of what was in the bathroom.

Needing to know if Dayna and the others had left in her car, he'd circled the Curran cabin. He'd first seen the fallen tree and then under that, the smashed sedan. Back inside, he'd noted that there were four cups in the sink. Perhaps, he reasoned, Dayna and Park had joined their guests in having something to drink, but then Park had died and the others had left.

On foot.

Cursing his inability to contact anyone, Jace paced into the kitchen where he opened a can of stew and set it in a pan on the stove to warm, but staying here wasn't an option because he'd gotten himself into this, he had to get himself out.

Besides, there was Dayna and the others—mostly Dayna who'd become more important to him than he'd thought possible. What made sense, what might allow him to hold onto his career and sanity was to go after them. Had he and Dayna begun some kind of connection, the start of a personal relationship? The only way to know was by talking to her again.

Only, where had they gone? Had he passed within feet of them or had they set off cross-country to Diamond?

Restlessness sent him into the nearest bedroom, but except for an extra set of male underwear, it was empty of personal belongings. He'd started to close the door behind him when he spotted a piece of paper on the floor under the dining area table.

"To whoever", the note began. The top of the page bore yesterday's date. It must have been left on the table but had blown off when he opened or closed the front door.

His meal forgotten, Jace backed up to the stove and began reading.

"Park is dead. Beacan and Kandi—they're the people who were at the other cabin—left before he died so they don't know. The weather forecast calls for more snow so I… If someone comes here before I get to Crater, please don't tell Scott that his father is dead. That's something I have to do. I can't stay here, not with my brother… The others, Beacan Jarrard and Kandi Ferber are from the Bay area. He's a pro baseball player. Kandi works at a hospital, but I don't know which one. They're—they too were heading for Crater."

She'd signed the note Dayna Curran, then added a P.S. which included what he assumed was her home address. She also gave an address for her brother along with the name of his business.

The stew began to simmer. Jace removed it from the stove, picked up a spoon and started eating. Heat snaked down him but not enough to master the deep chill he now felt. This was becoming last winter all over again.

* * * * *

Something had changed about her surroundings. Kandi struggled to make sense of that change, but she'd buried herself so deep that the effort of coming back to her devil world took incredible effort. She stopped, which was what she'd long wanted to do and listened.

The deep whine spoke of strength, of power, distant but coming closer. Fear wormed its way into her and met up with a wild and irrational hope, both emotions shattering a little. She wanted to suck in enough air to clear her head but was afraid too much would drop her temperature even more. If she froze, would she collapse, or would ice lock her legs and leave her a lifeless statue?

Her eyes lacked the strength to focus, but that didn't stop her from staring in the direction the sound seemed to be coming from. Like a blind woman trying to distinguish salvation from danger, she clamped her head between her numb hands and growled low in her throat.

No longer an uncomplicated whine, but a scream now. A machine!

"I'm here! Please, I'm here!"

The wind caught her pitiful words and tore them apart so she forced strength into her legs and willed them to return to life. They responded slowly, hissing in pain and weakness, nearly pitching her forward onto her face, would have if she hadn't refused to let the storm have her.

On puppet-string legs, she lurched to what she believed was the middle of the road and hung there exhausted. The approaching snowmobile—it had to be that!—enveloped her with its promise of power and salvation and despite her desperate order not to pin everything on the sound, she did exactly that.

Henri Lansky, who hadn't slept more than a couple of hours last night, was grateful both for the snowmobile's heater and the large windshield which protected him from all but a few outlaw flakes. Just the same, his eyes burned from the effort of trying to penetrate the relentless white that constituted his world, and, not for the first time, he cursed Jace for making him do this.

"You're a damn, stupid fool," he'd tell his co-worker. "Too damn stupid to be allowed to live. What the hell's the matter with you? You ain't got the sense God gave a—"

With no conscious command behind it, Henri twisted down on the throttle, slowing the four-year-old snowmobile because he'd seen—

The person standing in the middle of the snow-coated road was buried under layers of clothing, yet he could tell that he or she was slightly built and maybe five and a half feet tall. The person wore no skis or snowshoes and walked—

Hands hanging, head appearing too heavy to be held up, the figure lurched forward. Henri shifted into neutral and before the snowmobile stopped moving, jumped off it. The thick, loosely packed snow made running impossible, and, mimicking the other person's movements, he plodded forward. Finally he was close enough to see that he'd found a woman. "Dayna?" he asked. "Dayna Curran?"

The female shook her head, stared at him.

Henri took another step, and then gripped her shoulders and although she felt so stiff he wondered if she might crack, he drew her against him. "Who are you?" he asked. "Where did you come from? Are you alone?"

"Lake Wolf," she mouthed.

"You came from Lake Wolf?"

She nodded.

"By yourself?"

"Noooo."

Belatedly remembering the snowmobile's heater, he started to guide her to it, but after a few steps, she pulled back.

"Where are we —?" she asked. "I have — Beacan."

"Beacan? Who's that?"

She didn't say anything for long seconds. Then, "A man."

"What man?"

When she spoke, her words were jerky and incomplete, and she paused several times as if she'd lost her train of thought, but finally he understood that she and this Beacan person had started walking out from Lake Wolf yesterday after Park Curran had injured himself and two vehicles had been rendered inoperable. By then, he'd helped her onto the snowmobile where the heater's life-giving warmth could reach her. Now she sat hunched over as if trying to become one with the heat. She'd pulled back her hood enough that he could tell she was young and attractive — at least she'd been good-looking before the elements had scraped all color from her face and left the skin raw.

"I'm Kandi," she told him when he pressed her. She wasn't shivering which concerned him. "Beacan couldn't walk anymore because of his back so I-I told him I'd bring back help. But then I reached the rim road and there wasn't anyone around, just some truck someone had abandoned, and it hadn't been plowed and I didn't know… I kept on walking but I knew…"

She'd known she couldn't make it to park headquarters before the elements claimed her, but instead of giving up, she'd pulled courage and strength from somewhere deep inside and forced herself to keep going. If he hadn't come along, she would have died out here.

Still leaning into the heat as if drinking from it, she speared him with her gaze.

"We *have* to find him," she said. A shudder gripped her, stiffening her spine and forcing her arms and legs to become rigid.

"I will," he promised. He still couldn't comprehend what reservoir of strength had sustained her for so long. "But first I've got to get you to where you'll be safe."

"No!"

"Look, I know you're worried about the others, but you're hypothermic and you probably have frostbite. If you don't get proper care—"

"Later." She gulped in air.

"Kandi, I lost one friend to a storm and now another's out there. I'm not going to take the same chance with you. I understand—"

"He's helpless. If we don't find him, he'll—please. Please."

Instead of responding, he reached for the snowmobile's two-way radio and keyed it in. One of his fellow rangers answered, and he asked to speak to Paul. He told his boss he'd found a woman not far from where Jace had been working yesterday and wanted to bring her in, but she was insisting he look for her injured companion and he wanted all available personnel to join him. Paul had started to respond when Kandi shook her head.

"Dayna and Park," she said, sounding fierce and determined. "Someone has to go after them."

Feeling the weight of responsibility, Henri added to his report. The only thing he left out was what he knew about Jace.

"What the hell's going on out there?" Paul demanded. Then, "All right. I'll get things mobilized on this end, but if she's been out there since yesterday, she has to be in bad shape."

"She is."

"Henri, make her understand I can't allow her to risk her life looking for someone who might not make it, all right?"

Kandi stared at the radio, leaving Henri with no doubt that she'd heard and understood.

"Look," Paul continued. "I can send three, four men, but it's going to take time for them to reach you."

"I know."

"I'm sure you do. I'll also dispatch a couple of snowmobiles and a sled from Diamond to Wolf for the Currans. Henri?"

"Yeah?"

"You know where Jace is, don't you." It wasn't a question.

"Yeah."

"And he isn't going to be any help in this, is he?"

"No," Henri made himself say.

"Shit. All right, get her to tell you where she thinks she left the guy and call me back. Let me know if you think she needs an ambulance."

"No hospital," Kandi said as Henri keyed off.

"Listen to me. I know you're worried about the others," he told her. "I am too. But right now you're my primary concern. If you can just give me an idea how far you were from the junction to Wolf when you and Beacan separated—"

"I'm *not* going back. I can't!"

Before he could respond, she swung her leg off the snowmobile, stumbled and then righted herself. The snow on the front of her coat had melted, but fresh flakes had already replaced them. She looked too small and slight for this, and yet—

"I promised," she told him. Inside her gloves, her fists were clenched.

Chapter Twenty-Two

🙾

Dayna growled at the monster that was the storm, the sound low in her throat. Again and again she ordered her muscles to keep working and was only vaguely aware of how poorly they responded. She had no feeling from the knees down, but she'd relentlessly flexed and straightened her hands, thus pumping circulation through them.

She concentrated on that, tried to anyway. They might have to amputate her legs but at least she'd still have her fingers. No more running but a person could tend plants from a wheelchair, couldn't they?

Stupid. Beyond stupid. Why had she left the cabin? Why had—?

The rest of whatever she'd been thinking froze and cracked, and the wind escaped with the pieces. Her arms were so heavy. She'd tuck her hands back into her father's coat pockets for a while, yes, and then—

The coat's length provided needed protection for her hips and butt, but it was no miracle fiber. If her father had been influenced by some ad agency's pitch, the joke was on him. For once his suspicious instincts had failed him and—

That wasn't all that had failed him. His brain was gone.

Like hers?

Another growl rolled out of her, stronger this time and even less civilized. She wanted to bite and snap at the storm, attack it as a cougar attacks prey, but she was a mouse, not a creature of fang and claw.

A mouse! Ah shit, no! Not anymore!

When, belatedly, she slid her right hand into the coat pocket, her club fingers came into contact with a strangely shaped rock. Wondering how it had gotten there and how long she'd been carrying it and why, she finally and with great effort drew it out of its hiding place. The animal she was becoming felt strengthened by its heft, but only when she stared at it with eyes so tired and wounded that everything carried a red tinge did she realize she was holding her dead brother's gun.

His loaded gun.

She could shoot the storm, blast holes through it and watch it bleed. If the cougar—What cougar? Where had it come from? Got too close to the mouse she'd been for most of her life, she'd blow the beast apart.

The thought that a predator might be stalking her made her laugh. The sound, hard and strong, awakened a small part of her mind, and she stopped—or maybe she'd already given up walking—and wrapped both gloved hands around the weapon.

Take that, you motherfuckin' blizzard. Think you can pull me down and tear me apart? Take that you mother—

Her father would have beaten her unconscious if he'd heard her talking like that, reared back and hit her so hard that her neck might have snapped.

It would serve him right. Convicted of pummeling his daughter to death. Sentenced to life in prison, wife divorcing him and gone, money sucked up by the lawyers he hired to defend himself, son disowning him.

Only Park couldn't disown—could a son do that to a father?—because he was dead.

Park. Dead.

Her mother dead.

Only she and her father were left.

Her arms and shoulders screamed, pleading with her to put down the obscenely heavy weapon, but she didn't. Couldn't. Because the pistol was everything. The only defense she had against the storm that was destroying her.

Ordering herself not to think, to simply be, she squeezed. For a wonderful and frightening moment, the sound killed the wind. Sharp and powerful, it took no prisoners.

Was anyone out there? If there was, if the cavalry was on its way, they'd hear the blast and come running. Running through snow that sucked strength from leg muscles and drained all energy from every cell and blood vessel.

"Hear me!" she bellowed. "Hear me! I'm here! Alive. I don't want to die! Not yet. Not until…"

More thoughts, things she wanted to tell the rescuers she prayed were on their way piled up inside her, but she'd forgotten how to organize words or thoughts.

Instead, she put everything she had into firing off another shot. She'd recoiled the first time, but she didn't now. Instead, she leaned into power and sound and took those things deep inside her and made them part of her.

If people were looking for her…

And if there was no one and night came again, she'd turn the weapon on herself. Rob the storm of the pleasure of sucking the last of her life out of her.

* * * * *

Jace was glad he didn't have a watch because knowing how much of the precious daylight he'd wasted wouldn't change anything. Slow and steady. Slow and steady.

Of course slow and steady might not accomplish anything, and three people could die out here tonight, three people who counted on him just as Cherokee had—

Stopping, he shook his head and fought to get at what had distracted him, but although he made an effort to pull the storm's sounds and messages into him, he learned nothing new. Conditions changed constantly, making it impossible for him to gather a single, clear image of his world. The sky remained a dark, leaden gray, proof that the clouds held an inexhaustible supply of snow. Was more than him, more than any man.

Pig-simple old boy. You might not live until morning yourself.

There, he thought as he started again. He'd said it.

Had Cherokee come to the same conclusion? As the storm that eventually killed him raged, had Cherokee looked into its growling mouth and known?

"I'm sorry," Jace started to say but before he could, something without form or definition snagged his attention. Maybe another tree had crashed to the ground and he'd sensed the earth's vibration, maybe. He might have heard a snowmobile, but that wasn't right, was it, because a snowmobile whined and screamed and went on and on while this had been—

"Ah shit, Cherokee. What have I—?"

Something about his left snowshoe didn't feel right, but instead of examining it, he continued with what needed to be said.

"This storm's a bad one. Say all you want about the need for a deep snowpack and how the runoff's going to help come summer, that has nothing to do with now."

Cherokee didn't give a shit about whether there'd be enough water in the dams and reservoirs. If the atheists, of whom he was one, were right and there was no life after death, Cherokee didn't give a shit about anything.

"Are you out there? Any part of you?" he demanded. "Some molecule, some something?"

With his legs working and fear taking relentless nips out of him, he told Cherokee that if he enjoyed haunting him, he, Jace, didn't appreciate it.

"You're the damn idiot who made the mistake that got you killed," he told his best friend. A moment later the snowshoe's binding broke.

* * * * *

Could she kill herself? In a dim way, Dayna knew she hadn't felt anything except determination for a long time and determination could doom her if it blinded her to reason and logic. Wanting back emotion, she purposefully drew out her last memory of her brother, but he'd been an unliving lump, a useless mass to be disposed of, and today she felt no sorrow, no need or desire to cry. Even the thought of placing his pistol against her temple and squeezing the trigger and sending bleeding fragments of what she'd once been into the air elicited no response.

At first, she'd hated pulling up and discarding her plants when they died, but after a while she'd become hardened to the task because the dead had to be removed to make room for the living, it was as simple as that.

She'd survived one night out here, barely, but couldn't another. Her options were simple—she'd either tough it out until the bitter end, monitoring her vital signs and clenching her teeth against the agony of her system shutting down, or she'd speed the inevitable.

"Not a word, old man," she told her father. "This isn't your decision, and I don't give a damn what you think. You always thought I was a coward, a shit coward. The Currans are fighters, aren't they? That's what you drummed into me, but this is my life, what's left of it anyway. My decision how and when I choose to check out."

Speaking aloud exposed her teeth to too much cold so she stopped. Now, silent, she told Park she was grateful he'd given her control over the situation.

You, too, told me I was a coward, and you were right then. But not this time. Blowing out my brains takes courage.

Although she avoided horror movies and had little interest in medical TV programs, she had a fair idea what would happen to her skull if she plowed a bullet into it. She felt sorry for whoever found her, but by then, hopefully, the elements and animals would have pared her down to little more than bone. What she wanted was for the end to be quick, one moment thinking and breathing, the next gone.

And no fear?

She sniffed at the question, pulled its essence into her and tried to taste it. Nothing. After a moment, she put the gun back in her father's coat pocket and started walking again.

As she did, she sensed she was being watched.

And that the watcher's death had been far different from the one she planned for herself.

* * * * *

Kandi couldn't get enough of the heat blowing over her. Still, despite its life- affirming warmth, she gave it only scant attention because fatalism had settled into her bone marrow. The snowmobile fought the storm, not mastering it but showing no signs of giving in either. Still, it couldn't hold back the approaching night. When daylight faded, she'd demand that the ranger not give up, but she couldn't tell Beacan the same thing any more than she could keep the temperature from dropping.

Henri, who'd told her that his friend, another ranger, was out here somewhere, had assured her he'd have no trouble finding and then staying on the road to Lake Wolf, but what if Beacan had become disoriented and wandered off it or snow had covered him and he couldn't make his presence known as they passed within a few feet of him?

What if his inability to move and keep his blood circulating had made it easy for the elements to claim him?

She hated the questions drumming inside her, wanted to think about the blessed warmth in her legs, the strong and healthy presence behind her. When Henri used the snowmobile's CB to let others know what they were doing and that he needed them out here as soon as possible, her mind had fastened on that, briefly.

"Staff's spread all over the park," Henri had told her after his third conversation with his supervisor. "It'll take them hours to launch a concerted search. I wish…"

"We can't stop."

"We won't, yet. I just want you to know what we're up against."

"I do," she said. She felt a thousand years old.

After that, they'd said little as they made their all too slow way back to the Lake Wolf turnoff. She'd worked so hard to get beyond that point and hated having to retrace her steps, and yet this was the only way they had a chance of finding Beacan. Henri put a great deal of energy into studying what little they could see of their surroundings, but it didn't matter to her because Beacan wasn't anywhere on the rim road. She hadn't spotted the turnoff, but Henri had and now with every foot, every yard, they were getting closer to where she'd left the man she barely knew.

The man who'd given her the ring that meant everything to him.

The man who might already be dead.

Then, too soon, Henri stopped. "I don't dare go any further," he said. "We have to go back to the turnoff, be there when the others arrive."

"No."

"Do you think I want to do this? Hell, if there was any other way, any chance we'd find him in—"

"I promised."

"I know how you feel, believe me, I do. But I have my orders."

"I heard those orders."

"Look, as soon as everyone's together, we'll get organized. By dawn—"

"He'll be dead by then." *If he isn't already.*

Henri sighed and drew her against his chest. Both needing and resenting what he was offering, she stared through the Plexiglas windshield at what she could see of their world. She couldn't tell whether the wind had altered its tempo or if it was snowing any less than it had been when Henri found her, not that either of those things mattered.

Exhaustion was a living force inside her, and she'd never wanted to sleep more than she did at this moment. Henri would take her to a place of electricity and food and someone would loan her a car or drive her home because she wasn't a trained rescuer and would only be in the way. Surely the others wouldn't fault her for wanting to go home, and even if they wondered at her lack of compassion, what did it matter? Alone within her own walls, she'd have back the quiet and space she craved. She'd sleep and shower and fix herself something to eat and then go back to bed and not dream and finally, finally, she'd recover.

She'd done all she could for Beacan Jarrard.

"I'm sorry," Henri said, his breath warming the back of her neck. "Damn it, I'm sorry." He began a slow circle. In a moment they'd be heading back the way they'd come.

"Wait."

"I can't. The risk—"

"I know. I-I have to go to the bathroom."

"Oh," he said. "Look, I—oh hell, nothing I say's going to change anything, is it?"

"No, it won't. Please, this will just take a minute."

"What about you?" she asked once she was standing. Already cold had begun to seep into her newly revitalized legs.

"What?"

"Do you—have to go?"

He didn't answer her mother-speaking-to-a-toddler question, but as she stood staring at him, he swung his leg over the seat and stood. She thought he was going to touch her again, but he didn't.

"There." He pointed to a spot behind her. "The snow looks fairly firm over there. You should be able to—you know."

She started to turn away, then looked up at him. "I don't want you watching."

"All right," he said after a short silence. "I can trust you not to run off, can't I?"

"I won't run," she told him.

And she didn't. However, as soon as he started toward the spot he'd chosen for himself, she hurtled herself at the snowmobile and scrambled onto it.

She wrapped her fingers around the handles, praying for balance and twisting down on the throttle at the same time.

The machine bucked and threatened to throw her off, but she hung on, a cowboy riding his bull to the bell.

Behind her, Henri bellowed, but she didn't dare look around. Eyes wide and staring, she headed into the storm's teeth.

Chapter Twenty-Three

෨

"I will not have a quitter for a daughter."

"I can't stand in front of a room full of people. I wouldn't be able to say—"

Whap! "Don't question me, young lady! Don't ever do that!"

I hate you! Hate you!

Head pounding, Dayna pulled herself out of the past where she'd stupidly allowed herself to go. The day had been both too short and never-ending, dark gray. On that distant day when her father had forced her to face close to a hundred of his business associates and regurgitate what he'd force-fed her about the inadequacies of a public education, her world had taken on the same color. Even now she remembered little except a tidal wave of cynical eyes on her and her father sitting beside her, the tempo of his breathing telegraphing his reaction to what came out of her.

"You failed," she started to say, but instead of telling her father he'd been a miserable example of a parent, she twisted around so she could see the depression her foot had made in the snow. She didn't know where the strength to go on walking had come from, just that it had been *her* muscles, *her* stupidity, *her* determination. The same determination had gotten her to her feet in that long-ago meeting room and made it possible for her to return those cynical stares.

If that was true, if she'd been more courageous than she'd known, then maybe her father had passed on something worthwhile after all.

She'd never known his parents. They'd died while she was a baby, her grandmother succumbing to cancer, her grandfather drinking himself to death. If she'd asked about them, she couldn't remember, and her memories of what her father had told her revolved around his tight mouth and narrowed eyes. He hadn't known what his father was like, he'd told her—not sober anyway. His mother had been a shrew whose theory of child-rearing was to yell.

"You're lucky you don't have any memories of them," Park had told her once. "Their excuse for a marriage gave dysfunctional a whole new meaning. Dad would have been better off growing up in an orphanage or on the street."

Why couldn't she get her father out of her mind? This day, this moment was about staying alive, not wallowing—

He'd never had a chance, had he?

Her temple pulsed, pulsed again. She was getting close to something important here, or she would be if she could think. As it was, she was left with fragments—a small, frightened boy needing comforting arms but knowing he'd never find them, an adolescent needing direction and guidance but having to take those steps alone, a young man wanting to get married so he wouldn't be lonely anymore but finding a woman who couldn't see beyond the armor he'd erected around himself, a new father holding his son and not wanting to be like his father.

"You weren't," she whispered. "You never drank and you supported—"

It was a good thing she didn't have children, good Park had only had Scott and his mother was raising him.

She couldn't feel her nose. Her eyelids had been sandpapered and her cheeks weren't in much better condition. She, who could run a sub six-minute mile, hadn't managed one this afternoon. She didn't know where she was going or why because only a moron—and she hadn't yet sunk to that level—would think that they were accomplishing anything.

Park was dead. She couldn't help Dayna and Beacan. She had no children, no husband, few friends, and if she died, some agency would step forward to take care of her father. The world would continue to revolve without her. No one, really, would mourn her so why—

For herself.

But why?

She didn't dare stop and yet she did. Exhaustion pelted her. There was no game to be won and not a chance in hell heroics would save the day. She'd been on this path to death since morning, maybe since yesterday when she'd turned her back on her brother's body.

Was that what this was about? Was this some insane attempt on her part to atone for allowing herself to be ruled by revulsion at the sight of Park's body? Had she fled the way a child covers its eyes when the monsters come on the TV screen and was now determined to make up for that cowardice?

No, not a coward!

Then what?

The question hammered and hammered. There was no answer, only something or someone—in front of her. Waiting. The man, young and strong with old, old eyes, held out his hand to her. She stared at it, and then, although she knew deep down that she was alone, she reached out her own nerveless fingers.

"*You don't want to do this,*" the "man" said. "*Die the way I did.*"

"*What choice do I have?*"

"*Go out strong. Proud. On your terms.*"

* * * * *

Kandi blinked repeatedly, but no matter how she tried, she couldn't keep things in focus. The snowmobile's headlight sliced through the flakes and yet those same flakes stopped the light from penetrating more than a few yards. Although it was, she believed, still afternoon, it was already colder than it had been last night, either that or she no longer had the reservoir of inner heat that had gotten her through the night.

Henri would be all right. He'd walk back to the juncture between the two roads and wait for help to arrive. He might be cold by then, cold and upset, but alive.

"Beacan!" she yelled. "Beacan! Damn it, where are you?"

He didn't answer. Maybe she was nowhere near where she'd left him. She'd have to keep going then, belly growling and eyes burning. According to the gas gauge, she still had half a tank, but she didn't know how many gallons it held.

It didn't matter. She'd continue to jockey the unfamiliar machine and look, call out his name and —

She'd nearly told herself she'd pray but stopped herself in time. Still, praying was something people did in times of crises and if nothing else, a few well-worn words would have given her mind something to do.

However, she didn't know any prayers so as she chugged along, she told herself she was doing this insane thing because she wanted to make sure Beacan got his ring back and he'd better not be dead because she sure as hell didn't want to spend the rest of her life burdened with a hunk of jewelry.

"Beacan! Beacan!"

Frozen knives raked her throat. She clamped her mouth shut and tried to work up enough spit to ease some of the pain. Her arms ached from holding onto the vibrating handlebars, and she wanted to let go so she could place her fingers near the heater. She'd been going and going and going, trying to fit her too short frame to the big machine when she needed to crawl into the heating unit and stay there.

That's what she'd do, shut down and go into hibernation. She'd been out in this shit for more than twenty-four hours, doing what no sane person would do, looking for some man she barely knew. Beacan hadn't been able to go on. He'd given up, but instead of doing the same thing, she'd plunged on. She'd done more than anyone else would have, and now it was time for her to think of herself. Let the chips fall.

Time to turn around.

Something that sounded too much like a whimper clawed up her throat. Breathing hard, she fought to keep it where it belonged, and as she did, the snowmobile drifted to the right. It started to slide down a slope at the edge of the narrow path, and she yanked on the handlebars, adrenaline pumping through her.

Too late! Too little! As the snowmobile's slide accelerated, she catapulted off it. Snow pillowed around her and sucked her down. Fortunately, the slope was short, and the snowmobile stopped before it had gone more than fifty feet, but it now canted dangerously to one side.

Not quite believing what had happened, Kandi dug herself out of her snow bed and crawled on hands and knees to the machine. The downhill runner had plowed into the snow while the other hung in the air. The motor continued to roar, but she must have instinctively shifted into neutral because the track wasn't moving. The screaming, complaining howl chewed at her nerves, but even if she dared climb onto the snowmobile and turned it off, the alternative was the sound of the wind and maybe that was even worse.

Despite the danger, she made her way around the useless hunk of metal until she was on the downhill side. Positioning herself so hopefully, she could roll out of the way if it started to slide toward her, she pushed. Her muscles burned, and she ground her teeth, but even when she grunted and screamed, nothing moved.

Trembling, she fell back on her haunches and stared for a long, long time, felt nothing and everything—the only thing that mattered. She hadn't escaped the wilderness after all.

Barely aware of what she was doing, Kandi gathered up a handful of snow and put it in her mouth. The cold produced an instant headache, but she swallowed the small amount of water and then repeated the process.

The headlights, canting upward, illuminated nearby trees and turned their snow-blanketed branches silver. No artist could capture that clean, pure color, a shame because it spoke of timelessness, of something both frozen and alive. If she could find a dress with that iridescent quality, she'd wear it as long as the fabric held out. Instead, she was going to die beneath it.

* * * * *

The squalling hum rumbled through Beacan and pulled him out of himself and the nothing place he'd gone into. He'd been sitting with his back propped against a tree and his legs pulled tight against him for maybe fifteen minutes, watching it snow and the snow changing from white to gray and grayer and knowing he was seeing the color of death and now, when his strength was spent and he wanted only to bury himself in his world, something was trying to pull him out of it.

He'd been maybe seven the night his parents had rushed his gasping, blue-lipped sister to the hospital. Because there hadn't been anywhere for him to go, he'd stood in a corner of the emergency room while medical personnel worked over her. He'd hated her strangled breathing, wanted to tell her she was scaring him and not to die because he loved her even if she had eaten the last of the cookies Mom had made the day before. His parents' fear had tasted bitter and hot, and he would have cried if he hadn't somehow known that at that moment they didn't have anything to give to him. Wise in the way of children who love and are loved, he'd stayed where he was, been nothing.

He'd felt the same way when, barely twenty-two, he'd stood in another emergency room and looked down at his tiny daughter's ruined remains.

Today, however, he couldn't remain a nothing. He couldn't say what was pulling him back to a thinking place. Part of it was the unexpected sound, of course, but that wasn't all. Some element, some something had been beside him all day, keeping him company and goading him on, reminding him of the consequences of giving into pain and demanding he try. Try, damn it!

As a consequence, he'd crawled after Kandi then, a dog forcing his back to do things it couldn't until he'd exhausted himself. He hated, not being dependent on her, but this helplessness, and yet hatred hadn't changed anything,

Seeking answers swept away the hatred and fear and gave him something.

He thought standing would be torture, but his back must have gone to sleep because he felt nothing—not until he was on his knees and gripping the tree so he could pull himself erect. Then the coma ended.

Wailing, nostrils flared and sucking in snow, pain beat at him. He acknowledged gnawing fear and smelled his sudden sweat. Still, he refused to give in because the essence that had kept him company throughout the long hours wouldn't allow that. Now he stood, shivering again when earlier he'd been certain his body had been shutting down. In a dim and dumb way, he knew it was either do this thing or die, but he really didn't care.

Earlier, the only thing he could do was crawl, but now he found the will and way to walk. Still, he remained a dog thinking a dog's thoughts. Panting. Afraid and curious.

As he came close, the angry engine sounds took over the world. After endless hours of nothing except the wind and his body, the scream was an assault on his nerves, and he wanted to attack the unwanted newcomer. Kill it. Still it. Return the wilderness to what God had intended. He and others like him were intruders and didn't belong. The wild would never accept them, had every right to destroy—

Beacan stopped, pondered. His raging back demanded rest, yet death waited at the end of that decision. His life had been about making and achieving goals, proving himself, and yet what got him going again wasn't drive but the memory of a woman's voice.

Kandi's voice.

Spent, Kandi sank into the snow. As if mocking her, the snowmobile continued its useless howl. This machine that was to have been her—and Beacan's—salvation could keep her warm until it ran out of gas, but in the end, embracing its heat would only delay her death.

Beyond tears, she lifted her head and stared. Something or someone was out there, probably the same presence that had both haunted and sustained her earlier. She hadn't attempted to name or understand the presence. Maybe it was only a function of her imagination, yet because of it, she wasn't alone. Wouldn't die alone.

Cold gnawed at her thighs and buttocks, forcing her to stand. Leaning over the snowmobile's seat, she inhaled warm air. Pain from newly revived facial nerves forced her to rear back, but then the cold attacked again and she started to climb onto the machine. She felt it begin to slide and scrambled away.

Not fair! Not fair!

"Kandi?"

The voice turned her around, but no matter how much she strained to see, the wilderness refused to give up its secrets. Her system was shutting down, whether it was the cold or because her ill-conceived attempt to find Beacan was killing her, she didn't know, didn't care. In her mind, she saw herself again hauling on the snowmobile, finding a way to get it back on level ground and moving again. If she accomplished that, she'd head, not deeper into the wilderness, but to where she'd left Henri. In reality, she stood a foot from the beast and listened as it sucked gas out of its tank.

"Kandi?"

For a heartbeat, she embraced the word and a force that wasn't human, that couldn't be denied, whispered that the impossible had happened. Beacan had found her—had been led to her by that same force and she shouldn't question what was.

Then because she'd always been a realist and didn't believe in anything she couldn't see or touch, she clamped her hands over her ears.

"Kandi?"

"Stop it! Just stop—"

"Kandi."

If she was going insane, so be it, she thought as she turned her back on the snowmobile and made her laborious way up the slope. She wasn't sure what she hoped to accomplish, but finally, arms and legs trembling, she stood on level ground.

"Beacan?" The word hung on her lips, and then slid free. "Beacan?"

"Kandi?"

Snow had packed itself on his head and shoulders and his legs up to his knees were buried in it. She wanted him standing tall and strong, not hunched forward this way.

"Beacan," she repeated.

Then her muscles took over and she plodded forward. He did the same, his movement a curious, lurching thing like a child learning to walk. When he reached out, she leaned into him and they clung to each other.

Crying? She was crying?

"How?" she asked when, finally, she could speak.

"How?" he said at the same time.

More minutes ticked away and the snowmobile continued its insistent din, but she ignored it and stared into Beacan's red-rimmed eyes. The reality of him still eluded her and yet his heart beat and she felt his chest expand and contract.

"I can't move it," she told him finally, indicating the snowmobile. "Every time I try, it threatens to tip over."

"Oh."

"I'm sorry." She spoke with her head resting against his chest and loneliness seeping out of her.

"It isn't your fault."

"Yes, it is. I was careless, got too close to the edge and—"

"The way I did at the lake?"

"Yes," she admitted after a minute.

"Careless the way I'd been when my daughter died."

"Your…?"

"That's what I couldn't talk about. The thing I kept inside me. Kandi, I can't believe… You're alive. God, I prayed… What are you—thank God you're alive."

"Beacan. Your daughter—how old was she?"

"Eleven months and sixteen days."

"Oh God, Beacan, I'm so—"

"So am I." His voice vibrated. "She… This isn't the time to talk about…"

"When?" she demanded. "This might be all we have. I came back—I don't know why the hell I did, but I did."

He pulled her to him again and she could no longer see into his eyes. Didn't need to. "I was so afraid," she started. "Afraid you were dead. But I had to know… Beacan, how did she die?"

"How?"

He sounded like a small child and she longed to mother him, but if she did, they'd lose this moment when the miracle of their reunion was everything—when she was hungry for everything he could give her. Her voice gentle, yet insistent, she again asked him how his daughter had died. When he began speaking, she clung to him and sent him her scant strength.

"Amber's mother and I had been fighting," he said without emotion now. "We'd gotten married when she became pregnant, but it wasn't working out. We were—I was too young. The fight—I don't know what it was about, just that in the middle of it she said she wanted to go see her mother, spend some time with her while she thought about—about whether she wanted to stay with me. I put Amber in her infant carrier, but I didn't check to see if it was secure. I remember—remember thinking it felt loose and then…

"They'd-they'd only gone a few blocks when a garbage truck hit them. My wife — ex-wife — was fine, but Amber's seat came loose and she was thrown…"

"Was-was she killed immediately?" Kandi asked, not sure of anything except the need for this conversation.

"I don't know. The ambulance came and they did CPR and took her to the hospital, and Carol and I waited while they worked on her, but then this doctor told us we could come see her because…"

"Beacan? All the things that have been written about you, and this never came out, did it?"

He shook his head and she continued to hold him, refused to let him stand alone.

"I was still in college. Not making headlines. No one cared back then."

"No one except you and Carol."

"And our parents," he whispered. "It nearly destroyed them."

"And it destroyed your marriage?"

He nodded but didn't explain. Tears ran down her cheeks, cooling and then freezing. His pain was rough and raw and real but not, she prayed, everything. She couldn't stand to have him go through those emotions again.

"Maybe Amber's the reason you found me," she said, feeling stupid and yet unable to stop herself. "Because you wanted me to know this."

"Maybe." He rested his cheek on the top of her head for a long time, but she didn't think he was crying. Just the same, his every breath was shaky.

"I thought," he said finally. "That if I never saw you again, you wouldn't understand why I let you go the way I did. Why I didn't say more than I did."

"Telling me goodbye was nothing compared to what you had to do with your daughter."

"Wasn't it?" He sounded angry but only for a moment. "It felt...so much... You didn't have to come back."

"No, I didn't."

"Why did you?"

She didn't have the answer to that, not with his grief flowing through her, so she turned both of them toward the snowmobile. "It has not quite a half tank of gas," she told him.

"Enough. Maybe. Kandi, you know what has to be done, don't you?"

"Done?"

"So we can get out of here."

Suddenly afraid, she shrank away from him. "What?"

"Listen to me. I'm going to stand on the downhill side of it," he went on. "Push against it, balance it and keep it from sliding any more. You'll have to steer it back up this way."

"Push? You can't—"

"Yeah, I can."

"Your back."

"I know."

"Do you?" she raged, hating and loving him at the same time. "You could tear something, do something—"

"I don't have a choice, Kandi. Neither of us does."

The coming night lapped at them. The wind rumbled and pulsed, whispered of its cruel power. And the snow fell.

"I'm scared," she told him. "If this doesn't work—"

He took a long, long breath. "Why *did* you come back? Why?" he repeated when she said nothing.

"I don't know, all right!"

"Kandi? Don't."

She sucked in as much air as her lungs could hold. "Maybe," she whispered. "Because I know what it is to be alone, and I didn't want that for you. Maybe-maybe I don't want to be alone anymore."

"Dying together?"

Chapter Twenty-Four

๕ว

Dayna knew she wouldn't escape the forest today. As she struggled and rested, struggled and rested, the knowledge rode with her, but she continued to walk because the alternative meant admitting defeat. Still the question raged — why was she denying that defeat its inevitable time?

Her flashlight, which she'd have to turn on before much longer, would never last through the night, not that that was the greatest of her concerns. In truth, she had few, three, not that they really mattered. Number one, Scott should hear about his father's death from his aunt, not a stranger. Second, without her, her plants would die. Finally, overseeing her father's care should be her responsibility because he was, after all, a lot like her plants. The nursing home personnel might see to his physical needs, but would they open the windows and let in sunlight?

Sunlight.

She felt half drunk this afternoon. Still, she remembered what sun on her back and head felt like.

So do I.

Startled, she looked around, but if anyone was out there, the storm hid him.

Storm. And, soon, night.

And with it, death.

A smile touched her lips, but how could that be when she felt so miserable? It wasn't until she started clawing through what remained of her mind that it came to her. Along with the stupid things she'd done since yesterday had been a nugget of intelligence. Of brilliance really. Because she had Park's gun, she could face death on her own terms. Mold it to her needs.

She tried to take a step, but the snow refused to let go and she pitched forward onto her nose—hardly for the first time. Beyond cursing, she struggled to a sitting position and stared into the trees. If this had been a wet snow, her clothing would be soaked, but the flakes were like powder, which was good or bad depending on how one looked at it. A wet snow probably would have killed her by now, but she remained relatively dry which put the responsibility squarely on her shoulders.

The decision wasn't that hard. Go out now or later. But if she waited, maybe she'd lose what little strength remained in her. Incapable of holding the gun to her forehead, she'd die when and how the storm dictated.

But to actually blow a hole through her brain—

Are you afraid?

I don't know.

What do you mean?

All right! I'm fuckin' scared! Is that what you want to hear?

It's what you need to say.

She mulled on that for a few moments. As she did, the snow sucked at her, lapping the few remaining molecules of warmth from her bone marrow and shutting down more brain cells. She'd just admitted she was afraid to die and yet it wasn't the process itself that bothered her. Damn it, she hadn't really lived yet! Looking thirty in the face and never been kissed so—

Well, yes, she'd been kissed. Fucked and been fucked but not that many times and never the way she'd hoped it would be and never really falling in love because…

The because didn't matter.

I used to think I'd never get married, she told her companion. *Told myself I didn't want it, but that's a cop-out.*

Maybe the opportunity didn't present itself.

It didn't because I wouldn't let it.

Why not?

How the hell would I know? Maybe I didn't want to turn out like my mother.

There was no response, either that or along with everything else, she'd lost the ability to hear.

Are you still there?

Yes.

A mix of relief and dread washed through her. *What are you doing?*

Waiting.

For what, she wanted to know. Instead, she started to laugh. She'd insulated herself from the danger of falling in love so she wouldn't become trapped the way her mother had been and yet look where and what she was now?

No one could be any more trapped than this.

What was it like for you? she asked because the presence had to be Cherokee. *Waiting to die – what was it like?*

You don't want to know.

But I have to.

Scared. I was scared. And mad at myself.

Why?

Because I'd gotten myself into the mess, and there was no way out.

It's different for me, she told him. *I have an out.*

* * * * *

Jace had managed to tie his snowshoe in place using his bootlace, but with every step, he risked walking out of his boot. His progress had slowed, but that wasn't his greatest problem. Last night he'd done a fair job of conserving his headlamp, but he couldn't expect it to get him through another. It was all too easy to imagine someone — Cherokee — laughing at him.

At least I'm doing something. I'm not sitting there waiting to die.

Like I had a choice?

Shit! He didn't want, didn't need this! Seeking escape, he plunged forward but only a few yards. Then, accepting the inevitable, he stopped and waited. He thought he might have to say something to get the conversation going but —

Do you really think I'd have stayed out in that shit if I'd had a chance?

I don't know.

Don't you?

Because he had nothing else to do, because there was nothing except the wilderness to look at and nothing except the sound of his breathing, Jace drew on what he knew of his friend. Cherokee was — had been — a wild man, his emotions never subtle. He loved or hated. Laughed or cried. Most of all, he'd embraced the hand life had dealt him — a challenging and rewarding career in spectacular country, youth and health, good friends. A woman he was crazy about — had been crazy about.

You didn't go out there to kill yourself that day, did you?

You know the answer to that.

Yeah, I do. What happened then? Why didn't you come back?

I couldn't.

Not because his so-called best friend had failed him but because he couldn't.

What happened? he asked.

It doesn't matter. I screwed up, buddy. Big time.

You?

Yeah, me.

But – ? Jace started to ask. The question died unspoken because he'd just heard a gunshot.

With a grunt, he settled his weight over his snowshoes and struck out in the direction of the blast.

* * * * *

Pain screamed through Beacan, but he fought it. Kandi stood on the other side of the snowmobile and with one hand, worked the accelerator. With the other, she gripped the handlebar and pulled, grunted and swore. At first they didn't seem to be making any progress but inch by precious inch, the machine dug itself out of its grave. When it no longer tipped dangerously, Kandi climbed onto it. Beacan had no idea how he'd managed to push the way he had because something was tearing apart in his spine, separating, maybe dying. Holding his dead daughter hadn't hurt anymore.

"Gun it!" he screamed. "Give it – everything!"

If she answered, he couldn't hear over the machine's roar. The way she sat, she reminded him of a cowboy fighting to stay on a bucking bull. The track dug into the snow and sprayed him. Blinded, he turned away and listened. At first he couldn't tell what was happening but finally the sound leveled out and became steady. He tried to wipe his face, but his hands didn't want to work, and pain was drilling a hole through the top of his head. Gathering himself, he concentrated on his legs. Felt nothing.

"Beacan?"

There she was, a dark shadow above him.

"Beacan?"

He wanted to answer, but it took everything in him to fight the monster his body had become. As long as he didn't move, the monster remained nearly manageable but even the act of breathing resulted in hot brands of agony. Struggling to escape the pain, he began counting. He made it to ten and then twenty, pictured the numbers in his mind, and then imagined his daughter repeating them in her soft, sweet voice.

"Beacan," Kandi said. "Can you move?"

He didn't know how she'd gotten down to him, and although it should matter that she'd left the snowmobile to idle untended, it didn't.

"I'm going to put my arm around you," she told him. "We'll take it one step at a time. You can lean—"

"Leave…me…alone."

"I can't do that. If you have to cry, do it. If you need me to drag you, we'll get it done."

"You…aren't strong…enough."

"You want to make a bet on that?"

Talking to her had put breathing space between him and the worst of what his back was capable of, either that or the tornado had begun to recede. Instead of telling her that and running the risk of having his body declare him a liar, he looped a heavy arm over her shoulder. He fought to lift the leg closest to her, but it refused his order. Not saying anything, she bent down and helped him flex his knee. He didn't yell, but neither did he recognize the sound rolling out of him.

"Keep your back straight. I think—it might be easier if you do."

Left to his own power, he would have spent the rest of his short life staring up at the too-distant snowmobile, but because Kandi was there, he made himself do what had to be done. She was right. As long as he remained rigid from neck to hips, the pain didn't overwhelm him, but if he turned or twisted in any way, his fingers bit into her shoulder and he felt sick. Instead of trying to break free, she stayed with him and was the strength he'd lost and desperately needed. It took forever and longer to make it up the slope, and by then he was drenched in sweat and trembling, but the effort taught him one essential lesson—he wasn't paralyzed.

"I'll drive," she told him with her arm still around his waist and her breathing as hard and fast as his. "You'll have to sit behind me, hold onto me."

"Sit?"

"Unless you'd rather walk?"

"Don't…be funny."

"I'm not. Do you want to rest a few minutes?"

"Yeah. I think…I'd better."

After making sure he could stand on his own, she leaned over the snowmobile and wiped off the dials. "I wish I knew how far it'll go on half a tank."

He started to tell her he had no understanding of snowmobiles, and then stopped. "What are you doing with it?" he asked. "How—?"

She held up her hand, silencing him. Then, her words spare and matter-of-fact, she told him about coming to the rim road and finding it deserted but going on anyway, not knowing how long she'd been on it before a forest ranger found her. His mind snagged on the reality of that deserted road, but they'd talk about that later.

"They're going to try to get help to Park and Dayna," Kandi explained. "The man who found me made sure of that, but it's not going to happen until tomorrow."

Tomorrow?

"What are you thinking?" he asked as Kandi stared in the direction of Lake Wolf.

"Nothing. I just…"

"You're worried about them, aren't you? Park and Dayna." He shifted position, and although the movement stirred up a hornet's nest inside him, at least the top of his head no longer felt as if it was going to explode.

"I can't help it. We told them…"

"We told them we'd get help for them. But…"

Head turned to one side, Jace glided forward. Although he'd traveled perhaps three hundred feet, he stopped and called out. He half expected Cherokee to answer, but only the wind had anything to say. During those seemingly endless hours last winter when he'd searched for his friend, he'd become accustomed to the way the world narrowed down in a storm. It had been like that again last night, and yet this afternoon he felt trapped inside a shrinking, windowless room. He couldn't tell how much longer the sun might remain in the sky. When he'd left the cabin, he'd thought he'd easily make it back to his truck before nightfall, but then his snowshoe had broken. What preyed on his mind wasn't just the prospect of another wilderness night—although that was a major chunk of it—but where the others were and what he was doing to Henri.

Henri? Could his co-worker have come after him, fired a gun in an attempt to draw Jace to him?

"I'm here!" he called out. "Here!"

The wind chewed up his words and swallowed them. Angry, he strained to hear anything except the storm, and when that didn't happen, he started forward again because he'd been sure—nearly sure anyway—that the gunshot had come from somewhere beyond him.

He felt heavy, old and weary. In all his traveling today, he'd lost track of exactly where he was on the spur road. He'd tried to reassure himself that he'd covered a number of miles and thus wasn't that far from the junction, but cold had numbed his brain and taken him away from reality. If he'd been standing still—

Henri didn't own a handgun. Given the reality of a lone ranger coming across who knows who doing who knows what in the middle of nowhere, more and more of his co-workers had taken to carrying weapons, but Henri, who'd never hunted, had been a holdout.

Not Henri? Then who?

"Hello? Is anyone there?"

Night lapped at the sky. Right now it only tasted the day but before much longer, it would feed in earnest. When it did, Dayna, Beacan, and Kandi, if they hadn't been rescued, would be facing their second night out here.

"Why can't I think?" he asked. When no answer came, he repeated his question, louder this time.

"Why the hell can't I think?"

The snow blanket that was his world tightened its grip on him, and yet, off to his right, seemed to be a small tear. The spot didn't look that different from the rest of his surroundings and yet something...

Cautious because he didn't know who might be at the other end of that gun, he crouched and began moving again, a hunter on the trail of wary, perhaps dangerous, game. The air carried no telling smells and his ears were all but useless and flakes clung to his goggles, but bit by bit, he became convinced that what had caught his attention was more than a hole in the storm. It didn't move, was low to the ground.

"Who is it?" he asked although he wasn't sure he'd come across a whom at all. There was no answer, and his legs wanted to be still.

"Is anyone there?"

Nothing. Too damn much silence.

"Can you hear me?"

Still nothing.

Not bothering to speak anymore, Jace inched forward. His mind snagged on the way he'd dug in the snow earlier when he thought he'd found Cherokee's bones. This was different—but different enough?

The next time his legs rebelled, he gave into their insistent message and stopped. Now he judged the mound to be maybe twenty feet away and if it hadn't been for the dull blue color, he might have taken it for a boulder.

"Hello. Can you hear me?"

The mound seemed to shudder, but he couldn't be sure.

"Canyouhearme?"

"Y-yes."

Despite his overwhelming sense of relief, for several moments, Jace simply stared. "Who are you?" he finally asked.

The mound straightened, the movement slow and laborious. "Dayna. Dayna Curran."

Chapter Twenty-Five

❧

Dayna remembered, not Jace's features so much as the sound of his voice. His explanation of why he'd decided to go to Lake Wolf to look for her and her brother and what he learned once he got there seemed disjointed, but that might be because she hadn't been able to concentrate. When the ranger prodded for information about what had happened to her since she'd left the cabin, she told him what she remembered. Mostly she felt awed by everything he'd accomplished, the effort he'd been willing to go to for strangers.

"Gun?" she asked, struggling to concentrate on what he'd just asked. "It-it was my brother's."

"You were trying to attract attention?" He'd dropped to his knees beside her and was staring at her as if he couldn't make himself believe she existed. "You heard me?"

"No. I…

"What?"

Dragging her gaze off him, she reached into her coat pocket and drew out the weapon. "I wasn't going to let the storm win."

"I…see. What stopped you?"

"I don't know."

Jace shifted position so he now sat cross-legged. The storm continued to spit its endless flakes, and it struck her that there was very little difference between the two of them and not enough to distinguish them from their surroundings.

"I thought I could do it," she told him. "That whether I lived or died didn't matter that much, but it's not that easy."

He held out his hand and she gave him the gun. "It shouldn't be. Life's precious."

"I guess."

"You guess?"

"It's not as if I have anyone waiting for me, not really. This decision is mine. Mine." Why was she telling a stranger this? "But admitting this—" She swept her arms to take in their surroundings. "Is all there'll ever be takes awhile."

"I'm glad it did." He brushed snow off her shoulder.

"I kept thinking—about the risks Kandi and Beacan were taking. If they managed to get help and learned I'd—if they realized they'd risked their lives for someone who— Where are they?"

"I don't know."

"Don't know? Then they—"

"Don't assume anything," he interrupted. "It's possible they made it out."

"How?" she demanded. "I know what it's like, how hard—God, it's my fault!"

"I read your note, Dayna. It sounds as if what they did was their decision."

"It was," she started to say. "But if I hadn't been so worried about Park… He's dead and they risked their lives for nothing."

She'd been sitting for too long. If she didn't soon get to her feet, she might not be able to. Putting her mind to the task, she managed to kneel, but her legs refused to complete the task. After standing, Jace offered her his hand and drew her up beside him. She started to sway, and when he caught and held her, she made no attempt to pull away. The reality of him still came to her in fragments, and she had no idea how she'd ever thank him enough or if she wanted to.

"The rim road isn't being plowed," he said. "My work truck's not that far from where this road hooks up to it, but we'll never make it before dark."

"Oh."

"Do you understand what I'm saying?" he demanded. "We'll have to keep going through the night, otherwise we risk freezing."

"Oh."

He was staring at her, digging into her and finding things she didn't want him to know.

"You can't do it, can you?" he said.

"Do what?"

"Walk."

Of course she could! She had what, a good half dozen steps left in her. And then—and then what?

"No," she whispered. "Not really."

His sigh hung between them for several seconds before the wind silenced it. "All right," he said.

What are we going to do? she nearly asked, but this wasn't his problem.

"I'm sorry." She felt calm. "I wish I had more left inside me."

"All right." He again took in their surroundings, and she saw him as a trapped animal. Only that wasn't right because he wasn't trapped, she was.

"You know what you have to do, don't you?" she said in the same calm tone. "Take care of yourself."

"No!"

"Yes. You've already done more than anyone else would have. But I can't let you sacrifice…" Images of Beacan and Kandi surfaced in her mind but she wrenched free. "I won't let you— Jace, when you go, I want you to leave the gun with me."

"No!"

"Yes. Jace, I—" She felt dizzy. "I need that option."

No. Although his mouth moved, he didn't say anything.

"It has to be on my terms." She stared at the pocket where he'd placed her brother's weapon.

"I can't do this," he said. "You don't understand but I-I can't go through this again."

"Again?"

"The way it was with Cherokee."

He had a disturbing ability to punch out words and emotions she couldn't dismiss. "I'm not Cherokee," she tried to tell him, but before she'd finished, dizziness overcame her, and although she didn't want to, she again wound up letting him support her. "Not your friend. You don't owe me anything."

"The hell I don't."

"I don't want this from you. I won't—"

"This isn't about you."

Not to him it wasn't, but to her…

The fade wasn't total and it didn't last long, but by the time her head cleared, she was back on the snow and Jace was rubbing her cheeks with the hated stuff. She slapped at him, and then gave up.

"Don't you see?" she asked, wishing she could make her voice stronger. "I'm played out. I can't—can't do…enough."

"After you've rested—"

"By then it'll be too late for you, and I can't let you do that. I won't."

He placed her hands between his and began rubbing them together, the gesture so gentle and futile that it brought tears to her eyes.

"I didn't come all this way to abandon you," he said.

"You aren't abandoning me." *But when you're gone, I'll be more alone than I've ever been.* "You're saving yourself."

He said nothing, only shifted so less wind reached her and continued trying to massage warmth back into her fingers. She needed to tell him that no touch had ever meant as much as his did at this moment, but if she did, she might not be able to make him leave. She had to! There'd already been too many deaths on this mountain.

"You said…" She paused, gathering her thoughts around her. "You said they were going to send rescue to the cabin. Maybe you should go back there instead of trying to make it to Crater?"

"I don't know."

"You can't contact—"

"No! My damn PTT doesn't work."

She'd been without a way to contact the outside world for so long that it didn't bother her. In truth, she barely remembered what that world had been like.

"I keep asking myself what I should have done different," he told her. "Whether I should have stayed in my rig and done what I'm paid to do."

"But you didn't."

"No, I didn't. Once I realized you and your brother were at Wolf…"

Fighting cold had been an endless battle, but now it was over because she'd surrendered. She felt as if she was telescoping inward, becoming less and less of a person. Her lungs still pushed in and out, but maybe her heart had stopped because even when she tunneled deep inside herself, she couldn't find it. It was better this way, less complicated.

"Go," she told him. "While there's still daylight."

"God! God." He ran his hands up her arms, but if she hadn't been looking at him, she wouldn't have known because she had no feeling left.

"It's all right. All right. I just—I'm not going to watch you leave. Turn my back and think…think…Jace, the gun."

He might have repeated his plea to God, but she couldn't be sure because these few minutes of talking had exhausted her. She'd always thought a person would fight to go on living no matter what, but that wasn't always true, was it? There was something almost peaceful about knowing the end was coming, accepting it. When Jace curled himself around her and spoke earnestly, she tried to concentrate on his words, but only a few penetrated. She nodded and hoped that would satisfy him but if it didn't…

There. In her lap. Weight. Deadly and blessed.

His mind screaming at him, Jace stared at what he'd just done. He wasn't sure Dayna had the strength to grip the pistol, and if she didn't, her death would be slow the way Cherokee's had been. If she did, she might kill herself before he could return with help.

What help? Even if he put everything he had into the journey ahead of him, he couldn't possibly get anyone to her before nightfall.

"I'm sorry," he whispered. It didn't matter if she heard because this was for him. "So sorry."

She nodded. Her eyes were half-closed, holding her essence inside her.

"I'll be back. I promise. I'll be back."

"I know you will."

But will you still be alive?

Instead of asking the horrible, impossible question, he turned his back on her and started walking. Before he'd gone more than a half dozen feet, the storm sucked him into its belly and he lost touch with everything else—with her. His legs took up the familiar rhythm and he tried to make it everything and for a short while it worked but then an image of her, silent and spent, wrapped around her brother's pistol, filled his mind, and he tried to run.

The snow wouldn't let him. Instead, it mocked and challenged, all the time whispering that it was beautiful. It was. He'd never deny that, but beauty could also kill—not just Dayna and Kandi and Beacan but him as well.

If he got out of this, would he ever want to set foot in the forest again? And if not, where could he possibly go so the memories wouldn't haunt him?

Memories. Damnable memories.

Teeth bared, he snarled at his surroundings, then started to laugh because the winter monster was impervious to anything a single human being might throw at it. He'd started to lower his head when something like an electric charge touched his spine. Instantly alert, he trudged to the middle of the road and strained to listen. Something seemed to be rumbling in the distance, but the sound was so faint, so mixed into the wind that he couldn't be sure. He was still far from the rim road and couldn't possibly hear anything on it, but maybe something—a snowplow—had completed its work on the road around Crater and was heading this way.

"Dayna!" he yelled. "Listen!"

When she didn't answer, he turned around, shocked to discover he could no longer see her. Putting his mind to the task, he went back the way he'd come. Finally he spotted, not her really, but familiar terrain.

"Dayna? Dayna? Where are you?"

"Here," she said, but although her voice located her for him, it bothered him that she wasn't moving.

"Listen," he ordered.

Her head came up a few inches, but she didn't look at him.

"Listen," he repeated. "I heard—I know I heard… I'll be right back. I just—" He pointed. "Can you hear that?"

She didn't respond.

"It's—I'm not sure what it is, but it has—I have…" His voice fell away and although he strained to hear, only the storm's sounds came to him now. If he'd imagined—

"Dayna? Stay where you are. Just wait for me, all right?"

"Whatareyoudoing?"

"I'm not sure. I thought I heard—" No! He had to give her more than that. "I'm sure I heard something."

"What?"

"I don't know! Dayna, I have to try to find it—I want—" Torn between responsibility for her and something that might not exist, he turned this way and that. "Come with me, please. Together we'll—"

"I can't."

Of course she couldn't.

"Wait for me then. I'll only be a few minutes. I promise." He pointed in the direction of the rim road. "I think that's where it was coming from. It won't take long for me to find out—when I do, I'll come back. I promise."

Dayna hadn't responded the last time he'd spoken and more than anything her silence drove Jace. He cursed his patched-together snowshoe, and then dismissed it because there was nothing he could do about it. His mind played and replayed what he'd heard or thought he'd heard until he wasn't sure how to separate what might be fantasy from the truth, and although he struggled to regulate both his breathing and heartbeat, he couldn't do either. As a result, he only heard the loudest wind gusts, the complaining trees. His lack of progress ate at him and added to his inability to pace himself. His legs burned, and his head ached, but most of all, he thought about Dayna and the gun she held. He should have taken it from her, told her he wasn't going to leave her with it the way she was, but if he was on a fool's mission...

In the distance, barely visible through the darkening sky, the road curved to the right as it skirted a hill. He told himself that the hill and trees acted as sound barriers and as soon as he'd put them behind him, he'd have a clear idea of what had drawn him here, but his strength was draining away. Feeling like a racehorse being prodded toward the finish line, he focused on the curve, and then he was beyond it, looking at another straight stretch flanked by a wall of trees, the sameness of white, his pulse hammering in his ears. If he turned around, would he see his tracks. Maybe not, maybe he had no existence beyond this moment, this place.

Forcing himself to focus on what he could see of the road, he set a new goal. His knees and ankles had that much life in them but not much more if he insisted on this pace, and as he lowered his head and stared at his feet, the question he'd tried to run away from returned.

Sound was illusive in the wilderness. Trees and mountains to say nothing of weather conditions could twist and turn it, throw it one way and then the other, distort and even create what didn't exist. If he'd been wrong and what he'd heard had come from Lake Wolf, he'd nearly spent himself going in the opposite direction from what he should. And if there'd been nothing—

His legs slowed, stopped. He wanted to demand they explain themselves, instead he lifted his head and howled. The cry died almost immediately, a victim of the wind.

"God," he moaned. "God."

That, too, didn't survive the elements, and he fell silent. His surroundings ate at him, and yet he wasn't sure whether he hated or loved the forest. It was what it was, ageless, both simple and complex.

Had Cherokee seen its beauty? Even as the wilderness was killing him, had he understood that his dying was part of the rhythm of this place and thus right? Dayna didn't. Instead of waiting for the rhythm to overtake her, she held the means to dictate her own fate. Did she have the right to do that, would God —?

It built again, rumbling through him, pulling him out of himself.

"Hello!" he yelled, this time unmindful of how quickly the hungry storm swallowed the word. "Hello! Help!"

Heat rose in him, warming his chest and shoulders, bringing life back to his throat. The new sound battled with the wind, not vanquishing it but refusing to be silenced. It became real and powerful, called to Jace and pulled him into it.

"Help!" he repeated. "Help!"

Ahead of him, the storm parted or was pushed aside, and a snowmobile appeared in the opening. Jace started running toward it, but he'd taken no more than a half dozen steps when his right snowshoe fell off. It didn't matter because —

Because the snowmobile was coming closer, closer, and the two people on it were waving at him.

The driver, a woman he could now tell, brought the snowmobile to a halt a few feet away, and for a long time she stared at him while he held her gaze. Then, perhaps satisfied that he was real, she turned to look back at her companion. The man sitting behind her held himself stiffly, and his eyes appeared unfocused, but he was the first to speak, asking Jace who he was and what he was doing here.

"Jace Penix," he said. "I work for the Park Service. You—are you Beacan Jarrard?"

The man nodded, winced, then indicated Jace should get closer to the heater. He did so, his attention now on the woman. "You must be Kandi," he said.

"How did you know?"

"I was at Wolf," he explained as briefly as possible. "Dayna told me."

"Dayna. Then you've seen her?"

"Yes."

Kandi climbed off the idling machine so he could lean close and receive the heater's full benefit. At first he felt nothing but gradually the warm air began to penetrate the layers of clothing.

"You saw Dayna?" Beacan asked. He'd scooted back on the seat but made no attempt to stand.

"Yes." Warmth was incredible! His brain fed off it. "She's—I left her back there." He pointed. "Not far. When I heard—what are you doing here? She needs help." His words felt rushed but he couldn't help himself. "I didn't want to leave her but she couldn't—couldn't walk anymore. "

"Not far?" Beacan questioned. "Kandi?"

It seemed to Jace that Beacan and Kandi had developed a means of communication which needed no words, because after Beacan spoke her name, Kandi nodded and then climbed back on between the two men. Jace's fingers were slow to respond, and it would have been better if Kandi had continued driving, but his need for heat was so great that he didn't offer to change places with her.

The snowmobile complained and labored, making Jace wonder if he could have gone faster on foot, but that was a moot point because he no longer had both snowshoes. Despite the whining motor, he managed to ask the necessary questions, and he learned that this machine had belonged to Henri, but Kandi had taken it from him because she couldn't leave Beacan behind.

As for why Kandi and Beacan had headed for Wolf instead of Crater—

"We promised Dayna and Park," Kandi yelled in his ear. "We talked about leaving it up to search and rescue to find them but we—besides, Wolf is closer than Crater headquarters and we don't have that much gas and it's going to be dark soon and…"

He didn't say anything about their decision maybe saving his life because that went without saying. Besides, he wasn't sure he could get the words out without breaking down. Kandi filled in most of the blanks, explaining that Beacan had probably destroyed his back getting the snowmobile back on the road after she'd lost control of it, and although she'd asked Beacan if he didn't want to go to the first aid station at Crater, he'd told her that the damage had been done, and waiting wouldn't make that much difference.

"I'm worried about him," she admitted. If Beacan overhead, Jace couldn't tell. "If he's crippled—I knew he'd hurt himself when he was taking care of Park, but I—"

"Park's dead."

Kandi sucked in a breath and asked for details, but he couldn't concentrate enough to give her more than a summation of what he'd found. After relaying the information to Beacan, she simply sat with her arms warm around his waist.

Night hovered over and around them and challenged the snowmobile's light to keep it at bay. The beam caught and held the flakes and turned them into something beautiful, and yet Jace remained all too aware of the vast, frozen nothing just out of view. He thought he'd left Dayna no more than fifteen or twenty minutes ago, but she'd had no way of knowing what he'd found and that he was coming back to her. What if she'd been unable to wait, if she'd stacked reality around her and made her decision—?

Don't let her do it, Cherokee. Just the hell don't let her do it.

His plea, prayer, whatever, echoed inside him. His vision blurred and he had to struggle to find the road and he prayed again.

She's too young. Too damn young to die.

So was I.

I know that. Don't you think I don't know that!

Do you want to hear what it was like, not being able to move and it getting colder and colder and snow coming down, always coming down, and night—

No! I don't!

Why not? What are you afraid of?

Nothing, he wanted to tell Cherokee. Not a damn thing. But as he gathered the words inside him, the light caught on something ahead of him and he leaned forward, forgot to breathe.

Dayna.

Walking toward them.

Epilogue

๛

The old man sat motionless in the lawn chair Kandi had placed near the boat dock. Dayna studied her father, and then turned her attention to her surroundings. It was the middle of June, sunlight creating diamond sparkles on the lake where Beacan, Jace, and Scott were fishing.

"It's a guy thing all right," Kandi observed as she joined Dayna, iced tea glass in hand, near the bank.

"Fishing?" Dayna asked. "Hardly. I always thought that was something I'd enjoy if—" Shrugging, she indicated her father. "He hadn't turned it into something else."

"I wasn't talking about stalking some poor fish although there's nothing wrong with spending a day out there," Kandi said. "I'm talking about that boat. I swear, Beacan looked at a hundred of them before he decided on this one."

"He didn't have any trouble launching it?"

"Not with the setup he has. You'll have to get him to show it to you, power everything. I don't even want to know what that cost."

Despite Kandi's dismissive shrug, Dayna had no doubt that the other woman had a firm handle on Beacan's finances— Their finances now as witness by the modest engagement ring Kandi wore.

"He's doing much better than I was afraid he would," she said. "The physical therapy must be working."

"Because I'm there egging him on. I can't believe it, me, ready to say 'I do'."

"No second thoughts?"

"A million, but that's what life's about, isn't it?" Kandi indicated Dayna's father. "Do you think he knows where he is? Does he have any memories of this place?"

"I'm not sure. He lives pretty much in the moment, but I wanted to do this for him—for Scott to get to know his grandfather, at least as much as possible."

The three-day getaway at Lake Wolf had taken a good deal of coordinating what with Scott's schooling, her job at Sherms Nursery, Jace's park service schedule, and the fact that Beacan's coaching position with a double A farm team kept both him and Kandi on the road so much, but they'd all agreed that if a book was going to be written about their experience—and they were finally ready to take that step—they wanted to do it, not farm it off on a ghostwriter. Bringing her father along would have made for crowded conditions at Beacan's cabin if the new owners of the Curran cabin hadn't agreed to let them rent it. Dayna hadn't been sure she'd be able to step inside the walls where her brother had died, but Scott had needed the closure and having Jace nearby had helped.

"It's going to be a quiet wedding," Kandi said. "Just Beacan and me and a couple of witnesses."

"In other words, no press?"

"Exactly. They were so persistent when he had his surgery that it gave me an idea of what he went through when he was playing. No wonder he bought this place."

"How is he with not playing?"

Kandi shrugged and then smiled. "Better than I thought he'd be. He's pretty realistic."

"Like you."

"Like me. Ah, about those witnesses—we'd like it to be you and Jace."

Heat stung Dayna's eyes, and she let a nod serve as her answer. She wanted to tell Kandi that being asked was an honor, but for now she was content to let summer's wind sing to her. Tonight, once she'd gotten her father settled in for the evening, they'd lay the groundwork for the book. So far there'd been no major disagreements because they were willing to admit that errors in judgment had been made and those errors had led to one life lost and four others placed in jeopardy.

What they hadn't talked about yet was what they were going to say about Cherokee's role.

"There goes the neighborhood," Kandi announced. "The providers have returned. From the looks of things we'll be having fish tonight."

Dayna walked onto the boat dock with Kandi. As they stood waiting, her thoughts went back to the day her brother had stood in the snow on a dock similar to this one. "Kandi?" she asked. "Do you believe there's anything after we die?"

"A hereafter? I didn't used to but I'm not sure anymore."

The boat, under Scott's guidance, came in too fast, but because Jace was leaning over the bow, he managed to cushion the landing. Scott jumped out first and held onto the tie rope while Kandi offered her arm as support for Beacan. Jace handed the stringer with its five fish to Dayna, his smile open and free.

"That was great," he announced. "Absolutely great! Getting away from everything. Just being."

"What you needed?" she asked as he joined her.

"Better than all the shrinks in the world," he said and she believed him. So, she knew, would Cherokee.

Why an electronic book?

We live in the Information Age—an exciting time in the history of human civilization, in which technology rules supreme and continues to progress in leaps and bounds every minute of every day. For a multitude of reasons, more and more avid literary fans are opting to purchase e-books instead of paper books. The question from those not yet initiated into the world of electronic reading is simply: *Why?*

1. ***Price.*** An electronic title at Ellora's Cave Publishing and Cerridwen Press runs anywhere from 40% to 75% less than the cover price of the exact same title in paperback format. Why? Basic mathematics and cost. It is less expensive to publish an e-book (no paper and printing, no warehousing and shipping) than it is to publish a paperback, so the savings are passed along to the consumer.

2. ***Space.*** Running out of room in your house for your books? That is one worry you will never have with electronic books. For a low one-time cost, you can purchase a handheld device specifically designed for e-reading. Many e-readers have large, convenient screens for viewing. Better yet, hundreds of titles can be stored within your new library—on a single microchip. There are a variety of e-readers from different manufacturers. You can also read e-books on your PC or laptop computer. (Please note that Ellora's

Cave does not endorse any specific brands. You can check our websites at www.ellorascave.com or www.cerridwenpress.com for information we make available to new consumers.)

3. *Mobility*. Because your new e-library consists of only a microchip within a small, easily transportable e-reader, your entire cache of books can be taken with you wherever you go.

4. ***Personal Viewing Preferences.*** Are the words you are currently reading too small? Too large? Too… ANNOYING? Paperback books cannot be modified according to personal preferences, but e-books can.

5. ***Instant Gratification.*** Is it the middle of the night and all the bookstores near you are closed? Are you tired of waiting days, sometimes weeks, for bookstores to ship the novels you bought? Ellora's Cave Publishing sells instantaneous downloads twenty-four hours a day, seven days a week, every day of the year. Our webstore is never closed. Our e-book delivery system is 100% automated, meaning your order is filled as soon as you pay for it.

Those are a few of the top reasons why electronic books are replacing paperbacks for many avid readers.

As always, Ellora's Cave and Cerridwen Press welcome your questions and comments. We invite you to email us at Comments@ellorascave.com or write to us directly at Ellora's Cave Publishing Inc., 1056 Home Avenue, Akron, OH 44310-3502.

THE
☥ ELLORA'S CAVE ☥
LIBRARY

Stay up to date with Ellora's Cave Titles in
Print with our Quarterly Catalog.

TO RECIEVE A CATALOG,
SEND AN EMAIL WITH YOUR NAME
AND MAILING ADDRESS TO:

CATALOG@ELLORASCAVE.COM
OR SEND A LETTER OR POSTCARD
WITH YOUR MAILING ADDRESS TO:

CATALOG REQUEST
c/o ELLORA'S CAVE PUBLISHING, INC.
1056 HOME AVENUE
AKRON, OHIO 44310-3502

Cerridwen Press
Monthly Newsletter

News
Author Appearances
Book Signings
New Releases
Contests
Author Profiles
Feature Articles

Available online at
www.CerridwenPress.com

COMING TO A BOOKSTORE NEAR YOU!

ELLORA'S CAVE

Bestselling Authors Tour

MAKE EACH DAY MORE *EXCITING* WITH OUR

ELLORA'S CAVEMEN

CALENDAR

☥ WWW.ELLORASCAVE.COM ☥

Cerridwen Press

Cerridwen, the Celtic goddess of wisdom, was the muse who brought inspiration to storytellers and those in the creative arts.

Cerridwen Press encompasses the best and most innovative stories in all genres of today's fiction.

Visit our website and discover the newest titles by talented authors who still get inspired—

much like the ancient storytellers did

once upon a time...

www.cerridwenpress.com